HAIR TRIGGER

Peter McGarvey signature

Peter McGarvey

To Fred, the spider
is after you.
or at least Rip
& Wilma.

Pete

Cliff House Publishing

Cliff House Publishing
Huntington, New York

cliffhousepublishing.com

Cover design by Lesley Stodart

Photo by Giles Peterson

Author's Photo by William McGarvey

ISBN 978-0-9881396-3-3

FOR MY OLD FRIEND & MENTOR

DON HUTCHISON

Books by Peter McGarvey

FICTION

Dark Sunset

NON-FICTION

Baffled by Travel Guide to Toronto & Niagara Falls
The 10 Second Guide to New York City

ACKNOWLEDGMENTS

A special thank you to my editor **Amy Mark** for all her hard work and dedication to the process. She embraced Rip and Wilma and helped them to become better people.

Thanks to my brother, **Will McGarvey**, who has been an enthusiastic supporter of Rip and Wilma; and to **Steve Carlson**, **Peter Halasz**, and the **Second Tuesday Gang** for their suggestions and encouragement.

A special thanks to **Ellen Fine** and **Promod Sharma** for graciously lending their names to characters in this book.

And last, but not least, thank you to the **City of Detroit**. Your energy and spirit will persevere.

HAIR
TRIGGER

There are only two mistakes one can make along the road to truth; not starting and not going all the way.

Buddha

PETER LORRE
AND 1940S FILM NOIR

They were going to cut off my hand.

When I came to, I was tied to a chair. It was dark in the print shop and like a character in a 1940s film noir, I could see the distorted silhouettes of a tall man and short man standing in the shadows. I was dizzy and felt sick from the blow to my head. The two figures swam in and out of focus.

Leaning over as far as I could, I barfed on the floor at their feet.

"Feeling better?" the short one asked in a strained high-pitched voice that reminded me of Peter Lorre.

"Please don't say fuck you," the tall one added.

I didn't. I just vomited again.

After I finished whooshing whatever cookies were left inside me, I noticed my right hand was trapped under the clamping rail of a paper trimmer. This "guillotine" has a razor sharp blade with thousands of pounds of pressure behind it. It can make very neat cuts through thick reams of paper.

The short guy stood next to it, but I still couldn't see him clearly.

"It says here this thing can trim up to a thousand sheets of paper at a time," he read off the metal tag on the side of the machine. "Apparently the operator must have one hand on each of the side switches for safety." He looked straight at me. "Gee, I'd like to see how it works. Wouldn't you?"

The big guy walked to the wall and pulled down the breaker handle on the electrical panel. Machines around the shop started to power up. I could feel the vibration of the cutter humming through the metal surface under my hand.

The trimming blade gleamed wickedly.

"This is the part in the James Bond movie when I ask you to tell me what I need to know. If I don't get an answer I like, you're going to have to learn to jack off southpaw."

I have very few phobias. One, however, is my fear of dismemberment. I get queasy just thinking about it, let alone imagining what my life would be like without a vital appendage such as my gun hand. In feudal Japan, it was considered a sign of dishonor if a samurai lost a limb in battle. It showed everyone that he had failed in his duty as a warrior.

My heart started to hammer and my entire world compressed down to the gleaming blade poised a foot above my naked wrist.

"We're interested in a certain book," the short one said.

"Is it about whales?" I asked, my voice quivering in fear.

"Good boy," he said.

My hand was numb from the restricted blood flow under the clamping rail. He put his hands on the red buttons. He tapped them lightly, like they were flipper switches on the side of a pinball machine. As he did this, he leaned in close to me. I was tempted to throw my head back and slam it into his face, but I knew if I did that I could kiss my hand goodbye.

"I'd like to know where the book is," he whispered in my ear.

I hesitated, which was probably not a good idea in that particular situation. He pushed the buttons and there was a sharp whir. The blade came down a few inches. He lifted his fingers and it froze. It was now just six inches above my wrist.

I tried to form the words to tell him, but couldn't. My mouth was just too dry. All that came out were the kind of helpless squeaks a chipmunk makes the moment it's seized by the talons of a hawk.

He shook his head slightly, as if disappointed in me, and started to put pressure on the buttons.

I watched in horror as his fingernails turned white.

The blade descended.

I HAD MY HEART SET
ON A CONEY ISLAND

Let's rewind.

First, a little background might help.

Call me Rip.

It's not my real name, but it's the only one you're ever going to get from me. I work with a woman called Wilma, which is not her real name either.

Wilma and I are from the Detroit area. She grew up in Bloomington Hills and I come from Flint. In fact, I lived just around the corner from Michael Moore when I was growing up. For those of you who don't know, he's that guy who makes political films. While I don't like his politics, his movies are fun, especially the one about guns.

The Motor City has always been a tough place. If you know what's good for you, don't go off the beaten track. That would be like sticking your hand in a viper's nest and feeling around.

Most of Detroit's nastiness is directed inward. Crime here is mostly stupid stuff – dope deals that go bad, gangbangers who dis each other, grudges that simmer, and drunken rages. Eventually the guns come out, the bullets fly, and the victims go down.

And there's plenty of room for all at the Wayne County Morgue.

Well, maybe not.

A couple of years ago things reached a crisis level when unclaimed corpses literally began to stack up there. Hit hard by the recession, people couldn't afford to bury their loved ones. The morgue had body piled on top of body until they got it straightened out.

That's the way it's been going in Detroit for quite a while now. Fortunately, most tourists never get to see that side of our glorious city.

They visit the Art Institute, have lousy souvlaki in Greektown, and then watch the Lions blow it in the fourth quarter at Ford Field. Afterward, they jump on the Lodge or the Fisher and head back to the safety of their hotels in the suburbs.

I was double-parked on Lafayette waiting for Wilma to return. She had offered to get us dogs at American Coney Island before we headed up to the ferry in Ludington. It was six hours before the boat sailed so we had plenty of time. Once we got to Wisconsin, there would be another four hours of driving until we reached our destination – Iron City, Minnesota.

I was hungry. To distract myself, I ticked off time and tried to figure out just when we would arrive: Four hours to Ludington, three more sailing across to Manitowoc on the Wisconsin side – lose an hour for Central Time – and then four more hours driving through Wisconsin into Minnesota. That's eleven in total, and then if I subtract the lost hour in the time zone change, we should get there at …

I got lost somewhere in the middle of my calculations. Math was never my strong suit.

Wilma came out empty-handed and jumped behind the wheel. She was silent until we were on I-96 heading toward Lansing.

I finally worked up the courage to ask, "Where's my lunch?"

She slid her right hand into her handbag. This was not a good sign. There were two automatics inside; each nestled in its own custom pouch.

"Didn't feel right," she muttered.

We'd been partners for fifteen years, so I was used to Wilma's feelings about things. Actually, they verged on the outright paranoiac at times. Still, I trusted her and, more importantly, I trusted her feelings.

I call it her spidey sense, and it's helped us avoid some really unpleasant situations in the past.

I don't get weird sensations about things myself, which meant I would occasionally stroll into a dangerous situation. Luckily, Wilma has been there to watch my back, and to stop bad things from happening to me.

"I'm hungry," I complained.

"We'll stop at the next Wendy's then."

"I had my heart set on a Coney Island."

"Stop whining. You'd just make a mess of my upholstery with your hot dog anyway."

She was right of course. I would drip chili all over the seat, and Wilma liked to keep her car immaculate.

Wilma didn't like to drive all that much at the best of times, and got particularly testy on long road trips. Normally we'd take my car, a big bitching piece of Dodge muscle, but this time we had no choice. It was in the shop after its passenger door got torn off.

She kept looking in the side mirror, which made me nervous. Her spidey sense was definitely tingling. Of course, it might just have been restlessness. She hadn't shot anyone in over a month; maybe she was feeling edgy.

Come to think of it, I hadn't killed anyone in almost six months. Another reason I was happy the Iron City job came along when it did.

We were going to Iron City to fuck someone up good – and get paid for it.

I tried to lighten Wilma's mood. "You see *Antiques Roadshow* last night?"

She shook her head and continued to look in the side mirror. "*Storage Wars.* A stack of stuff fell over and almost crushed Barry." She chuckled at the memory.

Wilma is a high-functioning psychopath – well actually, we both are – and she gets off on the misery of others. She can't help it; it's her inherent lack of empathy. I share a similar deficit of feeling. It makes us ideal partners in our chosen occupation.

We kill people for profit.

Need to get rid of someone? We'll do it for you in a professional manner, and at a reasonable price. We don't care why you want the person dead, or whether or not the target is a saint or a rat bastard. It really doesn't make any difference to us.

If you have the money, we're happy to help.

We like to get in there and get the job done fast. I've heard about guys who spend days stalking their prey, getting to know their every move. They wait for the perfect opportunity. To us, time is money. Point us at the victim, and we'll go in with guns blazing.

Best of all, we charge affordable rates. If you can carry a mortgage in a good middle-class neighborhood, you can afford our services. You just need to know someone who has used us in the past. We aren't in the *Yellow Pages*, and we don't advertise on *Craig's List*. We're strictly a referral business.

The Iron City job came from one of our satisfied customers, Brett Maverick. Of course that isn't his real name. We use non de plumes.

Since a lot of our clients tend to be boomers, they prefer code names inspired by 60s and 70s television shows. In the past we've done business with Joe Mannix, Perry Mason, Matt Dillon, and a few less well-known names anyone born after 1972 would have to look up on Wikipedia.

Brett called and asked if I would meet with Barney Rubble. Brett vouched for him, so I agreed. He arranged for Barney to meet me in the bar of the Marriott at the Renaissance Center.

I was sitting by the window watching a freighter go under the Ambassador Bridge. This is the most nerve-racking part of the business, a face-to-face meeting with a total stranger to discuss murder. It's a real test of faith. There's always a faint chance the guy might be wired up to broadcast to the FBI.

Barney was easy to spot as he waddled into the bar from the hotel's lobby. His eyes darted around to make sure he wasn't being followed. Guess he hadn't been reading the local papers over the last ten or fifteen years. The Detroit Police Department barely had the budget to catch speeders, let alone slobs like him.

One look at Barney – balding, overweight, mid-fifties – told me he was the real thing. I pegged him as either an impatient heir or a cuckolded hubby. These are our two main food groups.

Just like Wilma has a feeling for impending danger, I have a good sense of character. Barney looked suitably uncomfortable.

He made a beeline for my table sat down across from me. "Rip Hunter?" he asked.

I nodded.

You probably don't remember a television character named Rip Hunter. That's because there wasn't one. My name came from an early 60s comic book – *Rip Hunter ... Time Master.*

My old man collected comics. He didn't drink or smoke like the other kid's fathers did. Instead, he spent all his cash, and most of his time, collecting comic books. They were sealed in plastic bags, and stored in special boxes. He had thousands of them locked up in his closet.

He spent a lot more time with his comics than he ever did with me. To compensate for his lack of attention, he promised that his collection would be "all mine" one day. When he finally died, he made good on his promise.

After the funeral, I went home and lugged all those boxes out to the backyard. We had an oil drum there where we burned the garden waste. His comics made one hell of a blaze.

Yeah, I know, I can hear you superhero fans grinding your teeth.

Fond memories …

Oh well, back to Barney.

I did not offer to shake his hand.

A waiter appeared – the Marriott has a very efficient serving staff – and Barney ordered a diet Sprite with no ice.

I sized up him while he drank. He was a slob, dressed in a wrinkled off-the-rack suit. His comb-over was so bad it made Donald Trump look like Fabio. I could tell he was working up the courage to get around to business. He seemed to be reluctant to broach the subject of murder.

I decided to hurry him along. "So?" I asked impatiently.

"A guy who knows a guy told me that you could help me out," he said, and glanced around.

Christ, I always hate when people talk like they're in the *Sopranos*. I mean who the hell do they think I am – a gangster?

"You need someone killed," I said in my quiet, no-shit voice.

He nodded. "My uncle, but more importantly, I need something of his."

"What? Like an ear or a finger? Sorry, I don't do souvenirs."

"No, nothing like that. I need a book."

"Sure, I'll pick you up the latest *Harry Potter* at Barnes and Noble."

"It's one of his books. A first edition of *Moby Dick*."

I leaned in. "So it has to look like a robbery?"

"That's right. The book is worth a fortune."

"I know. I watch the *Antiques Roadshow*. Why don't you just hire a thief?"

"Because my uncle is a cheap, lying prick."

Ah, the loving relative. Barney had that distinct whiff of desperation. He was the uneasy heir, terrified that he would be cut from the will. His uncle might decide to leave everything to his cats instead of his nephew.

Barney slid an envelope across the table.

"Here's ten to get you started."

I didn't touch the envelope. "I don't get out of bed in the morning for less than half down, which is twenty five thousand." I looked at him severely. "You're fifteen thousand short. Didn't Brett explain our payment policy?"

"He did, but I don't have the full twenty five right now. Once I have the book, I'll clear at least sixty and pay you the rest of your fee. I'll even tack on an extra five if you carry me." His voice slid up to an annoying whine which made me grind my teeth.

Money is one thing Wilma and I have never been flexible on. It's too easy to get stiffed, and I hate tracking down deadbeat clients to make them dead. It increases the risk. But we hadn't worked in a couple of months, and things were starting to get a little tight. I thought about my mortgage payment. The extra five was just the right amount of incentive.

Against my better judgment, I picked up the envelope and put it into my breast pocket. "Okay, but I'm holding the book. When you sell it, I go along."

"No problem," he said with a sigh of relief.

In my experience, when someone tells you it's "no problem", a problem is just what you're going to have. And it will probably be a big one.

Barney handed me a picture of his uncle. It had been taken at some family event. The old man stood apart from a group of grinning people. He looked like he just drank vinegar.

Among the details I learned from Barney was that his uncle owned a book binding business in Iron City, and lived in a condo overlooking the bay.

"A real classy place," Barney assured me as he gave me both his uncle's home and business addresses.

He wanted the job to be done on a Thursday evening because he bowled in a league in Troy. He would be surrounded by a group of close friends and, more importantly, good alibis.

I asked him to pay for the drinks, and left the restaurant.

Wilma picked me up outside the parking garage next to the hotel.

"Did you get them?" I asked as we turned onto Jefferson.

She nodded.

I picked up the Nikon from the seat between us. It had a long telephoto lens. There were half a dozen high-resolution pictures of Barney seated at the table.

Like I said, Wilma always has my back.

FUCK YOU, WOLF BLITZER!

"Fucking Iron City?" Wilma muttered as she fingered the five thousand I gave her.

"You're not superstitious are you?" I asked her.

What was I saying? Of course she's superstitious.

Things had not gone well the last time we visited Iron City. What was supposed to be a routine job had turned into a running gun battle across three downtown blocks before we made our escape.

Our target had been a pimp who'd gotten too greedy. His stable of girls chipped in to pay for the hit. They wanted it done in a public place to send a clear message to any other 'personal managers' who might come along.

We figured this dick for all swagger and no pomp, but when he saw my gun he pulled one of his own, a big pearl-handled job. He started blasting away. Although his marksmanship was as poor as his pimping skills, we still had to chase him down while dodging bullets. We finally cornered him outside a mini mart, and sold him a ticket for the *Oblivion Express*.

The only thing that had made me nervous was the number of security cameras covering our little war. Our luck held out; the security cams had only gotten fuzzy videos of us. We even showed up on CNN. They dubbed us 'a modern day Bonnie and Clyde'.

Fuck you, Wolf Blitzer.

"He's going to stiff us you know," Wilma muttered, and put the money in her purse.

I showed her a picture of the uncle.

"What's that, a birthday party?" Wilma asked. "From the look on his face, he must really hate his relatives."

"I like him already," I added.

"I don't feel good about this," Wilma said. "No shitting around. We just pop his eyehole. Get it over with fast."

Wilma hadn't "popped an eyehole" in a while. It's her preferred method if the target lives in an apartment. She had it down to an art. She would walk up to the door, knock like she meant it, and place the pistol's barrel right over the peephole. When the victim asked who it was she would pull the trigger, putting a slug straight into his brain.

No muss, no fuss.

Wilma lived in a luxury condo on the river. The view was spectacular, especially at night with the all the freighters going past. However, I couldn't see much because it was raining like hell. The wind raced up the river, making the windows shimmy in their frames.

"We can head up there before lunch, and stay over tomorrow and Wednesday. That'll give us time for a good look around. We do him on Thursday night, and get back here before dinner on Friday," I said.

She turned away from me, and looked at the rain as it battered the window. I thought I saw her shiver. "Iron City is bad for us," she said putting her fingers on the glass. She looked out across the river at the casino on the Canadian side.

I poured myself a couple of shots of her best vodka. Wilma has excellent taste in liquor, and the drink went down smoothly with no edge to it whatsoever. I made a note of the brand – Tito's. It sounded more like tequila than vodka but it was great.

I waited to see if she was going to invite me to stay over. Sometimes she did, but more often she didn't. Which was okay, it's the nature of our relationship. We have no hold on each other. Sex, when we did it, was just to scratch an itch.

I didn't feel like going back out in the rain, and having to find a cab. I was tempted to ask if I could sleep on her couch. However, she was so absorbed in her own gloomy thoughts, I let it go.

"See you in the morning," I said, still hoping for an invitation.

There was no response.

I let the silence speak, and left her brooding by the window.

I had reserved space on the Badger for a round trip across Lake Michigan from Ludington to Manitowoc, Wisconsin. We arrived an hour before the ferry was due to leave. I turned the car over to the attendants who would drive it up the rickety ramp into the belly of the ship. Wilma didn't want to trust her car to another driver, but there was no point arguing about it. We didn't need to draw any attention.

Even though the crossing would only take three hours, I booked us a cabin for privacy. It was better to keep a low profile when you can.

Wilma slipped into the lower bunk, and closed her eyes. I was feeling restless, so I went up on deck as the ferry sailed out of the harbor. The sun was just starting to set. It was a spectacular sight from the bow. A number my fellow passengers clustered near the front and took it in. I headed for the stern where I felt I could get some privacy.

The Badger was the last of a dying era – a coal-powered ferry boat. Its smoke stack belched out great black clouds that swirled over the back deck where I stood. My eyes stung from the cinders carried by the smoke.

Once a fleet of ferries like this one carried people and vehicles between the major ports on the Great Lakes. You could still see the rails sunk deep into the wood of the deck where train cars once sat.

Interstates killed off most of the ferries in the early 1960s. However, the Badger survived because it saves a lot of time if you're heading into the Midwest. By sailing straight across, you don't have to drive around the south end of Lake Michigan. It also means you avoid the traffic going through Chicago. That can shave hours off a trip west.

I lined up in the restaurant to get a burger and fries. The water was calm, and I could hardly feel the boat rock. Somewhere deep in the ship came the faint thudding of the engine.

The burger was tasteless, but I didn't have that much of an appetite anyway. Wilma's gloomy mood was contagious, and I found myself sinking into it. I could feel an unshakeable sense of impending doom.

I should have walked away from the job when Barney didn't come up with the full down payment. With all that was to follow, that would have been an extremely wise thing to do.

Two nights later, I copped a taxi at a self-serve gas bar on the outskirts of Iron City. We'd left Wilma's car in the hotel's garage, and taken a city bus into the suburbs. The station was large and busy, everything we were looking for.

Gas stations like this always have excellent CCTV systems monitoring the pumps to discourage the gas-and-dash crowd. They would also have a few cameras covering the front entrance and the cashier's cage, but they usually didn't include the washrooms around back. It's the perfect dead zone as far as camera coverage is concerned.

Wilma followed a cab driver, and clocked him outside the men's washroom. She dragged the body inside, and locked the door. That would give us at least an hour to get the job done.

Wilma handed me a dusty baseball cap along with the driver's keys. She slid into the back seat of the cab to make the scene look more natural, and it was hi-ho, hi-ho, off to work we go.

I would like to come up with some romantic description of Iron City but, in reality, it's a shit hole. When the last steel mill shut down in the mid-90s, all that was left was filth and crime. Detroit is the City of Light compared to this place. Drive down any street, and you instantly sink into a deep depression. Boarded up or burned out buildings litter every block.

Iron City citizens trudge along its streets with their heads bowed as if they're afraid to face the shame of what their community had become.

While I drove, Wilma prepped. The prospect of killing someone had perked her up a bit. She had a nicely matched pair of Kimber Solo pistols. Short and lightweight, each Kimber had a .9mm punch. They fit nicely into custom carbon fiber inserts hidden inside her purse.

She'd picked up a family pack of them at a gun show in Virginia. Though neither of us is what you might call a gun nut, we love gun shows. They're the last bastion of gun powder capitalism, where Second Amendment rights rule over any kind of common sense.

In our line of work, we go through a lot of guns. We have a hard and fast rule about them. We only use a gun once, and then toss it. Or, better still, leave it out for some local gangbanger to find so when the police pick him up, forensics matches it to our kill, and the poor schmuck gets condemned to life in prison, or the needle.

That's Darwinism for you.

Anyway, about once a year, we take a road trip down south to do the gun show circuit, and pick up our supplies. The further south we go, the less paperwork and fewer questions.

God bless the National Rifle Association.

This time out, I was also packing a Kimber – a Super Carry model. It's a big gun, easy to conceal and designed to blow huge holes in things.

I pulled the cab into the parking lot behind the target's building, and parked it next to a garbage bin. There were a lot of guest parking spots available, but what the hell. We were in a taxicab, and they can stop wherever they damn well please.

We'd already scoped out the apartment building, noting security cam locations as well as all entrances and exits. The apartment was on the fourth floor, so we could easily use the stairs. Not only did that promote good cardio, it meant we didn't have to depend on elevators. Using an elevator after you've killed someone is always a bad idea. A breakdown while trying to get away will gift wrap you for the cops.

Even though there was a peep hole in the door, we decided not to "eye hole" the old man. We needed to get the book, and there was a pretty good chance it wouldn't be sitting on the coffee table. In that case, Barney's uncle would have to get it for us before we killed him.

It was mid-evening, and we were pretty certain he was home. To make sure, I made a quick jog down to the garage in the basement. Conveniently, each parking space was labeled with a condo number.

That morning, after checking out his condo, we'd driven by his book binding shop. There was a grimy old boat of a Lincoln in the alley next to it. I figured it had to belong to him.

I was right. The Lincoln filled the parking space corresponding to his apartment number. He was definitely home. It was time to drop by and punch his clock.

Although it was a pretty good building, the stairwell had a distinctive fragrance of urine and damp cement. As we climbed the stairs to the fourth floor, I could felt my sphincter clench. This was usually the time I questioned the wisdom of my chosen profession.

If I worked on an assembly line at Ford or GM, I would know exactly what to expect every day. In contrast, each of our hits is an "undiscovered country" to quote Shakespeare, and *Star Trek*. A hit can go smoothly – knock on the door, the victim answers, and then BLAM. On the other hand, it might get bat-shit crazy – the target refuses to open the door, and starts blasting away with a shotgun. You just had no way of telling.

15

Our cardinal rule was to hope for the best, but prepare for chaos.

When we finally reached the fourth floor, I pushed open the fire door and looked down the corridor. It was empty, and the thick-pile carpet would help deaden the sound. We slipped into the hallway. As the stairwell door closed behind us, I thought I heard sounds coming up from below.

Wilma moved to the door of the old man's unit and picked the lock with her electric rake. The dead bolt slid back with a soft click and we were in. I eased the door shut behind us. Wilma had her gun out and moved quietly down the hall toward the livingroom.

I screwed the suppressor onto my pistol, although I didn't think I'd need it. Mahler thundered at a volume that told us the walls were well soundproofed.

The old man looked up in surprise from the book he was reading. He had a pen in his hand and was making notes. I couldn't believe our luck. We'd caught him totally off guard.

Barney's uncle must have been in his mid-80s. His skin was dry and desiccated, with a ruby-colored rash on his forehead. He wore a food-stained plaid shirt and a pair of black fleece warm-up pants. His feet were tiny and encased in a scuffed pair of leather slippers. His soupy yellow eyes were wide in surprise.

He closed the book carefully and set it on a side table. I could see it was a very old copy of *Moby Dick*.

"Is that a first edition?" I asked in my best gee-whiz voice.

He spoke with a soft German accent. "Yes, it is."

"Could I look at it?" I asked politely.

Wilma raised her gun and pointed it at his chest. He picked up the book and handed it to me.

I put my gun away and opened it carefully to confirm the publication date. I had done some online research and found images of *Moby Dick* first editions. I was definitely holding one.

I smiled and nodded to Wilma. She shot the old man in the chest. His mouth flopped open and his body slumped sideways in the chair. She stood over him and put a pair of shots into his head just above the ear.

I took a look around. There was a custom-made, wooden box lined with green felt that was obviously where the book was kept. I put it into its box and closed the lid.

Mission accomplished, I thought in satisfaction.

Then the door was kicked in and all hell broke loose.

However, a burst of automatic weapon fire inspired me to try. I motioned to Wilma to go over the edge.

"You first," she hissed.

I swung myself over the railing and dangled. My heart rate shot way up and my knees lost their strength. I felt my fingers loosening their grip on the railing. I was sure I was going to die.

I rocked back and forth to gather momentum and let go. Things spun around a bit, and I found myself sprawled in the middle of the balcony below. I didn't have time to consider my good fortune before Wilma landed next to me.

She immediately went to work on the balcony door with her lock pick. I figured we might have a few seconds before Mutt and Jeff discovered we weren't up there.

Wilma got the door open just as we heard boots crunching broken glass on the balcony above.

One of them shouted, "Shit!"

It wasn't going to take them long to figure out where we'd gone. Moving quickly through the dark condo, I peeked out into the corridor, which was reassuringly empty.

There were shouts from upstairs and the pounding of feet.

We ran down the hall and into the stairwell on the opposite side of the building. I was counting on them using the other stairs, the one they'd come up.

Since there was a good chance they'd stationed someone in the lobby to keep watch, we went down to the first level of the garage, and then ran up the ramp into the back parking lot. Keeping the cab's headlights off, I pulled away. There was more gunfire and one of the side windows blew in. I gunned it out into the street.

I dropped Wilma back at the hotel and she picked up our car. Heading west out of town, I passed a few malls. I found one with a good-sized parking garage and abandoned the cab on an upper level. I jogged down a few ramps, hoping the baseball cap would obscure my face on the mall's security cameras.

Wilma picked me up outside Macy's a few minutes later. She headed south.

"What the fuck was that all about?" I gasped.

"Trouble," she muttered, "and you only got ten grand upfront." She made it sound like it was my fault.

Of course it was. I'd forgotten another one of our cardinal rules – always get half the money up front.

"Promise me we'll never come here again," she sighed.

HIBERNATION IN SUNSET

After all the excitement in Iron City, the trip back was quiet and uneventful.

We debated whether or not to take the ferry and finally decided that it probably didn't matter. If they were after us, a watery grave was preferable to a shallow one in the woods somewhere.

How had it all gone so bad?

Wilma's spidey sense was still buzzing. She kept glancing nervously in the rear view mirror.

"We need to have a little talk with that treasonous fuck," she said through gritted teeth.

Barney Rubble *was* a treasonous fuck. It looked like he'd sent along another hit squad to kill his uncle.

What did he expect, that we would we kill each other and leave him free and clear to collect his uncle's estate? I wondered if he had stiffed the other guys on the down payment as well.

When we got back to Detroit, Barney was going to have some "splaining" to do.

We passed the hours planning which vital parts we would remove when we caught up with him. I favored toes while Wilma preferred fingers. Fingers or toes, it didn't really make much difference. When we were finished with Barney, he would never be able to count to twenty again.

It was prudent to lie low for a while and figure out our next move.

Over the years we had set up a couple of safe houses for ourselves just in case something ever went wrong. This certainly qualified for the going wrong department so we headed to our closest hidey-hole.

Sunset, a straight run up the coast from Ludington, was a quiet little town with great beaches that stretch on for miles. The population increases ten times with the influx of tourists during the summer, but goes into hibernation after Labor Day. So there were no other cars on the road as we drove along Main Street. We stopped at the 24 hour Glen's Market on the outskirts of town to pick up a few groceries.

We had a modest home on a quiet side street and visited several times a year to keep our cover intact. To our friends and neighbors, we were just another upper middle class couple from Detroit.

It was just after midnight when we finally got to the house. I was fairly certain we hadn't been followed.

"Good morning," I said from the carport where I was changing the lawnmower plug.

Our next door neighbor, Molly Parsons, worked for the Sunset Sheriff's Department. She was getting into her car – a sweet little green Austin Healey. She looked over in surprise.

"Hi, Fred. You guys up for a few days?"

Molly knew us as Fred and Bernice and believed we were the owners of an antique business in Bloomington Hills.

"Yeah, we took a few days off to get the place ready for winter."

Wilma joined me in the driveway and casually handed me a cup of coffee. Her usually cold blue eyes were sparkling. She gave Molly the perfect replica of an open and friendly smile.

"Molly, why don't you drop by for dinner tonight and we can catch up?"

"Sorry, Bernice. I'd like to, but I have an all-candidates meeting."

"How's the campaign going?" Wilma asked.

We'd noticed election signs on front lawns when we drove in. Molly was running for sheriff against the town's police chief, Kenton Sharpe. I'd met Sharpe a couple of times. He was an asshole.

"It's been a bit of a grind, but I'm having fun," Molly said.

"Well, you'll make a damn fine sheriff, Molly," I said in my best neighborly voice.

"We'd be happy to put a sign on the lawn and I'd like to make a contribution to the campaign," Wilma added.

Molly smiled and opened the trunk of the Healy. She pulled out a lawn sign.

"I'll put it up once I finished cutting the grass," I said.

"And I'll drop the check in your mailbox." Wilma continued to smile blissfully, which gave me the creeps.

Molly propped the sign up against the side of our house.

"And how are you guys doing?"

"Well, business is a little off because of the recession, but nothing to worry about."

Molly smiled encouragingly.

"Do they still have pizza at the Villager on Friday nights?" Wilma asked.

She casually maneuvered the conversation away from us. The less information Molly had the better. She had a reputation as a tenacious investigator and had solved a couple of fairly high-profile cases in the past year. We really didn't need her taking too hard a look at her next door neighbors.

Molly shook her head. "I really don't see what all the fuss is about. I think the pizza there sucks."

"I have to disagree with you," I replied. "We love a good pie and The Villager makes a fantastic one."

She got into her Healy and started it up. The car sounded rough, like it needed a tune-up. Molly must have been riding it hard and putting it away damp.

"Next time," she called over the noise. She drove off, leaving a trail of light blue exhaust in her wake.

It was nice having a cop for a neighbor. That meant the low-life types would stay away. Not that they would discover anything if they did happen to break in. If you looked in any ground floor window, it would look like a normal home. Wilma had hired an interior designer to give it a nice personality, complete with tasteful furniture and framed family photos on the wall.

I wondered whose family it was.

Our weapons cache was secured in a sealed vault behind a false wall in the basement. We kept it stocked with a good selection of large and small arms along with plenty of ammunition.

Wilma's encrypted laptop was hidden behind a panel under the kitchen sink. Even if it was somehow discovered, it would not boot up unless a USB drive with a unique key code was inserted before it was turned on. If anyone attempted to turn it on without the key code, a golf ball sized lump of C4 under the keyboard would vaporize the machine, and anyone holding it.

I watched as Wilma carefully set the laptop on the kitchen table. She made certain the thumb drive was firmly seated in the USB port. A green LED on the drive lit up indicating that it was properly connected.

However, being the superstitious type I moved out of range when Wilma turned it on. It always pays to be careful.

Wilma leaned down and brought her left eye within a couple of inches of the laptop's built-in camera so the security software could do a retinal scan. The laptop made a happy beep and began to boot up.

You might find this excessive, but extreme caution has kept us undetected since we began practicing our craft. Safe houses, false identities, untraceable weapons, and limited client contact keep us off the radar. Even when something goes wrong, our preparations usually minimize the damage.

Law enforcement agencies around the world depend on security cameras as a valuable tool. So do we. Over the past few years we'd hidden a network of wireless cameras inside and outside our Detroit residences. That gave us the ability to monitor them remotely from any location in the world.

We were curious to see if our friends from Iron City had followed us home. Wilma ran through the cameras at her place and didn't see anything suspicious. She did the same for mine.

"Don't you ever pick up your shorts?" she asked as she looked at my bedroom.

With the exception of my boxers, everything seemed to be clean at both places, which was a good sign. Just to be on the safe side, however, we decided to spend one more night in Sunset before heading home.

Besides, neither of us wanted to miss Pizza Night at the Villager.

When I set up the contract, I'd arranged to meet Barney at a motel in Inkster the following Sunday evening. I had deliberately chosen this location because it had excellent security camera coverage. We could hack in and keep an eye on things just in case someone was planning an ambush.

Isn't modern technology grand?

I didn't expect Barney to show up. However, on the off chance the ambush in Iron City hadn't been his doing, I thought we should at least check out the motel.

We headed back to Detroit the next day.

Wilma was in a better mood after checking the cameras that morning. Things were still quiet back home. There didn't appear to be any bad guys camping out on our doorsteps so they probably didn't know where we lived.

That was a good thing.

STRIKE ONE!

The Anchor Motel was at the far end of Michigan Avenue where Dearborn brushed up against Inkster.

It was a rundown pit of a place. Rooms rented by the hour and smelled of spent passion; it was the perfect spot for a clandestine meeting.

Barney and I had agreed to meet there at 10:00 on Sunday night. He'd register under the name of Barney Fife. Wilma hacked into the motel's computer. To our surprise, we saw he'd checked in at 8:00. He was in room eleven.

We sat at a window table in a diner a few blocks away. It had free WiFi and Wilma scrolled through the security cameras around the motel. All was calm and all was bright. We figured it would be safe for me to meet Barney. Maybe he could tell me what the fuck was going on.

Wilma dropped me on a side street a block away and I slipped into the back parking lot of the motel. I knew where the cameras were located so I kept out of their line-of-sight.

I reached room eleven; the door was locked.

I knocked.

There was no answer.

I waited a few seconds and knocked again.

There was still no answer.

I put my ear to the door.

It was silent inside.

That was not good.

I looked up and down the hall before I went to work with my lock picks.

Barney was a real mess. He'd been worked over with an aluminum baseball bat, which had been tossed into the bath tub. His body was sprawled across the bed and his head hung over the side. His face had been smashed in. On the floor, a wide pool of blood was soaking into the carpet.

Whoever had done this started on his feet and worked their way up his body. Barney was probably dead before they reached his head, but that didn't seem to matter. His features were almost unrecognizable.

As shocking as the mess was, all I could think about was the forty five thousand bucks that had suddenly grown wings and flown away.

I slipped on a pair of latex gloves I always carry for special occasions. I began to go through Barney's pockets looking for some clue as to who he really was. There was no wallet or any other ID on him.

My cell phone vibrated in my front pocket and I jumped. My hands were still shaking when I answered it.

"A car just pulled into the parking lot and a guy got out. He's heading your way," Wilma said urgently.

I pulled my gun and walked to the door.

The motel's construction was cheap. I could feel the vibration of footsteps climbing the stairs. Shutting the room door quietly after me, I ran in the opposite direction and ducked into a stairwell at the other end of the hall.

I propped the door open a crack and watched as a figure came down the hall and stopped in front of Barney's room. The light was poor, but I could see he was dressed in expensive clothes. He looked around casually, and then took out a room key, which he inserted into the lock. He entered the room.

A few minutes later, he came out of the room and scanned the corridor. The light wasn't good, but I caught a quick glimpse of his face. He looked really pissed off. I had a fleeting flash of recognition, and then it was gone. But I knew I'd seen him somewhere.

He turned and strolled away in an unhurried manner; a real cool character. I stayed in the stairwell until Wilma texted me that the coast was clear.

"What're we going to do now?" she asked once I was back in the car and we were on I-94 heading downtown.

It was a good question. We no longer had a live client to pay us for a job well done. However, we still had a rare first edition of *Moby Dick*. That had to be worth something.

"Let's see Donald in the morning. Maybe he can help us sell the book."

I kept flashing back on the motel room with the spray of blood on the ceiling and Barney's nightmare of a face.

Whoever had done that to him was even crueler than we were.

Donald Duchée was genuinely glad to see us when we entered his bookshop. I have no faith in anyone, but if I was forced to trust somebody at gunpoint, it would definitely be Donald. He'd been my very first client in the arson business.

The owner of an attractive little antiquarian bookstore just off the main street in Ann Arbor, Donald had specialized in rare first editions. He did big business with university faculty and wealthy clients. However, he'd overextended himself on some Shakespeare folios, and faced a severe cash-flow problem. That's where I came in.

He had carefully skimmed off the most valuable of his first editions and moved them into safety deposit boxes. Once he had the cream of the crop squirreled away, I did a Ray Bradbury on his store. The result was one of my most spectacular jobs. Books burn really well. People are still in awe of that fire.

The insurance settlement was huge due to the many rare editions that were supposedly lost in the fire. Insurers are not stupid. The company that made the payout had their best investigators keep an eye on him for months after the fire. But Donald was smart and knew how to play the part of the bereaved bibliophile who had his life go up in smoke. He spent months acting despondent and left the settlement alone, as if it didn't matter to him.

A couple years later, he opened a new bookshop in Grosse Pointe. When he was absolutely certain the insurance company had given up, he began to salt in the first editions he'd locked away.

Without a doubt, Donald was the most intelligent person we knew. He was a fount of arcane information – a human Wikipedia. We would go to him with the most obscure fact and he would flesh it out.

Apart from my abilities as an arsonist, I had also earned Donald's undying affection because I pronounced his name correctly as 'Dew-Shay' instead of saying 'douche' like some of his snickering customers did.

His shop was located between the Detroit Country Club and the river. It was on a quiet, residential street. It had once been a house like the others around it, but Donald had converted the main floor into a bookshop. He lived in an apartment on the second floor.

Antique wooden display cases held valuable first editions. Lesser valued books lined the shelves from floor to ceiling. Donald kept his most expensive tomes in a climate-controlled, walk-in safe in the basement.

His store had that distinctive smell of old books and no-limit credit cards.

Donald wasn't in the front of the shop when we entered. Security cameras followed us as we made our way to his office in the back. He was hunched over his desk repairing the torn dust jacket from a copy of Steinbeck's *Cannery Row*.

The cover lay flat on a piece of waxed paper. Donald wore a jeweler's loop and was carefully brushing what I assumed was glue along the length of a tear. When he was finished, he slipped another piece of waxed paper over the repair and set a heavy dictionary on top of it. He pulled off the loop and extended his hand.

"How wonderful to see you both," Donald said.

I shook his hand and he took Wilma's in his and kissed it. If anyone else had done this, I am sure she would have torn his ears off. But, like me, Wilma had a soft spot for Donald.

A long time ago we had tried to pin down his age. His face lacked the creases that came from a life of worry and woe. He had to be at least in his mid-sixties. Wilma thought he could be as old as seventy five.

He wasn't handsome; he was distinguished. His long gray hair still had a hint of the black it had once been. His face was elegant and he radiated a sense of authority. The only flaw in his features was acne scars that pitted his regal cheeks. I imagined this little defect made him even more fascinating to women, like a dueling scar.

Not that I had ever seen Donald with a woman, or in a duel for that matter.

When we could not determine his age from his physical features, we tried to pin him down with cultural references. Time and again he eluded us. He could discuss the aesthetics of 80s new wave music or the influence of 30s swing with equal knowledge. We finally gave up.

"How's business," I asked.

Donald shrugged. "Well, the market's down and that's always a challenge. The internet has kicked the hell out of bricks and mortar shops, but reputation still counts."

It also didn't hurt that he was one of the most respected antiquarian book dealers in the country.

"I've been thinking about retirement. A couple of more years of this and I'll have enough socked away to spend the rest of my life on a beach reading," he continued.

"We might have something here that could help move your retirement up a bit."

I set the box on his desk. He opened it and removed the copy of *Moby Dick*. He screwed the jeweler's loop back into his right eye. Turning the book over, he began to examine it.

"There's a bit of wear on the spine. Some rubbing on the front board." Donald set the book down on the table and opened it. "It's from the A lot. First edition, first printing."

"The 'A' lot?" Wilma asked.

He held it up and pointed to a circle engraved on the front cover. "This circle was only on the first printing of the book. The publisher, Harper and Brothers, only printed a few thousand copies in 1851, and many of those were destroyed in a fire in 1852. After the fire, they printed much larger quantities, but these first copies, or A copies, are the most desired by collectors."

"How much is it worth?" I asked him.

He frowned at the greed that underlined my question. "I have customers right now who would gladly pay between $70,000 and $80,000 for a copy in this condition."

As tempting as it was to ask Donald to sell it for us, the sale of a rare item like this would bring attention. We didn't need any more of that right now.

"Can you keep it for us for a few days?"

Donald smiled. "It would be a pleasure. I can do a more thorough examination to establish a more precise value for you."

"Please don't mention to anyone that you have it," Wilma said.

He nodded, looking like a child who had just unwrapped a very special Christmas present.

COUNT EYEGORE

We drove over to Dearborn and checked into the Hyatt next to the Fairlane Center.

I was beginning to be concerned about the expenses we were racking up on this job. Between the cost of the ferry, meals, and hotels, we had already spent almost $600, not to mention all the ammo we'd used. That cost between thirty and fifty cents a round.

I was at the point where I thought we should just walk away from the entire affair. We still had the book, and I was sure Donald could sell it for us after things settled down. With luck, after he took his share for brokering the deal, we'd get nearly all of our regular fee. Perhaps even a little more.

That only left a couple of killers who probably considered us a loose end. This job already had enough stress without having to deal with aggressive competitors like them. Unfortunately, we'd have to get on top of things before we could make a graceful exit with our money. That meant we were going to have to find out who killed Barney. To do that, we'd have to find out who Barney really was.

Therefore, we'd have to break another one of our cardinal rules: never contact a client after the job was finished and the bill had been paid in full.

It would be bad for business if it got around that we came back to clients for additional cash after the contract was finished. That was a serious breach of our ethics, and just too sleazy for words.

However, I was going to have to make an exception. Brett Maverick would certainly know who Barney was. I regretted breaking another rule, but we couldn't afford to stumble around in the dark when there were bad guys after us.

The face of the man in the hallway outside Barney's motel room popped into my head. I knew that face. I tried to remember where I'd seen him before. My brain began to ache from the effort.

Wilma ran through the security cam footage from the outside of the motel. She grabbed a frame and dropped it into Photoshop. She frowned. The resolution was too poor to get a clear image of his face. The car he'd driven was not clear either. We could only make out that it was a dark sedan, which could've been anything from a Chrysler to a Toyota.

Even though we used code names to keep our business discreet, I knew finding Brett Maverick wasn't going to be much of a challenge. He was a public figure. Any kid growing up in Detroit in the early 1970s would have recognized him.

Although thirty years older and not wearing his white face makeup when we met, I instantly made him as Count EyeGore, the host of *Chiller Horror Theater* on Channel 7. Each week he would rise from his plywood coffin. Turning to the camera, he would arch his eyebrows and say, "Welcome to Transylvania."

Indelible memories of rattling chains, spooky music, and clouds of dry ice fog filled my head as I sat across from him and pretended I didn't know who he was.

It was also common knowledge that in real life Count EyeGore was actually Channel 7's wacky weatherman Bert Lampree. Even though the Count had been off the air for fifteen years, Bert still continued to do the weather every night.

Local weathermen don't make a pile of money, so Bert was struggling trying to afford both his twenty-five-year-old girlfriend and his harpy of a wife. Mrs. Lampree was burning through their savings by donating them to one televangelist after another.

When he was at the end of his rope, Bert sold one of his classic wooden boats to get the money to pay us.

He was hosting a fundraiser for Children's Hospital when we took Mrs. Lampree into their two car garage and put her behind the wheel of her VW Beetle. I ran a piece of garden hose from the exhaust pipe and Wilma started the car. I'm sure she fell asleep dreaming of the glory that was to come.

Bert got a lot of sympathy from the local press because of the tragedy. There was even talk of bringing Count EyeGore back on Saturday afternoons.

Bert was a changed man when he came to pay me off. His life had completely turned around. He had a new spring in his step, likely put there by his girlfriend, and the Viagra he was getting from an online pharmacy.

I was really sorry I was going to have to intrude into his perfect world.

MRS. LAMPREE'S BEETLE

I almost ran into Bert's new squeeze as I was sneaking around the back of his house.

She came out the side door and got into a car that I recognized as the late, lamented Mrs. Lampree's Beetle. I approved of Bert's taste in women. The girlfriend was gorgeous. She whistled a happy tune as she passed by. It sounded like the sixth movement in the symphony of the satisfied.

Bravo, Bert.

I slipped into the hedge and waited patiently for her to drive off.

Vampire bats carved out of foam rubber hung from the ceiling of the master bedroom. Instead of being filled with expensive furniture, the bedroom had been decorated with Styrofoam tombstones and a plywood coffin, which I recognized from the show. It was the perfect ghoul's paradise.

I imagined all this stuff had been in storage while Mrs. Lampree had still been with us.

It was no surprise to find Bert sprawled across his king sized bed snoring loudly. He'd obviously had an energetic evening.

I reached over and shook his shoulder gently. He rolled away muttering and brought the pair of silk panties he was clutching up to his face.

"Bert," I whispered in his ear.

"Let me keep them, Elka," he sighed as he clutched them tighter.

"Bert," I said louder.

He woke up with a start and looked at me in terror. He recognized me.

"Fuck …"

I held up my hands and crawled off the bed.

"This isn't what you think, Bert," I told him.

He pulled himself up into a sitting position and stuffed the panties under a pillow.

"Yeah, then what is it?" he asked suspiciously.

"I'm not here to blackmail you or anything like that. Our business is finished."

"Damn right it is. I knew I should have worn a mask when we met. You're in my demographic."

"I was a big fan of Count EyeGore," I responded and waved at his props from the show.

"It was hilarious when you added silly sound effects to the movies," I added.

I remembered vividly a decapitation scene in some hoary old black and white film from the 60s. When one of the victims had his head chopped off, Count EyeGore played a track of loud cheering. I laughed so hard I almost choked on my Butterfinger.

Bert was breathing quickly and had started to turn red. He looked like he was having a coronary. I needed to get him calmed down.

"Very nice looking girl by the way," I said.

Bert nodded his head and continued to gulp air. I gave him a big smile.

"You're one lucky guy," I said.

"Thanks," he gasped.

"Look, Bert, I just need to ask you a couple of questions and I'll be out of your life again," I said sincerely. "I promise."

His breathing started to slow as he got himself under control. I sat down in a chair by the window to give him some space.

"Okay, what do you want?" he asked.

"The guy you sent to me, Barney Rubble. Who was he?"

Bert shook his head.

"I don't know."

I let menace creep into my voice. "You referred someone to me that you didn't know?"

Bert considered the implication of this and tried to back pedal.

"I met him in a bar in Dearborn. We were both pretty drunk. He was complaining about his financial situation and how his uncle was going to cut him out of his will."

"And you mentioned that you might know someone who could help," I said coolly.

I felt like killing Bert right there and then. He had stupidly referred a total stranger to me. I no longer felt guilty about invading his privacy. If Wilma had been around, she would have popped him.

But I was still a fan. I couldn't whack one of my cherished childhood icons, no matter how much of an asshole he'd turned out to be.

"I was just trying to help. I told him the number you gave me. You know, in case I knew someone who might need your particular services. Then I called you. He seemed like a nice guy. I thought I was doing you both a favor."

I sighed. I had given him the number of a throw-away cell. A good recommendation from a satisfied customer was worth gold in our business. Bert was just trying to do the right thing. He had just sent the wrong kind of client.

"So, are you going to kill me?" Bert had real fear in his voice.

"I should," I pulled my gun to emphasize this. I held it in my lap.

"So what else can you tell me about him? How was he dressed?"

Bert thought for a few seconds.

"He was wearing a red shirt with a number on the breast pocket and he had a small bag on the bar beside him."

He was really trying to be helpful now.

"Did you see what kind of car he drove?"

Bert shook his head.

"Sorry, I left before he did."

"Anything else then?" I asked in frustration.

"He had a round bag on the floor next to his stool."

"How big?"

Bert drew a circle in the air in front of him. From its circumference I could see it was about the size of a small volleyball. I recalled that Barney said he bowled in a league. Now I could see it – the numbered shirt, the round bag at his feet. It likely held his bowling ball. The small bag on the bar in front of him probably contained his bowling shoes.

"I wish I could remember more," Bert said anxiously.

I put my gun away.

"You've been a big help, Bert," I told him.

I walked to the door.

"Are you going to come back?" he asked fearfully.

"Nope. Not unless you invite me to the wedding," I said over my shoulder.

I shut his bedroom door before he had time to respond.

When I told her what Bert had done, Wilma wanted me to march right back and put a slug in his brain.

"So he's in a bowling league. That's no help. There are only a few hundred bowling leagues with a couple of thousand members in the Detroit area," she said bitterly.

"I think we can narrow it down. Barney told me he bowled in Troy on Thursday nights. If he's in a league, there's going to be a record somewhere. His team wears red shirts." Like a doomed ensign in *Star Trek*.

It turned out there were not that many teams bowling in Troy on Thursday nights. We got lucky real quick. Barney and his team won a championship last year. The Troy Bowling Center had a picture of their team – the Red Devils – posted on their website.

Barney was third from the left and caption under the picture identified him as Thomas Grande.

He was holding one handle of the trophy and looked pretty smug. Too bad it took an aluminum bat to wipe that look off his face.

"We need to find out all we can about Grande," I suggested.

Wilma nodded and got to work.

AND NOW LET US PREY

The Cadillac Building towered over the park where I was sitting.

Inside the building were the offices of the Detroit Planning and Development Department, which was an oxymoron if I ever heard one. Detroit appeared to be in two stages of development – torn down and about to be torn down. When the auto industry collapsed in the middle of the decade, it took most of what was left of the city with it.

When I was a kid, Detroit was an exciting place. I would come down from Flint every summer and stay with my grandparents. This was back in the mid-1970s. Everyone worked for a car company or a supplier to the automotive industry. My grandfather was a pipefitter at Chrysler. They all had jobs for life.

Or so they believed at the time.

In those days, there were great restaurants and fancy nightclubs all over downtown. Moms and dads got all dressed up for a night out on the town. It was a lot safer then. Kids would go downtown on the streetcar to shop for toys and records at J.L. Hudson's, grab Coney Islands and Cherry Cokes for dinner, and then go see a movie at the Madison or the Fox.

All that remains now are the ghosts of grander times. I looked at the office buildings around me. Half of them were sitting empty. The Blanchard Building, a classic Art Deco style skyscraper from the 1930s, was surrounded by hording. It was going to be brought down in a week or so.

I remembered when they imploded Hudson's. The entire city skyline changed in the two minutes it took for the dust to clear. I wondered how long it would take for the twenty seven stories of the Blanchard to come down.

Maybe I'd come watch if we got this mess sorted out in time.

So why was I here? Like a wildlife photographer, I was patiently waiting for my prey to emerge from the building. It was nearly time for lunch and I figured Matilda Barnes would either head for Domino's or, if she were looking for something lighter, to Subway.

Wilma had spent most of the morning researching Thomas Grande aka Barney Rubble. I wondered about the pronunciation of his last name. Was it Grand or was it Gran-dee? Detroit's hippest rock club in the 60s and 70s was the Grande (Gran-dee) Ballroom, though I doubted he was any relation.

We learned Thomas Grande spent his life toiling as a mid-level functionary in the Personal Property Tax Division of the Planning Department. Digging deeper, we found out his personal assistant was Matilda Barnes.

Matilda had a rich life on Facebook, which gave us a lot of information about her. She listed herself as a "devout Christian" and her main activities seemed to revolve around something called the Detroit League of Christ. There were lots of pictures on her page.

She wasn't quite a knockout, but still very pretty. While most of her pictures were taken with her church group, there were a couple where I thought I detected a hint of sexiness. From my experience, religion seemed to do one of two things to a woman. She would either turn into a prude who protected her chastity behind an impenetrable holier-than-thou façade, or she would throw off her religious strictures in a frenzied burst of sexual passion.

Of the two types, I preferred the latter.

Matilda Barnes finally came out of the building around 12:00 and went into Subway.

It was time for me to go to work.

Matilda was standing ahead of me in line. There were a couple of people between us so she hadn't noticed me. I was surprised the restaurant was nearly empty. There was lots of available seating; another unfortunate by-product of the recession.

A couple of years ago, you would have had to fight for a table at lunch in a restaurant like this. Now, many office workers were brown-bagging to save money.

I made a mental note to check my portfolio and sell any fast food stocks I held.

Matilda ordered a tuna on whole wheat and a small soft drink. She found a spot next to the window. If the place had been crowded, I would have asked to share her table. Because it was almost empty, that would look too suspicious. In this situation, I would have to bring her to me.

I sat at a table that was directly in her line of sight. When I was sure she was looking I bowed my head. I spent a minute saying a mock prayer and hoped she would notice.

She did.

As I raised my head she smiled at me. I looked away feigning embarrassment.

When I looked back, she stood at my table grinning down at me.

"Don't be ashamed," she said and sat down across from me without being invited. She glanced at my left hand and smiled when she saw there was no wedding band there.

Matilda was as easy to read as *Goodnight Moon*.

Half an hour later I was ready to scream. She had not stopped talking, except to take a short sandwich-chewing break. I sat and listened while I finished my turkey sub.

I don't understand why every born-again type is compelled to tell you every intimate detail of what an awful person they were before they found Christ. I prefer the Catholic system where you confess your sins in private to a priest. Not the evangelicals though. They stand on street corners shouting out their faith to total strangers.

That type of religion was just too loud and gave me a massive headache.

I felt a splitting one coming on when Matilda finally rose from the table and announced that she had to get back to work. I swallowed back my pain and went for it.

"I found our conversation delightful," I told her.

Of course we had not really had a 'conversation'. Matilda had talked at me for almost half an hour.

Matilda replied that she had enjoyed our talk as well.

She smiled and there was no mistaking that she was attracted to me. Matilda ran her tongue across her upper lip in a gesture that was hard to miss. She obviously had some devil in her after all.

"Maybe we could continue over dinner tonight," I suggested. "That is if you're not busy."

"Well, I've got choir practice at 7:00, but I'll be finished by 8:00, if that's not too late."

I flashed a smile and assured her it wasn't.

She gave me directions to the League of Christ Church where I could pick her up. She also wrote her cell number on a napkin and stuffed it into my top pocket.

Matilda had obviously learned all her romantic gestures from Meg Ryan movies.

I stood up and took her hand. She gave me a quick hug and a kiss on the cheek. During the hug she brushed me lightly in a way I could not mistake – it told me she would not let religion get in the way of a good orgasm.

"God be with you."

Amen, I thought as she left the shop carrying the remains of her sandwich. I watched her go, her hips swinging in an exaggerated motion. I could feel Little Rip stirring down below in anticipation of the evening. He was excited about the possibility of finding religion.

Motor mouth aside, she seemed like a nice lady. I'm sure we would have some fun. My only regret was that I would probably have to kill her afterward.

While I was mulling over that thought, the most beautiful woman I had ever seen passed the window. She was impossibly tall and blonde and moved with a lithe gracefulness.

All homicidal thoughts danced out of my mind. The brewing headache disappeared as sexual energy shot down my spine straight into my crotch. Little Rip jumped to attention and I bent over at the waist to hide his presence. Even though I only caught a glimpse of her, I knew she was truly the girl of my dreams.

Fantasies filled my head – staring into the deep green pools of her eyes, kissing her high cheekbones flushed with desire. I raced through dozens of my favorite fantasies: the countess and her chauffer, the naughty candy striper, the Turkish dominatrix, the shy concubine. She starred in them all.

I ran from the restaurant. I could not let her get away.

But reality returned.

I had more pressing priorities. I cursed Barney again for getting us into this cluster-fuck. She was a block down the street. Then she turned a corner, and disappeared from my life.

"Wow, what's gotten into you?" Wilma said back at the hotel as I entered her.

I had a tough time keeping it together on the drive back to Dearborn. It was a long way when you have a hard on. I swept into the hotel room and grabbed Wilma. I was so consumed by lust that she didn't have time to protest.

Spontaneous was always her favorite type of sex anyway. We fell onto the bed half undressed.

After we finished, I told her about my lunch with Matilda, and then about the woman of my dreams.

"I just hope you have something left for Matilda tonight," she purred as I ran a hand along her naked hip.

"But she's a good Christian girl." I replied.

"Sounds like she's really repressed. All you have to do is push the right button and she'll probably go nuts," Wilma said as she reached over and pulled me to her.

And then it was Wilma's turn to go nuts.

The League of Christ Church was north of Troy off I-75. It was a long drive from Dearborn. If it was any farther I'd be in Canada. I picked up Matilda in front of the church and we headed to a nearby Fuddruckers for dinner. Throughout the entire meal she kept up a steady stream of conversation. It felt like my head was being squeezed in a vice.

By the time dinner was over I knew every mundane detail of her life right back to kindergarten. I managed to keep an expression of interest frozen on my face the entire time. The only compensation was when her leg brushed against mine several times. It delivered a slight electrical charge that told me she was ripe for the plucking.

We decided to go back to her place.

It was a little awkward at first. I played the part of the slightly shy suitor not certain what to do next. I deliberately wanted Matilda to take the lead and to feel that she was in total control. After all, I reminded myself, I was here for a higher purpose – to learn everything I could from her about the late Mr. Grande.

Matilda moved over next to me on the couch. She took my head in her hands. Her lips parted as we kissed, and I let nature take its course. Before I knew it we were naked and under the covers in her bed.

Regretfully, she did have limits and going all the way was one of them.

"I'm still a virgin," she told me and crossed her legs. "I'm saving myself for my wedding night."

You might think this would be overwhelmingly disappointing. However, Matilda had many other tricks up her sleeve, among other places. When she finished me off, I kissed her down the full length of her body, and used my tongue to get her to take the Lord's name in vain.

Afterward, we cuddled together. It was nearly midnight when I rose to leave. She put a hand on my wrist.

"Do you have to go?" Matilda had a slight note of pleading in her voice.

"Don't you have to get up for work in the morning?"

She frowned.

"It's okay. My boss has been away for the past couple of days and I haven't been able to get in touch with him. If he makes it in tomorrow, he'll have no reason to be angry if I'm a little late."

I didn't think Barney was in any shape to complain about her tardiness.

She slid off the sheets to reveal a body flushed with a rosy glow. She took Little Rip in her hand and gave him a playful squeeze.

That got my undivided attention.

A few minutes went by before she was screaming the Lord's name again. Only this time, I couldn't hear it very well because her ankles were wrapped around my ears.

I wondered if that was what they meant by "speaking in tongues".

Matilda was snoring softly when I slipped the wallet from her purse and took the security access card for her office. I cloned the card in the bathroom and put it back. Nudging her awake, I offered her a glass of water before we started again. The Rohypnol I put in it worked its magic; fifteen minutes later she was down for the count.

I tucked the copy of the access card in my pocket and left. Matilda would wake up around noon with one hell of hangover, and only spotty memories of our night together.

I hoped what she did remember would be pleasant.

MOBY DICKLESS

I left my car in the Greektown Casino garage and walked to Cadillac Square.

There were already businessmen on the streets trudging to work. The sun was just starting to come up and infused them with the warm pink glow of dawn. These were the early riser keeners who believed their absurd dedication to their jobs would give them magical protection when lay off time came.

I blended in with them dressed in my best Joseph E. Banks suit and tie. I carried a leather briefcase to complete the subterfuge. A pair of horn-rimmed glasses and black wig gave the impression that I was just another office drone climbing the ladder to nowhere. I hung the fake access card from a lanyard around my neck.

Most offices today have this wonderful thing called flex hours, which meant I could get into the office really early. The security guard in the lobby paid more attention to stirring his Starbuck's latte than he did to me.

I was reasonably certain that no one else would be in the office when I arrived. After all it was a government department and most public sector workers liked to arrive late and leave early.

I was right; the floor was empty. It took me less than five minutes to find Grande's cubicle. It was a space no larger than a washroom for the handicapped. I stood in the middle of it and snapped a series of digital pictures. Wilma had this great piece of photo software that would allow us to stitch them together into a single panoramic image. Later we would be able to view his office from every angle in high definition.

Barney's cubicle was pretty pathetic. Not only was it repressively small, it was also devoid of any personality. The only thing that showed a real person dwelt there was the same picture of his bowling team that was on the website. It sat slight askew on a metal shelf next to a miniature version of the bowling trophy they had won. A tiny brass plaque on it proclaimed "We Are the Champions".

There were no pictures of any women or children so I assumed Barney was single.

No surprise there.

After I finished taking pictures, I slipped a USB thumb drive into a port in the front of his computer. The drive blinked a friendly green and then automatically downloaded a little program that would give Wilma remote access to his PC.

The top of the desk was covered with a large stack of unopened mail. A bright yellow sticky note was stuck to the phone. On it **SEE ME** was written in large, unfriendly letters. It was signed with a capital "**L**", which I assumed was from the first name of Barney's supervisor.

Earlier I had smeared my fingertips with rubber cement so I would not leave any prints. At some point, Barney's body would be discovered and law enforcement would drop by his office to ask questions. Fingerprints would be taken off his desk and computer. Though mine were in no existing database, I didn't believe in taking chances.

I picked the lock on a metal file drawer.

From my experience, I knew no one hid anything of real value in their office. Any juicy stuff would likely be buried inside his computer, which Wilma was busy downloading right now. When I slid open the desk drawer, I noticed a cheap nylon laptop bag stuffed between his desk and the wall. I pulled it out and opened it. Empty.

I was more interested in the tag hanging from the bag's strap. It had his name and home address neatly printed on it. I snapped a picture of the tag and replaced the bag between the desk and the wall.

His top drawer held a collection of pens, pencils, and miscellaneous trade show premiums. I slid the drawer out as far as it would go. There was a small blue book stuffed in the back. It was some sort of catalogue. A woodcut picture of a whale with *Spring 2012* in fancy script caught my attention. On the bottom of the pamphlet *Bauman Rare Books* was stamped in gold.

There was a strong temptation to take it, but I figured I could find it online somewhere. No need to raise suspicion in case someone knew he had it. I snapped a picture of the cover and closed the drawer. Next I checked the drawer below; it only contained files. I thought about going through them but, like I said, no one keeps anything of real value in their office. I backed out of the cubicle and took one final look around. I chalked it up as a waste of time. However, I did get to spend a lovely evening with Matilda, if that was any consolation.

I vamoosed before the real workers arrived.

My nocturnal activities had been exhausting. When I got back to the hotel, all I wanted to do was sleep. I tried to flop down on the bed, but Wilma grabbed my arm.

"Donald called. He wants to show us something."

She was ready to go. Obviously, she'd had a good night's sleep. I, on the other hand, had spent the entire night selflessly probing Matilda for information. Wilma led me to the shower and when I came out I felt a little more human.

We ran into heavy rush hour traffic on the way into town, and I was happy Wilma had agreed to drive. It gave me time to catch up on some sleep while we crawled toward Grosse Pointe.

"See this little dot?" Donald said as he handed me a magnifying glass.

In my exhausted condition, the text on the page seemed to swim. I managed to get my eyes to focus and looked where Donald was pointing with a small rosewood baton. He was right; I saw a tiny dot under a letter 'r'. However, it could have been anything – a speck of dust or a tiny splash of printer's ink.

"Yeah, I suppose I see it. So what?" I said, putting my head down on Donald's desk. Sleep was the only thing on my mind.

Wilma examined the dot. Donald turned a page and pointed to a spot in the middle.

"And here," he said tapping another tiny dot.

He flipped page after page and pointed out more dots under the text. Some pages had dozens of dots; others had none.

"The dots were put here recently. I took a look under the microscope. If they were there when the book was printed, the fibers of the paper would be compressed from the metal type of the printing press. These dots sit on surface of the paper."

"So what does that mean?" I asked.

"I believe these dots were added after the book was printed," he replied, "and from the lack of fading, I would say quite recently."

"Will that hurt the book's value?" Wilma asked.

"Well, some dealers would definitely count it as defacing and reduce the price."

"Shit," I muttered. "Can you erase them or something?"

Donald shrugged. That probably meant he couldn't and the book would be worth even less if he tried.

Could this get any better?

"It's interesting, don't you think?" Donald said.

"So are ball peen hammers to people who use them," I snapped.

"What are you trying to say, Donald?" asked Wilma. "Why would someone risk hurting the value of the book?"

Donald held up a sheet of grid paper. He'd transferred some of the letters above the dots to it. He had amazing handwriting. Even though done by hand, the letters looked like they'd been typed. I stared at the book, and then at the grid, unsure of what I was supposed to be looking for.

"I think it might be some sort of code. It's very subtle and would have taken a long time to do it," Donald said.

"Can you make sense of it?" Wilma asked.

"Cryptography isn't one of my strengths, but I'll give it a try."

"How long ago do you think the dots were added," I asked.

"Quite recently. I can smell solvents in the dots in the later part of the book."

"Solvents," Wilma said.

"Yes, from the ink in a fine-liner type pen – a Pilot Precise V5 extra fine, if I was to guess. It has a tip like the point of a needle and can make very small marks like these."

This latest disappointment only added to my exhaustion. It felt like the world was pressing down on me. I lay my head down on my arms and closed my eyes.

"So let me understand this," I groaned. "You think we're dealing with a *Moby Dick* code here? I'm not really interested in the Holy Grail."

"Oh, I don't think it's anything like that. However, someone went to a lot of trouble to hide something," Donald said.

I thought of Barney's uncle and the two guys who had tried to kill us. Then once again, I thought of Barney's pulped face.

"If I had to guess, I think that whatever the hidden message is, it has to be something more valuable than this book," Donald said as he drummed his fingers on the cover, "or else why take a chance and hurt its worth?"

"Can you make sense out of it?" I asked.

"Well, I do love an intellectual challenge," he said with a broad smile. "I'll certainly try my best."

We left him feverishly transferring letters from the book to the grid.

"We should go over to Grande's place and take a look," Wilma said as soon as we were on the road back to Dearborn.

"I can't," I pleaded. "I need sleep."

Wilma nodded and drove us back to the hotel. When we reached the room, I staggered to the bed and fell face down. I must have fallen asleep before my head even hit the pillow.

When I woke up fourteen hours later, it was too late.

BLAMMO!

Barney lived in a house south of Grand River in Novi.

It was mid-morning when we arrived. His street had a deserted suburban look. All the moms and dads were at work and the kids in school.

Just in case there were some Neighborhood Watch types peeking out their front window, we pulled into Barney's driveway like we belonged there. Wilma took a **FOR SALE** sign from the trunk, and I hammered it into the middle of the front lawn.

This was a bit of theatre for anyone who might be curious about two strangers prowling around inside Barney's home. They would assume we were real estate agents. And just in case someone was taking down license plate numbers, Wilma had lifted a couple of plates from a car parked at the Fairlane Center and put them on her Ford.

I raked the lock and opened the front door.

I wasn't worried the cops might be watching the place. Even if they had found Barney's body, the overworked Detroit PD probably hadn't figured out who he was yet.

The cops hadn't found Barney's house, but somebody else had. It had been tossed by experts. The living room furniture had been tipped over and the upholstery slashed. A drift of cotton wadding spilled out of the sofa cushions, covering the carpet like snow.

I pulled my gun and went into the kitchen. The refrigerator had been pulled out from the wall and tipped over. Its door was torn off and the contents were scattered all over the floor. The room stank from a pool of sour milk.

This went way beyond just searching the place. It was pure vandalism. They had even cranked the furnace up to hasten the spoilage. It was at least ninety degrees in the room. Wilma turned down the thermostat, and opened the window over the sink to let the some of the heat out.

"Well, they certainly weren't subtle about it, were they," Wilma muttered as she stepped carefully trying to avoid the mess.

I went to check the basement.

Same thing – boxes thrown everywhere, their contents spread all over. Dozens of jars of homemade preserves had been thrown and shattered. Streaks of tomato sauce had dried like blood on the walls.

My throat went dry when I saw what was hanging from the furnace. A pair of wires was attached to the thermostat control. They ran out of it and down to a small package taped to the gas supply.

Jesus!

I ran for the stairs, shouting for Wilma to run.

We were four blocks away when the house blew. A few seconds after the blast, we felt the concussion rumble through us like a freight train. The sound of car alarms swelled up from the direction of the explosion.

Thank God I'd kept up on the tools of the trade.

Though we prefer the intimacy of guns and knives, sometimes high explosives were necessary in our line of work. Barney's furnace had been rigged with a simple device wired to the thermostat. When the temperature fell below a certain level, the furnace would kick on and complete the circuit.

Then BLAMMO. The house and its occupants would be blown halfway across the state.

"This is nuts," Wilma grumbled as she started the car and headed back to I-96.

There was a great chorus of sirens heading toward the scene of the blast guided by the pillar of black smoke that had once been Barney's home.

"I think it was meant for us. That's why the heat was up so high. They figured we'd come in and turn it down before we started searching," I said. "They're one step ahead of us."

"Think they know about the book?" Wilma asked.

My stomach roiled. "Donald," I said.

She floored it and we headed toward Grosse Pointe.

Wilma hacked into Donald's security system at the shop. The exterior cameras displayed a view of the quiet street. There didn't appear to be any cars full of thugs in the immediate vicinity.

There was no one inside the shop. Unfortunately, there were no cameras to show us his office or the basement.

Wilma used her laptop to override the back door alarm.

We were going in blind.

Donald had a pretty heavy duty lock on the back door. It took me almost thirty seconds to open it. I looked over my shoulder, suddenly paranoid that I was being watched. The shop backed onto a patch of woods which were part of a golf course. Hidden among the trees, Wilma watched my every move through the scope of her trusty high powered rifle.

"Donald?" I called softly.

No response.

I stepped into his office and turned on the light.

It looked the same as it had yesterday, with two notable exceptions. His chair lay on its side on the floor, and there was a large smear of blood next to it.

The copy of *Moby Dick* and his grid were gone from the desk. I felt damp fingers of dread move along my spine.

Down in the basement, the large safe was securely locked. An angry looking red LED above the dial told me I wasn't going to get into it anytime soon. I hoped the book and the grid were locked inside, but I suspected they were with Donald. Most likely he'd been snatched by the same guys who had killed Barney.

It was now time for recrimination.

We should have headed to Barney's house right away. There was a good chance we might have gotten there first. We could've ambushed Barney's killers. Now they had Donald, and the book.

It's time to even the odds, I thought as I left Donald's shop empty-handed.

Wilma was not happy when I told her what we were going to do next.

"Iron City?" she said, "Haven't you had enough of being shot at?"

"If these guys have the book, we lose."

"Yes. Well then maybe it's time we did. We just let them have it."

"Somehow I don't think they're going to let us walk away from this."

Wilma couldn't argue with that logic. We were screwed either way.

"Next time, just get the full amount up front," Wilma spat. "That will spare us this kind of bullshit."

No ferry this time. Instead, we drove into the Upper Peninsula, then headed west on Highway 2 out of St. Ignace. The road was dangerous after dark, but I didn't care. Running the car head-on into a moose was preferable to whatever the thugs who were after us had in mind.

We avoided moose entanglements and arrived in Iron City just after lunch. I'd managed to get a little sleep in the car. Wilma did not. She was in a particularly bitchy mood.

"Great," she snapped. She was looking out the side window, not at all pleased with what she saw. "It smells like shit."

I had to admit that she was right. The air had an unpleasant sulfurous odor from decades of steel smelting. The mills were all gone now, but the smell lingered on. No amount of rain and scrubbing could completely get rid of it.

"Let's check into a hotel and nose around," I suggested.

Wilma shook her head and said sarcastically, "Why not. We might as well burn up what's left of the down payment. I can while away my time staring out the window and watch the air eat the paint off my car."

I picked up the *Iron City Star*. The old man's murder was still on the front page, though it had moved down below the fold. I read the story, but didn't learn anything new. The police had a shot of us careening through the streets in our stolen cab. They suggested the "Bonnie and Clyde killers" may have been responsible. They identified the dead man as Walter Randolfo, the owner of a local book binding business.

Since we wouldn't be going back to Randolfo's apartment, I suggested we take a closer look at his book bindery.

Wilma finally lost it.

"Are you out of your fucking mind?"

"Why not? There's a chance that no one else looked there," I said.

"I think that's pretty remote. I'm sure the cops did. And those guys who were shooting at us probably did."

"Maybe, but I think it's worth taking a peek."

She looked at me as if I had three eyes. She was about to say something, but held it back. When she finally spoke, her tone was deadly serious.

"I've been really careful with the money I've made. It's invested well and I've gotten a really good return, considering the market. So you know what I'm going to do?" She didn't wait for my answer. Not that I had one. "I'm going to the airport, catch the first flight out of here, and retire to wherever the plane lands."

Wilma gave me a look that told me she was extremely serious.

I tried to imagine what life would be like without her covering my back. Probably much shorter.

"Look, I know you think I fucked up by not getting all of the down payment up front …"

"Yes, you did," she snapped. "The only reason we've stayed out of trouble for all these years is by sticking to our rules. Client negotiation is *your* responsibility and you made a mess of it. And now look where we are."

She was really angry now. I decided not to push it. Wilma could be impulsive – and she carried guns.

When I left the hotel room, she was on Expedia looking at flights.

I went for lunch.

Wilma was gone when I came back to the room. She hadn't left a note, not that there was anything else to say. She had left her pair of Kimbers in the top drawer of the bedside table. Her car keys were in there as well. This was a sure sign that she had made good on her threat.

Wilma did not make empty promises.

I briefly considered heading for the airport myself. Maybe I could catch the same flight as Wilma.

She was right of course. I was being stupid. This was probably not worth the risk, but if there was a slim chance, I had to go for it. We had managed to stay off the radar by minimizing our risks and following our own set of rules. I had fucked it up.

Now I had no choice but to try and make it right.

Randolfo's book binding shop was located in a part of Iron City where no one should go after dark. It was midnight, and I had been watching the building for the past hour. Other than a brief distraction when a hooker took her John into a doorway across the street for a quick blow job, nothing else happened. I decided it was safe.

Of course, I was wrong.

There was a side door off the alley next to the shop. The lock was cheap. I popped it in about four seconds and slipped inside. After Wilma left, I had an uncomfortable sense of impending doom. Without her, I felt vulnerable.

I used my flashlight to look around. I was in a large workshop. Bindery tools lay on a long wooden work bench to my right. Some sort of hand operated letter press was pushed against the wall off to the left.

I had burned down a few print shops in my time. Their owners had been hurt by the rise of digital media. No one wanted to print anything anymore.

Some of the equipment in the shop was familiar to me. There was a two color press and some bindery machines. The large paper trimmer in the center of the shop looked like something from a medieval torture chamber.

The walls were lined with shelving that held paper and binding supplies. There was a row of ledger books along one shelf.

If I was Walter Randolfo, what would I have to hide and where would I hide it?

The answer came to me in a flash of insight. I started toward the shelf of binders. I had almost reached it when someone rapped on my skull with a blunt object.

I went down for the count.

BEN CANDLE

I looked in horror as the blade of the paper cutting guillotine continued its merciless descent toward my wrist.

I braced for the searing agony that would follow the amputation of my hand.

The short guy, an evil dwarf if I ever saw one, grinned at me as he kept his fingers on the buttons operating the machine. The blade was an inch from my arm.

There was a brilliant flash and the tall man staggered away from the electrical panel, shielding his eyes as it exploded in flame. A pair of booms from a high powered rifle filled the shop a millisecond later. A third bullet smacked the wall next to his head and he ran for the door.

The short guy pushed the buttons on the machine, but without electricity it had stopped functioning. A fourth shot chased him from the room.

I took the opportunity to faint.

"I can't believe you left my car in this neighborhood at night," Wilma bitched as she released me from the cutter.

She tested the sharpness of the blade. "That would have cut your sex life in half."

I massaged my hand, feeling the pins and needles that came along with the increased blood flow. She pulled me to my feet, and picked up the rifle from where she had left it leaning against the cutting machine.

"Come on, let's go."

I broke free of her grip and ran to the shelf containing the ledgers. I took them along for some light reading.

I dropped the ledgers on the backseat while Wilma stored the rifle in a hidden compartment in the trunk.

I wondered why Wilma had come back for me. I never asked and she never told me. Every time I look at my right hand, I'm very happy she did.

I could tell from the expression on her face that she was glad to put Iron City squarely in her rear view mirror.

Instead of spending more of our dwindling supply of dollars at the Hyatt, we headed for another of our safe houses. This one was located in a high rise apartment building south of the state fairgrounds. We leased a unit on the fourteenth floor. For security, the apartment was rigged with hidden cameras and an alarm system that would send us a text message if anyone tried to enter. We store guns and other tools of our trade here. It had two bedrooms and lots of secret panels. There was also enough C4 planted in the walls to take the top of the building off. Needless to say, we felt safe there.

The ledgers went back to the 1960s. They contained records of bindery orders. Occasionally, one of them would be listed in some sort of shorthand or code which I could not even begin to figure out.

The most interesting discovery I made was a brown accordion file jammed inside the 1973 accounts book. It was stuffed with bills of lading going way back. It looked like Randolfo had been receiving shipments from all over the world. I noticed a couple for large shipments from New Zealand and one from Australia. In both cases, they were from a company called Beach Associates.

I went line by line through each subsequent ledger. After a couple of hours I paused on a name I knew. It was in the 1986 ledger.

The name I recognized was Ben Candle.

"Ben Candle? He must be dead by now," Wilma said.

Randolfo had listed seven more transactions with Ben Candle in the next few pages.

In the notes column beside each entry, he had printed an **A**. I back checked through the previous ledgers and found a number of entries all with an **A**.

"Do you think it's drugs?" I asked.

"Well, if it's the same Ben Candle, he controlled them, along with just about every other type of crime in the city during the 70s and 80s."

I remembered reading about his exploits when I was growing up. One of the *Free Press* reporters had even written a book about him a few years ago. It was a best-seller around Detroit.

As a criminal, Ben Candle had no equal. He ran gambling, drugs, and prostitutes, and made a fortune off autoworkers who had limitless amounts of money to blow in those days. The local Mafia left Candle alone after he tossed a pair of their enforcers off the top of the Ambassador Bridge just to show what a hard-ass he was.

Wilma went online to look up Candle and found a lengthy Wikipedia entry on him.

"He went to prison in 1989 for conspiracy to traffic and served twelve years. There's nothing after that," she said.

"So he might still be alive?"

"Well if he is, he'd be pushing eighty."

"I'll give Del a call and see if he can find out for us."

You could not get very far in our business without having at least one contact in the law enforcement community. Ours was Detective Sergeant Delbert Newell of the Detroit PD.

Del was a weasel, but we had his nuts in a vise. Once upon a time, he'd been a bad boy. We know where the body is buried. We also have some incriminating pictures tucked away just in case he ever tries to double cross us.

I arranged to meet him for pizza at Supino in the Eastern Market.

Since Del was a vegetarian, we split their Red, White and Green pizza with extra spinach and capers.

Del had a face that looked like the business end of an axe blade. His eyes darted around furtively while we ate. When he finished, he brushed the spare olive oil off his fingers by combing them through his thinning blond hair. He was what you might call hygienically challenged and I always tried to sit down wind from him.

Despite the fact he was a vegetarian, he still managed to weigh over three hundred pounds. He laid his massive hands on the table and I noticed his finger nails were filthy and broken, like he had clawed his way out of a grave.

He certainly smelled like he had.

"Ben Candle," he said quietly. "Yeah, I think he's still around somewhere."

"Is he still in the game?"

Del laughed. "He did a long stretch up in Jackson and by the time he got out, the world had passed him by."

"When did he get out?"

"Sometime around 2001," Del replied.

"Is he still on parole?"

"I don't think so." He laughed again. "He must be about a hundred years old by now. His days as a crime lord are long gone."

"Why don't you make yourself useful and check for me, Del." I said.

He picked at a tooth with a dirty fingernail. "Sure, why not. I'll see what I can find out. Call me in the morning." He got up from the table and let out a loud belch. "Thanks for lunch."

I paid for the pizza and walked across to Rocky Peanut and picked up a big bag of mixed nuts. I was thinking about what Del told me. He was right. Candle might be ancient, but in his day he had been the most intimidating gangster this city had ever seen. And that's saying a lot.

Detroit had a very long and proud history of organized crime going back to the 1930s when the Purple Gang controlled the liquor traffic along the river and killed anyone who got in their way. Even Al Capone didn't want to take them on, so he made a deal to be their muscle in the Motor City.

When the Purples ended up in the big house, it created a vacuum and the resulting gang war lasted for years. Finally 'Black' Bill Tocco emerged as the undisputed mob boss and ruled over Detroit until he died in the late 70s.

Things changed and gangsters like Ben Candle started to whittle away at the edges of the Mafia, taking a lot of the ghetto action from them. In time, even Candle's era passed and ruthless crack gangs like the Chambers Brothers took control of the city.

Del was right; Ben Candle was most likely history.

MOBYZILLA

Wilma was out when I returned to the safe house after meeting with Del. I was kind of relieved.

Things had been so hectic lately and I could use an undisturbed nap.

Maybe it was the pizza, or the mixed nuts, but I had a really vivid and disturbing dream.

I was standing somewhere downtown looking up at the skyscrapers when they started to shake. Something big was coming toward me. Office towers began to sway like trees in a strong wind. I turned to run away, even though I sensed it was hopeless. I knew that whatever was approaching was coming for me.

As I looked up at the Blanchard Building, it began to crumble. Large pieces of stone and steel crashed into the street around me, but I couldn't move.

There was a piercing noise, like a metal file was being dragged across the strings of a cello. It was the sound Godzilla makes. I recognized his distinctive roar from the dozens of films Count EyeGore showed on Saturday afternoons.

The building continued to shake. I expected to see the giant Nipponese lizard eyeing me, but it wasn't Godzilla; it was a gigantic white whale. Standing on its tail, it pushed the building down on me.

It threw its massive head back and laughed.

"I don't think they have the book," I told Wilma.

We were eating a delicious salmon she had poached in white wine. I'm convinced that if Wilma had not found a satisfying career in contract killing she might have been a celebrated chef like Gordon Ramsay. She had the culinary skills and the killer instinct for it.

"Who doesn't have the book?" she asked.

"Those two guys from Iron City. Why threaten me with amputation if they already had the book? They could have just killed me."

Wilma cocked an eyebrow. "I think you're delusional. You heard them wrong. After all you were under a lot of stress."

I flashed back to my hand trapped under the blade and had to agree with her about being stressed.

"Still, they were searching for the book. I'm sure of it."

"If they don't have it, then who does?"

That was a question I would have to sleep on.

The next morning Del and I met at the food court in the lower level of the Renaissance Center. The place was crowded with office workers from GM grabbing a quick bite before heading into their towers.

Del set down a cup of organic green tea. "Ben Candle's no longer on parole. It finished seven years ago."

I took a big bite of my Egg McMuffin.

"No one seems to know where he went," Del continued. "After he got out, he apparently stayed clean and met all his parole terms. I pulled the PO reports and took a look. Candle was a model citizen."

"What about a job?" I asked.

"That's where things get interesting." Del took a sip of his tea. "He worked as a janitor at the Blessed Resurrection Church over on Mack. You know the place, it's near Elmwood."

I didn't know the church, but I knew the area — street after street of discount liquor stores and burned out houses. Definitely not a high rent neighborhood. If we had to go over there, I would be sure to pack some extra bullets.

"According to his sheet, Candle would be eighty three years old if he's still alive."

I nodded.

Del pointed to the Egg McMuffin in my hand. "Those things will kill you."

I looked at it and smiled. "Ronald McDonald will just have to get in line if he wants a piece of me."

After leaving Del in the food court, I took the elevator up to the hotel level. For some reason, the hotel lobby was two stories above street level and you had to take an elevator down to the main entrance. As I waited for it to come, I glanced around and saw her again – the girl of my dreams from the other day.

She was standing right beside me.

"I hate this thing. It's way too slow," she said and smiled.

I loved how she dragged the word out so it became "waaaaay". It made the electricity race down my spine again. Little Rip was standing at attention and I was glad I wasn't wearing tight jeans.

"Here for a visit?" I asked casually.

"No, I'm working."

Since she was dressed in a pair of designer jeans with a loose white cotton top, I assumed she was not some sort of high powered executive type.

The elevator door opened with a ding and we got on. There were no other passengers in the car and I decided to break the few moments of uncomfortable silence.

"What type of work do you do?" I asked.

"Most of the time I model, but I'm trying to break into acting. My agent got me a couple of days on a training film for Delphi."

The elevator door started to open, and I decided to go way out on a limb. "Look, if you've got any down time, I would love to show you around."

She smiled again, in a way that can only be described as radiant. "Sure, I'd like that."

She took out a business card and scribbled a number on the back.

"That's my room. My cell number is on the front. We'll likely go late tonight, but I have a short day tomorrow. I should be back here by four."

I borrowed one of her cards and wrote a number on it. I keep a few throw away cell phones for business. They are cheap to buy at Walmart, and completely untraceable.

I arranged to pick her up at 5:30 the next day, and watched as she got into a chauffeured minivan with dark tinted windows. I gave her a quick wave as the van drove off.

Afterward, I realized I had not introduced myself or even asked her name.

I looked at her business card. It had been printed on an elegant linen stock. 'Cinnamon Slade' was embossed in the center with a single phone number on the lower right-hand side. I flipped it over and saw her room number printed in neat letters.

Little Rip was singing an aria. He was looking forward to settling into a new home.

I shifted around in the passenger seat so my erection would not be so obvious.

"You look particularly smug," Wilma said. "What's up?"

"Nothing," I replied. "We need to go see Lightbulb."

Without another word, she turned right onto Jefferson and headed east toward Mount Elliott.

LIGHTBULB LUGOSI

Lightbulb Lugosi was hunched over a small fire in an empty lot on the corner of Charlevoix and Beaufait.

He was drinking from a large bottle of Colt 45, the champagne of malt liquors.

If you needed to get the 411 on what was happening on the mean streets of Motown, he was the guy. Del had introduced me to Lightbulb a couple of years ago. Lightbulb was still under the mistaken impression that I was a cop.

He smiled when we pulled up and toasted me with his bottle. I explained what I was looking for and his smile got even wider.

"Ben Candle. What you want with that old motherfucker?"

I showed him a hundred dollar bill.

"Two things, Lightbulb. Is he still around and, if so, where can we find him?"

"Well he was still alive last week when I saw him over at the Blessed Resurrection Church. They got some kind of seniors' center there and he was sitting by himself off in one corner. They say he was a tough motherfucker in his day. He owned this town."

I shrugged like this was old news and passed him the hundred.

Wilma leaned over, "What's he look like?"

Now, it was Lightbulb's turn to shrug.

"He's old, wrinkled, and has very little hair. What the fuck do you expect?" He laughed and slapped the side of the car.

"This him?" I asked handing over a picture Del had given me.

It was from Candle's PO file and had been taken about twelve years ago. Candle was looking straight ahead and holding up a number for the camera.

His face was gray, like he had spent a lot of time indoors. He had that hangdog posture of a con. However, it was his eyes that really got me. They were totally lifeless.

I shuddered when I had first looked at them.

We wasted almost three hours parked on Elmwood watching the Blessed Resurrection Church before we spotted Ben Candle.

Lightbulb was right. Candle was a wrinkled old man. He moved slowly, shuffling his feet carefully like he was walking on a large patch of ice. We held back a couple of blocks to trail him. He went into a corner store, and came out a few minutes later carrying a small plastic bag.

It was dark by the time he entered a small, decrepit house. The structure was the only survivor on its block. The other homes had either been burned up or torn down. It resembled a single crooked tooth in a ravaged mouth.

We parked down the block. The street was gloomy and somewhat sinister because scrappers had stolen all the streetlights off the poles for their aluminum. Scrap metal thieves were like termites in this city. Entire houses collapsed because they chopped up the joists to steal the copper pipes and wiring.

Candle had not bothered to lock the front door. There was a single light on in the back of the house. I assumed that was where the kitchen was since I could smell tomato soup coming from that direction.

We moved quietly along the hallway. Our biggest mistake was not having our guns out.

The kitchen was empty; a pot of soup was coming to a boil on the stove. The stove was in rough shape; the oven door looked like it was ready to fall off. However, the rest of the kitchen was surprisingly tidy. All the dishes had been washed and were neatly stacked on the counter.

Ben Candle stepped into the hallway behind us.

"I don't suppose you're from the City, are you?" he asked in a deep voice.

I did not have to turn around to know he had a gun pointed at us.

"We must really be slipping when an eighty three year old gets the jump on us," Wilma growled under her breath.

We turned around. His gun looked gigantic in his tiny, skeletal hand. It was a canon of a .44 magnum, a real 1970s piece. From shine on the barrel, I could tell it was well looked after. He flicked the gun toward the living room and stepped back to let us pass.

"No, you ain't from the City. I can see that."

He sat in an overstuffed chair and put his feet up on a stool. The gun did not waver. We planted ourselves on a stained couch facing him. I could feel bugs crawling around inside the cushions.

"You two have that killer look about you. That what this is? Some old score that needs settling?"

I shook my head, "No, nothing like that. We just need to ask you about Walter Randolfo."

"Wally? He's dead. Someone put a bunch of bullets in him. I read about it in the *USA Today* last week."

"So you knew him," I said.

"Yeah, I knew him. A long time ago."

"You were in the trade together?"

"The trade? What the fuck's the trade? You mean drugs? Wally didn't have nothing to do with drugs."

A strange look passed across his face, like a curtain had been pulled. He set the gun down on the floor next to the chair and got up. He sniffed the air.

"Is there soup?" Candle said as he headed for the kitchen.

I exchanged a what-the-fuck look with Wilma and scooped up his gun. There were no bullets in it.

We followed him to the kitchen.

"Tonight's movie night I think. They're going to show the one about that little girl with the devil in her." he muttered.

"What about Wally," I said. "Tell me about Wally." I tried to get him back on track.

However, it was obvious Ben Candle was riding the dementia express. Wilma took his hand and led him back into the living room. I turned off the stove. When I joined them, Candle was sitting passively in his chair staring off into space.

"I'll stay here with him," Wilma said, still holding Candle's hand. "Why don't you take a look around?" She added, "See if you can find any ammo for the .44 while you're at it."

I went upstairs and started to search.

One of the necessary skills we developed in our craft was the ability to figure out where people hid things. There were only so many places: in fake walls; under false floorboards; behind dummy electrical receptacles. I used a circuit tester on each of the second floor sockets and found a fake one in the small bedroom. I shone a small Maglite into the cavity. There was a fairly good-sized space stuffed with several cloth bags. I took them out and replaced the receptacle cover.

There was also a false floorboard in the bathroom. Under it was a bundle of cash wrapped in plastic, a nickel plated .38 special, and several boxes of ammo, including bullets for the .44.

Things were looking up.

When I returned to the living room, Wilma was talking to Candle, who continued to look like he was in some sort of catatonic trace. I passed her the box of .44s and she loaded the magnum. I went into the kitchen and poured the soup into a bowl on the counter for the cockroaches to enjoy.

There was a loud, flat bang from the living room.

I glanced in to see Ben Candle slumped in his chair with the magnum hanging out of his mouth. His brains dripped from the wall behind him. Wilma patted his knee tenderly. If she was capable of it, I would swear she was showing some sort of emotion. There might have even been a tiny tear in her eye.

I opened the front door. The shot had not attracted any attention, but then if a tree falls in the forest …

The street outside was dark and sinister, like our mood.

We drove back to the apartment in silence.

THE STATE OF MITTEN

The plastic wrapped bundle contained $4,567.

Not much to show after a career as the most feared crime boss of a major city. However, finding the money put us back in the black. I put five hundred in my wallet. I would definitely show Cinnamon Slade a good time.

We dumped out the contents of the two sacks onto the kitchen table. There was an address book filled with some sort of code. From the yellowing on the pages, I figured any names in it were people who died a long time ago. I put it aside.

"He said something about whales when you were upstairs," Wilma said quietly as we sorted through his treasures.

"What? Like *Moby Dick*?" I asked feeling a twinge of excitement.

"Maybe. I don't know. He just muttered about whales for a few seconds and then went silent again."

There were several small baggies with a white powder in them, which I assumed was heroin, and a day book with more cryptic writing. Wilma picked up the bags.

"I'll dump these down the toilet."

A few seconds later there was a flush. She carefully washed out the baggies in the kitchen sink and tossed them in the garbage. Meanwhile, I held up an intriguing item. It was a piece of stone about eight inches long. I guessed it weighed about half a pound.

Like the money it had been carefully wrapped in plastic. I could see through the wrapping that it was a chalky gray.

"What do you think this is?"

Wilma looked closely at the rock.

"I don't know. Maybe some kind of ore."

Thoughts of gold or other precious metals did a conga line through my brain under a huge sign that flashed MOTHER LODE.

Wilma took it from me, obviously thinking the same thing. She unwrapped the plastic and bounced the rock in her palm. Finally Wilma held it up to the light and sniffed.

"It smells good."

I put it close to my nose. She was right. It did smell good. It had a complex scent, sweet and rich like a bouquet of flowers.

"Yes, it does," I said and scratched it with a fingernail releasing more of its fragrance.

"What the hell is it?" Wilma wondered.

I shook my head. I had no idea.

"I bet Donald would know."

I thought of the pool of blood on Donald's floor. I shuddered as a goose walked over my grave. I pictured him with his hand jammed under the guillotine while they forced him to decipher the Moby code. Donald might be the smartest guy we knew, but I doubted he would be able withstand much torture. Once they had squeezed what they needed from him, they would chop him up and dump the pieces in a ditch somewhere.

I slammed my fist down on the table. We had to find the guys who had taken Donald and make them pay.

"Fuck this. It's time to go home," I declared. "I'm sick of running away."

If they were still following us, it would be the best way to lure them out. And it might be our only chance to get Donald back in one piece.

If it wasn't already too late.

Wilma and I spent the next hour cleaning up the apartment. As usual, we scrubbed all the surfaces with bleach and bagged up the bed sheets and pillow cases. The apartment was again DNA-free.

Just before we left our hidey hole, Wilma reset the detonators on the plastic explosive. On the way home, we dropped the garbage bags full of sheets into a Salvation Army recycling bin.

It was nearly 2:00 when I walked in my front door. I had a few hours to kill before I picked up Cinnamon. I called the Whitney House to make a reservation for dinner. Hopefully she would be impressed with its old world elegance. The wood paneled walls and high ceilings, coupled with a delicious dinner and fine wine, would be the perfect setting for seduction.

Wilma called around 4:00.

I did not mentioned Cinnamon Slade or our date.

"I have an idea about the rock," she said.

Before I could ask her what she had in mind, my other cell rang. It was the one that I had given Cinnamon the number for.

"Give me a second," I told Wilma and put her on hold.

I picked up the other phone with a sinking heart.

"Hi there." It was Cinnamon. "Sorry, I didn't get your name yesterday."

I told her.

"I'm sorry, Rip, but my day got a little backed up. Could we take a rain check?"

I tried to keep the disappointment out of my voice. "Sure."

"I've got one more day's work on the video and my agent called to ask if I could stay over and do a photo shoot. That won't start until Saturday so I'll have the entire day off on Friday."

I cheered up. It looked like I wasn't getting the high jump after all. It was just a temporary postponement.

Another twenty four hours of delicious anticipation.

"That sounds fine. I could pick you up before lunch and we could make a day of it."

Christ, I was starting to sound like a character from Jane Austin.

"Wonderful." She sounded sincerely excited. "Let's do it."

Joy was returning to my life. Little Rip was only going to have to wait another day.

Crap – I remembered Wilma was still on hold.

"Sorry," I said when I was back on the line with her.

She had had an epiphany and it was called Samantha Stevens.

I had only met Samantha Stevens twice; once when she hired us to kill her partner and a second time when she paid me for our services. That was four years ago.

She and her late partner had started Golden Labs. They had built a thriving business providing medical evaluations for insurance companies and chemical testing for industry.

As the business grew, so did their animosity toward each other. Samantha saw her partner as petty and narrow minded, with no vision for the future.

He refused to let her buy him out.

However, they did have a substantial buy/sell agreement in the event of a partner's death. It would pay a large chunk of cash that the surviving partner must use to purchase the deceased's share of the business. There was also a key person policy that would pay $500,000 to compensate for any financial loss that might be caused to the business by an unexpected death. At the end of the day, Samantha would be the sole owner of Golden Labs with a lot of cash for her expansion plans.

When Samantha decided it was time to get her partner out of the way she called us and gladly forked over our $50,000 fee.

Her partner died while working alone in the lab a few weeks later. He failed to notice he had accidently mixed two volatile chemicals.

The resulting blast, I understand, was quite spectacular.

Conveniently, Samantha was in Boca Raton at a medical convention when it happened. She faked genuine shock when she was told about her partner's untimely death.

It was the kind of job we loved. All it required was a simple label switch on a couple of bottles.

There was no real investigation. The partner's wife hated him almost as much as she loved money so she took the ample life insurance settlement and gladly sold her share of the lab to Samantha.

Everybody was happy, which made us happy.

Golden Labs had seen better days. The bold illuminated lettering that spelled out the name had faded over the years. The letter **L** in Golden was askew and leaned against the **D**.

When we pulled into the parking lot, I saw Samantha Stevens leaning against the front door smoking a cigarette. I was shocked. When she settled up our bill she had been full of energy and enthusiasm for her business. She was going to do great things now that she was free of the yoke of an unimaginative partner. She had been young, vibrant, and rich.

The intervening years had not been kind to her. I wondered what had happened. I suspected the tough economic times had something to do with it.

She looked as tired and worn as her building. Her silky black hair was now dried-out and streaked with gray. She wore a loose fitting lab coat in a vain attempt to hide the sixty pounds she had gained. Sharp wrinkles spiked from the corners of her eyes, which had faded from their once deep jade color to a milky aquamarine.

I doubted she would recognize me after all this time, but I took the precaution of wearing a pair of thick rimmed glasses and a heavy mustache. I decided to let Wilma do the talking. Wilma spun out a story about finding the rock among her late uncle's things when we were cleaning out his house.

"A hunnerd," Samantha said after Wilma asked her how much to do an analysis on the rock.

When I listened to Samantha speak, it was like fingernails screeching along a blackboard. She had that peculiar Michigan accent I had spent years trying to lose. Her speech was riddled with words like 'tuh' instead of to and 'ruff' instead of roof. Somehow the English language had gotten mangled in the State of Mitten. Linguists claimed it was the result of multiple influences – the influx of southerners, our proximity to Canada, Scandinavian immigrants, aliens from flying saucers, Bigfoot.

She looked uninterested and flicked her cigarette out into the parking lot. Samantha led us inside and passed Wilma a form to fill out, which gave me time to look around. The couch in the reception area looked lumpy; the magazines on the coffee table had ripped covers and were at least three years old. An old copy of *People* heralded "Michael Jackson's Comeback!"

The place smelled like a toxic waste dump. I could understand why she stepped outside to smoke. Samantha didn't want to risk joining her late partner in the ether.

She put the rock in a clear specimen bag and printed out a label on an ancient dot matrix printer. She stuck the label on the outside of the bag and put in a plastic bin along with the paperwork.

"How long do you figure it will take?" Wilma asked.

"Dunno. We don't do rocks here. I'm gonna haf to call in a geologist to take a look. It'll be a couple days at least. I'll call ya."

Wilma thanked her politely. As we turned to leave I thought I saw a glimmer of recognition in her eyes. However, I put it down to my paranoiac nature.

Samantha followed us outside and lit another cigarette.

As I pulled out of the parking lot, I was glad I had put false plates on the car that morning.

"I think she remembered me," I said to Wilma.

"Good, I hope she did. She'll think twice about pulling any kind of double cross."

Wilma was naturally suspicious and firmly believed in the badness of most people.

I suggested we get dinner before I dropped her off. I had a hankering for seafood and we decided on Fishbone's in Greektown. Wilma had Crawfish Étouffée, which she deemed as passable. I had fried lake perch and a big mug of St. Pauli Dark.

"Were you really serious about getting out?" I asked her over dessert.

She dug a large dollop out of her bread pudding and let it steam on her spoon.

"Probability," she replied.

"Probability?" I mimicked.

She frowned.

"Probability. It's working against us," she said and put the bread pudding in her mouth.

"Not necessarily. We take precautions to limit the risk," I protested.

She lifted her eyebrows in an *oh really* fashion and swallowed.

"Doesn't matter. Airlines take precautions and planes still crash."

"But the odds are really low. They fly millions of miles without anything bad happening."

"Tell that to the grieving widows and orphans after their loved ones didn't beat the odds."

"So what are you saying? You're finished?"

She ate another spoonful of the bread pudding, which I remembered was the dessert I had ordered.

"We have a few hiccups in a job and suddenly you go chicken shit?" I blurted in frustration.

Wilma's eyes went cold at this and I realized I had stepped way over the line. The last word I would normally use to describe Wilma was 'chicken shit'.

I was tempted to use the expression 'panties in a knot' but that would have gotten me shot.

I kept my mouth shut for a few minutes and let things cool down. I took her hand in mine. To anyone in the restaurant we would look like lovers in the middle of a serious conversation.

"I'll admit we've had some stuff go wrong, but can put it behind us and go on."

I could tell she was not convinced.

"Let's just get this over with and then we'll see," she said.

Her voice had an ominous finality to it.

Probability was a bitch – and then you die.

HAULING MY ASHES

I picked up Cinnamon at the hotel just before noon and took her to Red Smoke for a barbecue lunch.

It was as crowded as always with lots of Motor City movers and shakers making deals and political compromises. Just another day of selling Motown down the river. However, the food was really good and, from the way Cinnamon tucked into her white chicken chili soup, it was obvious I had made a good choice.

It was a beautiful afternoon. We spent it in Dearborn exploring Greenfield Village. She had a real love for antiques and excitedly pointed out one priceless piece of furniture after another. I was strongly attracted to her unabashed enthusiasm. I began to fantasize about some other things I hoped would make her just as excited.

Later that afternoon, as we walked back to my car, she took my hand. When I opened the door for her she kissed me.

"Thanks for the nice afternoon," she said softly, with a hint of promise that definitely got Little Rip's attention.

In the 1800s Michigan's lumber industry created more wealth than the California gold rush. Ruthless lumber barons systematically stripped the forests in the upper part of the state and created huge fortunes for themselves.

The wealthiest of them all was David Whitney, who built the grandest house in Detroit – 52 rooms occupying over 21,000 square feet. It was opulent and made with the finest materials, including pink granite from

South Dakota that gave the outside an impressive rose color. The Tiffany stained glass windows alone were worth more than the house.

Back in the 80s it was converted into one of the finest restaurants in the country. The Whitney was a place designed to impress. And it certainly achieved this effect with Cinnamon. After we finished our dinner, she slid her hand across the table and rested it on mine.

We had exhausted all our small talk. I had recited my phony biography with just the right amount of sincerity. She complained about the horrors of modeling and high fashion.

"It all depends on whimsy and desire," she told me as her fingers stroked the back of my hand. "One day, you're *that* special type and on everybody's call list. And then the next day, well …"

She let the sentence drain away, looking sad. I suspected she was already on the next day in her career, which explained why she was trying to make the move into acting. She had done a few commercials in New York, but so far she had not made much progress.

"Acting is even more fickle than fashion," she said, in a bitter tone. "At least designers have a sense of style. With acting, you're at the mercy of casting directors and agents."

I had to admit it didn't sound very romantic. She paused, a frown crossing her face. I could feel a horrible confession coming.

"I just want you to know that I'm married," she said.

I nodded and left her space to continue.

"Felix is a nice guy, though he's insecure and it can make him a little crazy."

"Define a little crazy for me," I said.

"Well, there's a twenty year age gap between us. At first I found him charming and sophisticated. He had a great sense of humor. Over the past few years he's become progressively more obsessed."

"He isn't here is he?" I looked around the restaurant.

She laughed.

"No, he's back in New York. But I think he's having me followed."

I almost pulled my hand away – until her ring finger slid suggestively between my second and third fingers.

"Don't look so nervous. I bet you can take care of yourself."

Little Rip took firm control of the situation and began to shut down all outside stimuli except the sensuous feel of her finger stroking mine.

"Look at those eyes," he shouted, "they're deep pools of desire ... And how about those lips ..."

With impeccable timing, the waiter brought the check and I paid it. All I could think about was getting the hell out of there and back to Cinnamon's hotel. From the way her finger moved and the look in her eyes, I knew we were thinking the same thing.

They say anticipation always trumps reality. They are not always right. Having sex with Cinnamon Slade blew my expectations out of the water.

It started with a playful tease. As we entered her room she began to strip. She pushed me back on the bed and pulled off her blouse. I caught a glimpse of a lacy black bra before it disappeared, revealing the most perfect pair of breasts I had ever seen. She unhooked her silk shift and let it drop to the floor. The thong she wore matched the color of her bra. And then it was gone as well.

Naked, she leaned over, unzipped my pants and tugged them down. She looked at me with a blissful smile and I knew I was going to happy land.

Cinnamon was more than promise; she was pure, unbridled passion. At first she took control, astride me, grinding her hips, head arched back, moaning, as I squeezed her nipples and tried to match her thrusts.

Next, I was on top while she screamed and thrashed, bunching the sheets around her as I bore down. She had a hunger that made me curious about how long it had been since she had been laid.

Finally, when the overwhelming lust was vanquished, we faced each other and gently rocked into another orgasm. When it was over, I lay in her arms and fell asleep.

It had been one hell of a first date.

Later I crawled from bed trying not to disturb her. I left a note on the pillow telling her how much I had enjoyed our day together. I hoped it didn't sound too tawdry, like I was sneaking out on her.

I promised to call her later that day.

A parking attendant brought my car around from the hotel's garage while I sipped a coffee poured from the complimentary urn in the Marriott's lobby. I had put my cell phone on silent. I took it out to check for messages.

"Everything alright at home?" a voice beside me asked.

I felt a firm grip on my right elbow and almost dropped the phone. At the same time, I sensed a second, taller, presence on my left side. I was firmly jammed in between the tall man and the short man. Shorty dug a Glock into my ribs. It was hidden from view by a sweater he had casually draped over his arm.

They walked me to a black Chevy parked out front. The tall one got behind the wheel while the short one followed me into the back seat. He reached around and pulled my .45 out of its special pocket on the inside of my jacket and dangled it between two fingers.

"Careful, that's a priceless family heirloom," I said.

He tossed it out the window.

"So, folks, what's on the agenda? I know a great spot for breakfast," I said cheerfully.

Shorty growled, "I hope you got your ashes hauled really good because from now on it's going to get really painful."

FAREWELL TONSILS

It was not quite dawn when they pulled into an alley off Woodbridge near the river.

It used to be the warehouse district, but was now mostly clubs and restaurants. It was also remote and quiet at that time of the morning.

Lurch came around and dragged me out of the car. Shorty walked over to a pile of construction debris and rooted around. He found a length of two by four and banged it once on the ground to knock off a coating of plaster dust.

While Lurch held me firmly from behind, Shorty walked up and whacked me on the forehead with the piece of lumber.

"Now that I have your attention, let's have a little talk," he said. Then swung the board up and brought it down again. I felt blood on my face this time. The force of the blow temporarily derailed the synaptic impulses in my brain.

Up to this point, I thought the night had gone rather well. I had a nice dinner with the woman of my dreams. I had gone back to her hotel room for some fun and frolic. And I had been stupid and let my guard down. Now I was paying the price.

Shorty raised the piece of wood again. I caught a movement out of the corner of my eye.

Wilma Tasered Lurch. The jolt went straight through him and into me. I felt my entire central nervous system do the Watusi. Lurch and I fell to the ground writhing in the grip of an electric seizure. My head filled with bright flashes that made the entire scene strobe.

When he turned on her with the piece of wood, Wilma calmly shot the munchkin in the throat. His body flew backward and out of my line of sight. In one smooth move, she put her gun and Taser back into her handbag.

"Well that was exciting," she said as she tried to help me to my feet.

I still could not control my muscles and flopped around spastically. She dragged me back to her car which she had parked across the mouth of the alley. Wilma opened the passenger door, pushed me in, and handed me a wad of tissues.

"Don't get any blood on my upholstery," she ordered.

I slumped down in the passenger seat. My teeth vibrated with an electrical hum and I felt like a toaster oven. With every ounce of muscle control I could manage I jammed the Kleenex against my forehead to stop the bleeding.

Back in the alley there was howl. Lurch staggered to his feet. Like a character out of a cartoon, his hair stood on end from the voltage. He slumped against a wall and looked at his buddy. There was a large pool of dark, red blood flowing from the ragged hole that had been punched through Shorty's Adam's apple. Wilma carried a large-caliber pistol and at close range it made quite a mess.

"His battering days are over," she said in a satisfied tone.

"Why didn't you shoot the big one?" I gasped.

"It's the little ones who are always the most trouble. Trying to make up for their inadequacies I suppose," she explained.

She put the car in gear.

I tried to make sense of what had just happened, but in my shattered condition it was impossible. Every nerve-ending in my body felt like a paper cut and my head was leaking all over Wilma's front seat.

She jammed her foot to the floor to put distance between us and the alley. At the next intersection, she turned sharply to the right and my head slammed against the side window. I could see a smear of red where it hit the glass. Nauseating pain shot through me. I slumped back against the seat.

Wilma slewed the car around another corner and gunned it.

"You should have given me time to ask him some questions," I stammered, feeling another nauseating wave of pain.

"He wasn't going to tell us anything," she spat.

I flashed back on Shorty spread-eagle in the alley with most of his throat blown away. I was still tingling from Wilma's Taser, but seemed to have regained control of my limbs again.

"Could you please slow down?" I pleaded. "I think I'm going to be sick."

Instead she speeded up. We were flying north on I-75.

"The rock," was all she said.

Shit. I had forgotten about the rock and Samantha.

Of course that was not too surprising. I had not thought about much the past couple of days, except getting into Cinnamon's pants.

"If they found you, chances are they know about her," Wilma said.

"Fuck. You were following me," I said. "Don't I rate any privacy?"

"They followed the two of you everywhere yesterday. You were so entranced with her you let your guard down. Sometimes you do all your thinking with your little head. Someone has to watch your back."

I thought of the scene back in the alley and was glad Wilma had.

"Next time you decide to take a little R & R, wait until the job is finished."

I couldn't argue with that so I held my tongue and watched the blood drip onto my shirt.

STRIKE TWO!

There were no lights on at Golden Labs when made our first drive by. It was just a little before 6:00 in the morning so that made sense.

Wilma jacked the alarm system and I jimmied the back door. We entered Golden Labs with our guns drawn.

Samantha Stevens lay on her back on a stainless steel workbench. She was dead.

Broken test tubes and other lab equipment were scattered around. Blood sprayed across the ceiling in wide arcs. It looked as if they had given her the Barney Rubble treatment with a baseball bat.

I thought of the pounding the munchkin had given me with the two by four. I was glad again Wilma had killed him.

We searched the lab for the rock. It was gone. The plastic container it had been in was lying on the floor. The form Wilma had filled in was on the floor beside it.

I tried to rub the pain from my eyes and dabbed at the drying blood on my forehead.

We both jumped when the phone rang. Did someone know we were here? We let it ring until it finally clicked over to the answering machine. A man's voice came from the unit's speaker. He sounded desperate.

"Connie, if you're there pick up," the voice said and waited a few seconds.

So Samantha's real name was Connie. Funny, she looked more like a Samantha.

"What the fuck is going on? Two goons showed up at my place last night."

"The geologist," Wilma said quietly.

"Whatever this is about, I don't want any part of it," he continued. "You can have the sample back. Meet me in the parking lot outside the Ford Mansion at 8:30."

I looked at Samantha, eyes open in death, focused on the ceiling.

"And have my fifty bucks or I keep it," he threatened and then hung up.

The Henry Ford mansion was butt ugly as far as I was concerned. Even with all his money it looked as if Ford could not make up his mind what architectural style his home should be. The result was a mish-mash of different influences from early Georgian to Frank Lloyd Wright. What do you expect from a guy whose favorite color was black?

Figuring we would likely have to kill the geologist, we left Wilma's car in the parking lot at the Fairlane Center. The mall wasn't open yet, but there were a number of cars parked on the outer fringes of the lot.

It was nearly 8:30 and the Ford Mansion was over a half mile away. I considered hot wiring one of the cars, but we decided it would be safer to approach the mansion on foot. We began to jog toward it.

The geologist had sounded really scared on the phone. I hoped he was patient enough to wait.

The Ford Estate was on the edge the University of Michigan's Dearborn campus. The only car in the parking lot was a tan Honda. It was almost desecration parking a Japanese car there. Poor Henry would roll over in his grave if he saw it. But then he might have been impressed with its mileage.

A man stood next to the Honda. He was only about five seven, but weighed at least two hundred and fifty pounds. The geologist looked scared and glanced around nervously. We approached through the woods and he did not see us coming.

Wilma stepped into the parking lot. She held a clipboard and appeared very official.

"I'm sorry, Sir, but the house is closed to visitors right now," she said smiling at the geologist who hardly paid attention to her.

"I'm just waiting for someone," he mumbled.

"You can walk around the grounds if you'd like, but please stay away from the river. The banks have been eroding, and we wouldn't want you to fall in."

The distraction gave me time to move up behind him and pin his arms to his sides.

"Samantha's dead," I said in a deep, menacing voice.

"Who the fuck is Samantha?" he cried, wriggling in my grasp.

"Sorry. Connie's dead," I corrected myself.

He slumped in my arms.

"She gave you a rock the other day to take a look at," Wilma said.

He nodded.

"It wasn't," the geologist sobbed in fear.

"It wasn't?"

"A rock," he said.

I almost released him.

"Then what was it?" I asked.

"Whale shit," he gasped.

Something sizzled past my ear and his head exploded. There was no sound of a shot. Someone used a high powered rifle with a suppressor.

What the fuck is going on here?

I had no time to think about it because a second slug slammed into the Honda's rear door between me and Wilma. I let the geologist's body fall. We dived for cover under the car.

As the MythBusters proved on an episode not too long ago, automobiles provide lousy protection from someone with a powerful rifle. However, it was all we had and whoever killed the geologist was not likely to hang around for too long.

Wilma lay under the front axle while I hugged the ground under the rear one.

"What did he tell you?" she asked as we lay there.

"Nothing. He called me "whale shit" and then vaporized."

"What is that, some sort of insult? Like pig shit or something?" Wilma sounded exasperated.

"Odd choice of words don't you think?"

She ignored my question.

"Think he left the key in the ignition?" she asked.

Wilma slid out on the far side.

I heard the door open and then slam. The sound of the engine starting nearly deafened me. I jumped into the back seat and Wilma slammed the pedal to the floor, spraying gravel in a wide fan behind us.

I glanced back at the geologist's body.

We dropped the Honda off in the parking lot of a medical clinic on the far side of the mall. I used Wet-Naps to clean as much of the blood off my face as I could along with bits of the geologist's gray matter. There was still a lot of blood on my shirt and pants, but there was nothing I could do about that. They were ruined.

Wilma took me home. I desperately wanted a shower and a shave. Most of all, I needed some answers. It had been a rough night.

Wilma smiled over at me, "Was she good?"

"Yeah," I groaned.

"You are so boringly predictable. A romantic excursion to Greenfield Village followed by a fancy dinner at Whitney House. I probably didn't even need to follow you," she said.

I had started bleeding again. The cut on my head would likely need stitches and spoil my movie star looks. I leaned my head back and pressed a hunk of Kleenex to the gash.

"Well, at least we've gotten rid of half of them," I groaned.

Wilma smiled at the memory of Shorty lying in a pool of blood in the alley.

She shook her head.

"Get real," she said. "There has to more than just those two. They smell like lackeys to me."

That made me think about the man I'd seen in the motel hallway. Was he behind all this? And where had I seen him before? I knew him from somewhere. I wished I could remember where.

IF IT BLEEDS, IT LEADS

It came to me when I was showering off the blood and gore.

His name was Felix Frame.

I had seen him not that long ago on one of those late night fashion magazine shows on cable. Felix Frame, the fashion impresario – the king of the New York designers. I even owned one of his sports jackets, a black silk one that always made an impression.

He was rumored to be in his 60s, but good plastic surgery and Botox kept him looking eternally young. I remembered the story was about his spring collection. He strutted down the catwalk and flipped his gray pony tail arrogantly to the applause of the audience. I got the impression that he was a real prick.

I jumped out of the shower and shouted at Wilma to look him up online.

Meanwhile, I went to work on my wounds. Liquid bandage took care of the weeping cut on my head. I rubbed in a tiny bit of foundation makeup over the scratches and bruises on my face.

Thank god I was a metrosexual.

When finished, I looked like a reasonable facsimile of a human being. I changed into jeans and a tee shirt and joined Wilma in the living room.

My home was located in East English Village, northeast of Grosse Point. It was on the kind of quiet suburban street where strangers got noticed quickly. My neighbors believed I was a business executive who traveled a lot. They kept an eye on the place for me.

It was a two storey brick house with three bedrooms and two and a half baths. After I bought it, I had one of the upstairs walls knocked out to make a master bedroom that covered half the second floor.

Like our place in Sunset, the basement had a false wall where I kept my more precious possessions. Since we were strictly a cash business I had a large Chubb safe down there. It held almost three hundred thousand, just in case going on the lam was necessary.

Wilma said my house gave her the creeps and it was too much like the one she grew up in.

She paced the living room nervously, staying away from the windows even though they were made of ballistic glass and could stop almost anything short of a .50 caliber round. The outside doors were reinforced with armor plating and had heavy duty hinges to support their weight.

I had paid an unscrupulous contractor cash to install them along with other special modifications, including an escape tunnel in the basement behind the washing machine. The tunnel ran for fifty yards and ended up inside my neighbor's garage.

I had no problem dealing with the contractor. He did the work by himself at night and I helped out when I could. After six months, the work was done and so was the contractor.

His wife had paid us to make something bad happen to him. A week after he finished my renovations a trailer full of concrete pipe flattened him at a construction site in Livonia. As a result of this horrible accident, the state tightened up construction safety standards.

There is a silver lining in every cloud.

Wilma was monitoring the security cams outside my place. "I can't believe they don't know where you live," she said.

I flopped down on the couch and turned on the television. Channel 4 news was just starting and the lead story was about a murder in the parking lot of the Henry Ford Estate.

If it bleeds, it leads is the mantra of Detroit television.

A blue sheet covered the body which the reporter identified as "Gerald Moore, fifty years of age, from Pontiac. Mr. Moore was a geologist and taught at Wayne State University. His car had been stolen in what police believe was a robbery. The abandoned car was later found near the Fairlane Center Plaza."

"Why do you want to know about Felix Frame?" Wilma asked.

"He's the person I saw in the hallway outside Barney's room."

"I doubt if he was staying there. According to Bloomberg, he's worth close to a billion."

"So why was he interested in a middle manager at Detroit's Planning and Development Department?"

What connection they could logically have to each other? From the way Barney had dressed, he did not have much fashion sense. Not unless red bowling shirts were the new black.

Maybe Frame was doing a property deal in Detroit and needed someone to grease the wheels for him. But that did not make a whole lot of sense. Detroit real estate was worth maybe fifty cents an acre, so anyone coming to town with money to invest would probably get a blow job from the mayor.

"Did you find anything unusual in the files we took from Barney's computer?" I asked Wilma.

"Just routine stuff. His career was less than fulfilling."

"Still, there has to be some reason why a big deal like Felix Frame would be interested in Barney Rubble's welfare."

"So why don't you go find out?" Wilma suggested.

"Oh yeah, and where do you think I start?"

When she told me, I had a mixed reaction.

THAR SHE BLOWS

I called Matilda Barnes the next morning, explaining I had been out of town on business and would love to get together with her that evening.

She sounded a little petulant at first, but became more enthusiastic as the conversation moved along. We agreed that I would pick her up after work in front of the Cadillac Tower.

Matilda had obviously been crying. "Mr. Grande's dead," she said and began to sob.

"Mr. Grande?" I asked.

"The man I work ... worked for."

Barney Rubble had been found. Funny, there hadn't been anything on the news about it.

"That's terrible." I reached out and took her hand. "Was it an accident?"

"No, he was murdered and do you know what's even worse?"

Worse than being murdered? Let's see ... How about being ground up and fed to hogs ... being forced to sit through a Glee marathon ... or Windows Vista?

I kept those responses to myself and just shook my head.

"Somebody killed his uncle in Iron City as well," she sniffled.

"That's tragic," I said in my best consoling voice.

"And he was such a nice man."

"His uncle?"

"No. Mr. Grande. I didn't know his uncle." She added, "The FBI came to the office today."

While the Federal Bureau of Investigation might strike terror into the hearts of evil doers everywhere, I knew from experience they were basically inept. It was a good thing they were involved. The Bureau would certainly muddy up the investigation.

The FBI was a joke in my experience. J. Edgar Hoover used the media and his political clout to create a myth of a crime fighting machine that used technology and high standards to get their man. In reality, the FBI was a dismal failure. Their computer systems were antiquated and their investigative methods produced little in the way of results. They were famous in law enforcement circles for investigating crimes to death.

Anyway, the Detroit field office was pretty much focused on terrorism and spent most of its time in Dearborn camped outside of the Islamic Center. Unless the murders of Barney and his uncle led back to al-Qaida, the Bureau would quickly lose any interest.

"So was it like a family vendetta or something?" I asked.

"No one is saying anything."

Matilda began to sob again. I suggested we have dinner at Sinbad's.

I chose fish and Matilda had a burger. Much to my surprise she also had a draft beer which she downed in a couple of massive gulps. I ordered her another, wondering what she would be like when she was drunk. Hopefully, her tongue would be looser.

Three quarters of the way into the second draft her words began to slur.

"Did I tell you he was a nice man?"

Matilda held up the mostly empty draft glass and got the waiter's attention.

"Yes, you did."

"Well, he could also be a real prick."

Her choice of words shocked me. She was, after all, a proper church-going gal.

"I guess we all have our bad sides," I said.

She blinked hard as if trying to figure out which one of the two images she was seeing was the real me.

She pointed a finger at the wrong me. "It was usually after his bowling team lost a game. He would be nasty for days."

She swallowed the final dregs of beer as the waiter set down another glass.

"But he could also be really sweet. When my mom was sick he got me a little teddy bear from Hallmark. It said **HANG IN THERE**."

Matilda started to blubber and I looked around nervously to see how much attention we were attracting. The waiter brought over the check, making it obvious that it was time for us to leave. I took her arm and guided her out of the dining room.

Back at her place she pawed my clothes off in the front hallway. By the time we reached the bedroom her tongue was so far down my throat I thought it would set off my gag reflex.

A sober Matilda Barnes was a wildcat in bed; a drunken one was a wolverine. She clamped a hand over each of my ears and forced my face down into her nether regions.

Lubricated by beer and my tongue, she let it all hang out. I hoped her apartment walls were thick enough to withstand her barrage of profanity. Luckily it did not take too long to get her off. When she came, she flew off the bed like she had been jolted with ten thousand volts.

I joined her on the floor and held her close. After a minute I felt her mouth moving down my chest. I did not object.

Once she was finished, I rested my head between her breasts.

"I needed that," she purred.

"You must have had a hard week," I said tenderly.

She looked confused for a second.

"With your boss's murder and all."

She sighed.

"You don't think it would have had anything to do with his work, do you?" I asked.

"I don't think so," she replied. "We really don't do anything that someone would kill us over. Mostly we take proposals and summarize them. Right now, with the way things are, there isn't a whole lot for us to do. We're lucky if we have a few hours of real work in a day. The rest of the time we just try to look busy."

She giggled as she remembered something.

"I remember one day I came back from lunch and found him on the internet."

"Looking at pornography I suppose," I said.

"No," she said with a laugh, "he was on a website about whales."

"Whales," I said nonchalantly.

"Yeah, like sperm whales and humpbacks." She ran her tongue along the inside of my thigh. "Don't you find whale names really sexy?"

I had to admit that I hadn't until that moment. Matilda must have found them a real turn on though. I felt her hand crawl down my chest and across my belly. Little Rip tried to get my attention and Matilda helped him along.

Whales?

"Like Moby Dick?" I whispered in her ear.

"See, didn't I say whales are really sexy?" She giggled again and wrapped her hand around me.

Well blow me down and shiver me timbers.

And she did.

I wondered how Matilda reconciled her Christian beliefs with the kind of casual sex she enjoyed having with me. Other than her declaration of "saving herself for marriage" she didn't seem to be interested in anything but sex; albeit of the non-penetrative kind.

I took a close look at her bedroom for the first time. An entire menagerie of stuffed creatures stared back at me. At some point she had also lit two votive candles which made a teddy bear look extra sinister in their flickering glow.

She had some sports trophies on the upper shelf and a pennant from a softball tournament. The framed picture of Jesus staring down from the wall made me feel uneasy. He seemed to be leering at her naked body which was curled up next to mine.

I was still debating about whether or not I needed to kill her. However, right now I just wanted to admire her beauty. She was still young and things had not started to sag. Her breasts were full with dusky rose areolas the size of silver dollars.

I felt the urge to reach out and run a finger along her belly. Instead I lay back and thought about whales. I realized I knew next to nothing about them. I had seen a full sized fiberglass reproduction of one hanging from a museum ceiling once. I stood under it marveling at how unbelievably huge it was.

From watching numerous nature documentaries, I knew whales were on the brink of extinction and that sometime in the future a space probe would arrive and call out to them. When it did not get an answer, it would destroy Earth.

It was a shame really. The biggest animal on the planet hunted out of existence by a much smaller organism. I figured we must be like a disease in the whale's scheme of things. Too bad they didn't carry guns.

"You look so serious. Whatcha thinking about?" Matilda put a finger in my ear playfully.

"Whales," I replied.

"Sperm or humpback?"

I slid over and spooned against her, feeling her spine along my belly.

"Ohhh, humpback," she squealed in delight.

Matilda gently nudged me. Slivers of pink light were coming through the blinds. "Get up, sleepyhead," she said with a giggle.

I rolled over and tried to go back to sleep.

"Sorry, lover, but I've got a busy day. I have to be at the church by 9:00."

"But it's not Sunday," I groaned.

"I know, but it's Mr. Grande's funeral today."

That woke me up. I started to get out of bed. She slid the sheet down unveiling her naked body.

"You don't have to leave right away. I just wanted you up," she said smiling.

And I was.

RIDING THE COFFIN

Wilma and I had breakfast at a Bob Evan's in Novi.

It was across the street from the church where Barney's funeral service was being held. We waited in the parking lot while the church bell tolled forty six times; once for each year of his life. Outside the church, a bored looking hearse driver stood waiting. However, I was more interested in the black Chevy parked down the block.

I pointed the car out to Wilma. "FBI."

"Yup," she said as she put a stick of peppermint gum in her mouth.

When I first met her, Wilma had been a voracious cigarette smoker. She had given up her habit five years ago. There is nothing more terrifying than a psychopathic woman with guns going cold turkey.

From the other direction, a gray Mercedes cruised past the church. I caught a glimpse of the driver and instantly recognized Lurch. The rear windows were tinted and I could not tell if there was anyone else inside. I had a feeling there was.

Wilma chewed reflectively. She had seen the tall man as well.

"Figures," she muttered snapping the gum in a way that really annoyed me.

We waited for the Bureau agents in their black Chevy to pass before we pulled in and followed the funeral procession up Novi Road and into Oakland Hills Memorial Gardens.

After parking the car on the other side of the cemetery, we watched from a safe distance as members of Barney's bowling team gave him an eight pin salute. A nervous-looking boy scout played Taps as the coffin was lowered into the grave. I caught a glimpse of Matilda Barnes walking arm in arm with a female colleague. They dropped roses into the open grave.

Wilma slipped away for a few minutes. Somehow I did not think she had been overcome by the emotional scene.

"Done," she said quietly when she rejoined me.

Wilma got her iPad from the trunk and brought up a Google satellite map on the screen. She zoomed into the area around the cemetery. She had secured a GPS tracking device under the Mercedes, which was parked near the hearse, and had put another under the Bureau's Chevy.

The Mercedes was now a red flashing dot superimposed on the map while the Fibbiemobile was a bright yellow one. We left the cemetery and parked a few blocks away while she monitored the iPad.

At long last we had an edge.

THE HERKY JERKY

Not really caring much where the FBI was heading, we stayed with the Mercedes as it headed back downtown.

With the GPS, we could remain blocks away and easily follow them. They would never even know we were there.

Wilma had a great trick that would keep them from finding the tracker. She installed it in the space between the exhaust pipe and the muffler. Hot gases from the engine heated up the pipe so the likelihood of someone feeling around there was nil.

When we realized where they were heading, I speeded up and beat them downtown. I parked on the second level of the garage on Randolf right across from the main entrance to the Marriott. We had a good line of sight to the hotel's vehicle drop-off.

Two minutes later, the gray Mercedes pulled up. A parking attendant rushed over and held the door as two figures got out of the back. The first I recognized as Felix Frame, the fashion designer. When I saw the second, my heart sank. Cinnamon Slade accepted Frame's hand and elegantly stepped from the car.

Then Lurch joined them and they continued into the hotel.

"Well that's a kick in the head, isn't it," Wilma said sarcastically.

"Let's go," I responded bitterly.

I spent the afternoon in a funk watching old game shows on television. I wondered what sick mind came up with the idea for an entire cable network to broadcast reruns of them. I found myself sucked in by The Price is Right and Supermarket Sweep and did not think about Felix Frame or Cinnamon Slade for a while.

It came to me that she had mentioned Felix was her husband's name. However, from the way she had looked at him when getting out of the car, it did not seem like she was concerned about her husband becoming "progressively more obsessed".

Trying to fit everything together made my head hurt. Why would Frame, with his multi-millions, be so homicidally determined to get a rare book that might fetch only eighty thousand bucks at a good auction? And why would his goons torture and kill Barney, Samantha, the geologist, and possibly even Donald?

And where did Donald's *Moby Dick* code lead?

I chewed my way through a big bowl of microwave popcorn and contemplated all this. Nothing made sense.

My phone rang. It was Wilma and she sounded like she was in the car.

"They're on the move," she said. "Let's go."

She was waiting in my driveway. I grabbed my jacket and locked the door behind me.

I took over the wheel while Wilma balanced the iPad in her lap. They were heading along Jefferson and then crossed the bridge to Belle Isle. I had fond memories of the area. My grandparents used to take me there on really hot summer days. We would jostle with crowds of other families in the Aquarium or the Nature Center and then cool off in the fountain.

"Maybe they're having a picnic," Wilma said.

The Mercedes stopped.

"Park near the Aquarium and we'll go on foot," she said stowing the iPad under the front seat.

We left the car in a lot and walked toward where the Mercedes was parked.

They were over near the Yacht Club. There was a large dressing room trailer, like you see on film sets, with a group of gorgeous women milling around. Frame was obviously in control. He barked orders to the photographers and their assistants who had set up their lights and reflectors facing the river.

A freighter going up river hooted its horn as it passed the island. Several of the models waved back at the sailors.

"Looks like the circus is in town," I said.

103

We had hid in the trees and watched the scene through binoculars. I could see there was a rack of clothing under a canvas gazebo-style tent next to the trailer. The fabric waved in the breeze.

Occasionally an assistant would pick one of the outfits from the rack and climb the stairs into the trailer. A few minutes later a model would emerge wearing the dress. Little Rip was making it difficult for me to concentrate. At last, Cinnamon came out of trailer and took my breath away. She was dressed in a sleek black silk number that hugged her like a lover. I felt a shard of longing.

Wilma took the binoculars from me and looked for a few seconds.

"Where's the tall man?" she asked as she scanned the scene.

Before I could reply, I felt a knife blade against the side of my throat.

He walked us deeper into the woods.

"Move, bitch, or I cut hubby's throat," the man with the knife commanded.

Wilma looked at him with her mouth open and eyes wide in fright – all feigned, of course.

"Please don't hurt him," she pleaded.

The punk turned me around and held the tip of the blade an inch from my right eye. I was relieved to see my attacker was not the tall man, who I imagined might still be holding a grudge. He was a plain, old-fashioned street thug; a junkie looking for a quick tourist score.

"Throw your purse over here lady," he demanded.

Wilma remained frozen in place playing the terrified spouse to the hilt. From inside the purse came a sharp rising whine.

"What the fuck is that?" he asked.

Wilma shook her head frantically, "I think it's the flash on my camera."

She opened the purse and stepped forward offering it to him.

He shifted to face her, still holding the knife at my throat. I stepped effortlessly to one side, grabbed his wrist, and gave it a quick twist. I felt the radius bone snap. He screamed and dropped the knife. I let go of his wrist, picking up the knife as Wilma Tased him.

Amateurs.

He fell to the ground and did the herky-jerky. I stepped in and kicked him once in the temple with a steel toed shoe. I felt his skull crunch and he stopped moving. Wilma moved quickly to the edge of the woods. We had not attracted any attention.

I wiped the handle of the knife on my jeans and dropped it next to his shattered wrist. Chances were good his body would not be found for a couple of days and by then he would be a bit of a mess after the wildlife used him for a smorgasbord.

Oh, well. Live by the switchblade; die by the boot. That's nature's way.

"I just saw the tall man," Wilma reported, lowering the binoculars. "It looks like they're going to be here for a while."

Lurch stood next to Frame, shadowing his every move. Frame and his fashion minions ignored him and I guessed he was a permanent fixture in the fashion designer's entourage. At one point, Cinnamon approached him and they stood away from the group having what appeared to be an intense conversation.

After watching the action for forty five minutes, we decided nothing much was happening. It was probably not a good idea to hang around much longer, just in case someone discovered the punk's body. While it was pretty unlikely, there was always a possibility. City cops on bikes patrolled the park on a regular basis. Today, though, they seemed to be more interested in ogling the models.

Wilma dropped me back at home and I resumed my game show marathon and tried not to think about Felix Frame and Cinnamon Slade. When I did, it made my gut ache. Leave it alone. Just walk away and forget about it, I thought. But I couldn't.

It made me furious that she had played me, especially because I thought I was playing her.

Richard Dawson yelled something on *Family Feud*. Reflexively I threw my coffee cup, which just missed the plasma screen.

Goddamn it! I was not going to leave it alone.

PERRY IS A PIXIE NAME

I expected Cinnamon to at least look surprised when she saw me sitting in an armchair in her hotel room.

My gun sat on the table next to me with the barrel pointing in her direction. Wearily, she set an expensive leather overnight bag down on the floor. It clinked loudly, probably from cosmetics and other tools of the modeling trade.

"I've had a long, very tiring day. So if you're going to kill me, do it now," Cinnamon said as she sat down on the edge of the bed.

She still looked gorgeous, even in the baggy sweatshirt and well-worn jeans. I flashed back to her writhing under me in this very same bed. It seemed like decades ago.

"Where's hubby?" I asked in a deadly serious voice.

She shrugged, "Last I saw him, he was chatting up one of the girls from the shoot. Some photographer's assistant, I think. They're probably up in his suite doing the nasty right now."

She flopped onto her back and looked up at the ceiling.

"And before you ask, I didn't know. He told me to get your attention. When your defenses were down, Mark and Perry were supposed to grab you."

"Why do I have a hard time believing you?"

Cinnamon pouted. "I don't really care whether you do or not. Anyway, you shot Perry so what's the difference?"

I remembered something my uncle Jack said to my father in the middle of a heated discussion about the merits of DC comics versus Marvel. He said, "Perry is a pixie name." I found that hilarious. My dad ended the discussion by punching Uncle Jack in the face. Dad was a dyed-in-the-wool

106

DC man and couldn't abide anyone insulting Perry White or Superman. He chased me out of the house for laughing.

"The midget was Perry?" I asked her.

She did not respond and for a moment I thought she had gone to sleep.

"So what do you think this is all about?" she asked.

I was starting to believe that maybe she did not know that much after all. Perhaps she was just the honey trap.

"Did he tell you to fuck me?" I asked.

"You know, fuck is such an ugly word. I was supposed to get close to you, intimately, and learn whatever I could before Mark and Perry took over," she said and added, "and then they would really fuck you."

I shivered remembering Perry, with that crazed look in his eyes, bringing the two by four down on my skull.

"If it's any consolation, I really liked it. You're a gentle and considerate lover. You thought about my needs before your own. Most other men just want to get inside as quick as they can so they can go home and brag to their friends that they banged a fashion model."

"Is that the way Felix treats you?" my voice was beginning to soften.

"Felix? No, not really. It's different with Felix."

"How so?"

"He owns me," she said sadly.

I swear I was only going to comfort her, but I fell into her liquid eyes. I stripped off her jeans and sweatshirt and a frantic few seconds later we were joined at the hip. A few minutes later, I held her tight as she came in a series of whimpering gasps.

I felt the cold barrel of my gun behind my ear.

Shit, not again.

I opened my eyes.

Wilma passed me my pistol and put a hand over Cinnamon's mouth.

"She's coming with us," Wilma said and pushed a syringe full of something into the crook of Cinnamon's arm. She instantly went limp.

I didn't argue with Wilma about what a bad idea this was. I got back into my clothes and helped her put jeans and a sweatshirt on Cinnamon. When she was dressed, we dragged her to the door and Wilma checked the corridor outside. It was clear. Holding Cinnamon between us, we hustled her into the service elevator and got off at the lower lobby.

I assured the parking attendant that I was okay to drive, but the ladies were way over the limit. We had perfumed ourselves with a liberal dousing from a bottle of cheap Scotch Wilma had thought to bring with her; the Marriott did not have minibars in their rooms. The attendant looked at an unsteady Wilma who was propping up Cinnamon and seemed to accept it.

He certainly did not raise any objection when I tipped him ten bucks to help me put them in the back seat of the car.

"How long will she be down for?" I asked.

"Six or seven hours," Wilma said as I floored it.

We figured it would be smart to get out of Detroit for a while. We headed up I-75. Six or seven hours would give us plenty of time to get up to Sunset and square Cinnamon away in a special room we had in the basement of the house there.

A .45 ON YOUR PILLOW

Deputy Molly Parsons knocked on our side door the next morning.

"Wow, twice in one week," she said.

I invited her in and offered her a toasted bagel.

"A pipe burst in the shop so we had to shut down for a couple of days while the plumbers sort it out," Wilma said.

Molly frowned at the news. "Was there much damage?" she asked with concern.

"Not a lot. Anyway that's what God made insurance for," I said and handed her a cup of coffee.

"How's the campaign going?" Wilma asked.

Molly took a sip of the coffee and smiled.

"It's going well," she replied. "Thanks, by the way, for the contribution. It was really generous."

I wondered if Cinnamon was awake yet. This was the first real life test of our sound-proofed room and so far it seemed to be living up to our expectations.

We spent the next few minutes in relaxed conversation with Molly. She really was a great neighbor and we were lucky to live next door to her. She brought us up to date on all the happenings in Sunset. The election was the hot topic around the county with the citizens pretty evenly split between Molly and her opponent, the former chief of police Kenton Sharpe.

Sharpe had been Molly's boss before she switched to the Sheriff's Department. He had made her life hell for a while and I hoped the bastard did not win. I wondered idly if Molly had a spare fifty thousand she would like to put to good use. If she did, we could make sure the race would not even be close.

A few minutes later Molly excused herself.

We promised to get together for dinner after the campaign was finished and waited until we heard Molly's car leave. She still had not had it tuned.

Wilma went into the living room and opened up the security cam monitoring program on her laptop. She flipped through the cameras in and around our Detroit residences. All was clear. Then she switched to the camera in the room downstairs. Cinnamon sat on the edge of the narrow metal cot holding her head in her hands.

I clicked on an intercom button on the screen.

"Would you like a pain killer? We have Advil or aspirin."

Cinnamon shook her head.

"If you feel like something, to eat I have some very nice bagels and cream cheese."

"You mind telling me where I am?" she asked.

From her tone it was clear that she was really pissed.

"Right now you're in a secure, soundproofed room. How about coffee?" I offered.

"You think this'll make any difference to Felix?"

"I hope so," I said. "He has a couple of things that belong to us and we're hoping he's willing to trade."

"What things?"

"A friend of ours named Donald and a very rare edition of *Moby Dick*," Wilma said.

"I don't know what you're talking about," Cinnamon said. She looked confused and was on the verge of tears.

"I'm sure that Felix does," I said. "You don't happen to have his personal cell phone number handy do you?"

Cinnamon took a few minutes to weigh her options and finally gave us the number.

I turned off the intercom and Wilma switched the view to the Marriott's lobby security cameras. Meanwhile, I slid a doctored SIM card into one of our burner cell phones. I dialed the number that Cinnamon had provided.

After a couple of rings a gruff voice answered.

"Yes?" He sounded pissed off.

"Hello, Felix. I'm not sure if you noticed, but your wife appears to be missing."

I heard him say something while muffling the receiver.

"I tell you what, you and Mark go check. We left you a little present on the pillow in her room. Be down in the main lobby in ten minutes and I'll call you back."

I hung up. I wondered how he would react to our little going away gift. Especially when he discovered it was a .45 hollow point.

It would tell him we meant business.

Eight minutes later, we watched as he and Lurch entered the Marriott's lobby and looked around. Felix Frame did not hide his anger as he glared defiantly at the people around him. I rang his cell phone.

"Okay, so you've got her. For all I know, you've already killed her."

"Felix, I'm surprised at your lack of faith," I said hoping my light tone would make him even angrier. "Just to show that you that I'm a man you can trust, I'm going to give you proof of life. Do you have a pen handy?"

On the screen I watched him root through his jacket and pull out a pen.

"Is that a Mont Blanc? Very classy."

Frame looked around at the people mingling in the lobby.

"That's right, Felix, I could be anyone," I told him in a mocking tone.

"Take down this URL," I instructed him and then recited a long internet address and asked him to read it back to me.

"See that PC over there by the concierge desk?"

He walked over to a rental PC and sat down. He spent a few moments reading the onscreen instructions and then swiped his credit card. He now had internet access. He frantically typed in the URL I had given him.

Wilma angled the camera. Frame was staring down at a live feed of Cinnamon in our basement. Isn't technology amazing? I held my cell phone close to our PC and pressed the intercom button.

"Why don't you say hello to Felix, dear?"

I was touched by her pleas to Frame to help her. Finally, I turned off the feed.

"Okay, you bastard, what do you want?" he demanded.

"You know what I want," I said.

"No, I don't," he growled.

This guy had serious anger issues. For a second I thought he was going to put his fist through the PC screen. The concierge was looking at him nervously. Frame got up and walked across the lobby.

"Look, quit playing games. Just tell me how much you want and where and when you want to do the exchange."

"How do I know if Donald is alright?" I asked.

"What the fuck are you talking about? Donald who? Trump? I don't even know that blowhard."

"Not Donald Trump, asshole. Donald Duck."

"The cartoon character? Are you on meth or something?"

"Donald the book dealer. And we want our copy of *Moby Dick* back, too."

He froze, "I thought you had it."

Frame looked genuinely confused. What the fuck is going on here?

He looked around and then figured it out. He looked directly at the security cam.

"I don't have the fucking book." Frame looked dismayed.

However, he was not half as dismayed as I was.

"I'll get back to you," I said and disconnected the call.

Wilma looked at me incredulously.

"Is this a good time to remind you how much you've fucked up this job?" Wilma said.

She was right. This was getting way too complex.

"What do you suggest then?" I asked.

"I think we should take Mrs. Supermodel back to where we got her."

"And then what?"

"Remember that vacation I was going to take? Well now would be a good time to sit under some palm trees and drink white rum all day long."

"And what about Donald and the book?"

She poked me gently.

"We cut our losses," she said quietly.

"No way. Frame has more money than God. At least let's get a ransom."

She shook her head. "We're contract killers, not kidnappers. It's not our expertise."

"So we diversify a bit. Kidnapping can have a killing component," I said.

"Only if it doesn't go according to plan."

We went back and forth for a few minutes and finally she reluctantly agreed that we might as well pick up a few bucks to help defray our expenses.

A CROSS BETWEEN
BRAD PITT & JERRY LEWIS

"Five hundred thousand in non-sequential $100 bills loaded into a gym bag from the Detroit Athletic Club.

"I'll call you back in four hours and tell you the time and location of the exchange," I said and abruptly hung up.

Frame turned and glared at the security camera.

Wilma and I agreed that five thousand $100 bills would not be that much of a burden. We would end up with a tidy profit. Wilma was still dubious, but she went along with it anyway.

Cinnamon looked a little better when I opened a panel in the door and slid in a cup of coffee and a pair of pills on a saucer. I watched her swallow the tablets and drink some of the coffee. She must have thought they were painkillers, but they were actually Ambien and by dinner time she was sleeping soundly in her snug little cell.

Wilma went over to Molly's to see if she wanted to join us for cocktails, but she was on her way out to a campaign event and wouldn't be home until late.

Once it was dark, Wilma gave Cinnamon another shot and we carried her out of the house and dropped her in the trunk.

I figured Frame would have contacted the FBI by now and they would be monitoring all incoming calls trying to get a fix on the nearest cell tower to my location. However, with our specially modified SIM card, all our calls would appear to come from Nome, Alaska.

"So, have you got my money?" I asked when Frame answered.

He was sitting in the food court of the Renaissance Center as I had requested.

He nodded to Lurch who stood beside him and he held up a DAC gym bag.

"Good boy," I said with just the right edge of menace. "At 6:30 tomorrow morning I want you to take it to the east parking of the Hamtramck Cadillac assembly plant. Just drop it next to the fourth car in the first row and walk away.

"I'll call you later to tell you where you can pick up Cinnamon."

We left a note on Molly's door to let her know we had to return to the city unexpectedly to meet with the insurance company.

We stopped for coffee near Frankenmuth at 4:00 in the morning. Wilma checked on our passenger in the trunk and gave her a sedative top-up. Cinnamon would still be in oblivion when we dumped her off.

Wilma took over driving.

"We haven't got any margin for error," she said staring at the road ahead.

I knew she didn't like driving at night. When we were still students in Ann Arbor, Wilma had hit a deer on a dark country road. The experience had left her tentative behind the wheel once the sun went down.

We had no time to plan this one properly. Our strategy came together on the fly. However, it was a good one.

"What the hell are you worried about?" I said. "I'm the one on the firing line."

"Yes," she said with a grim smile, which I thought carried a faint hint of satisfaction.

A lot of what would happen in the next few hours came down to trust. I had to trust that Frame would pay the ransom in the way I had demanded. I also had to trust that I correctly anticipated what he would do next. Most of all, I had to trust that Wilma would have my back.

I felt a coffee-fueled worm wiggle around inside my belly. Maybe we should have just walked away like Wilma suggested. It was still not too late. We could just drop Cinnamon in a park somewhere and keep going. Fuck Frame, fuck the book, and fuck Donald.

However, the temptation of $500,000 trumped all that.

The Hamtramck Assembly plant was a zoo. It was 6:15 in the morning and the shift change was just beginning. Thousands of workers were pouring into parking lots around the plant. They would soon be joined by thousands more coming off the night shift.

Wilma followed the blinking red dot as it moved up I-75 and stopped in a traffic jam at the East Grand entrance to the plant. I was wearing my trusty horned-rimmed glasses and false mustache. I was dressed in a set of gray GM coveralls and had an insulated lunch pail under my arm.

Wilma poked me. "Time."

They had arrived and were driving slowly down the first row counting cars. I could see Lurch behind the wheel. Frame was in the passenger seat beside him. The car stopped and Frame jumped out lugging the DAC bag. He slid it into the space between the cars. Then he got back into the Mercedes. Wilma followed their progress as they joined the long stream of traffic out of the lot.

I got out of our car and joined a group of workers heading for the front entrance of the plant. When I was parallel to the spot where the bag was hidden I slipped sideways out of the group and ducked down as I moved between the cars and grabbed the bag.

I had to work quickly. I unzipped it and looked inside at neat stacks of hundred dollar bills. My heart hammered a little harder. Riffling the bills took longer than I was comfortable with, but it had to be done. We could not take the chance the FBI had put a tracker in a dummy bundle of bank notes.

Three minutes after the bag was dropped in the space, I stood up and walked away carrying it. I headed toward the plant, but then veered away and joined a group coming off shift. We walked toward the west parking lot. I got into a stolen GMC pickup I had parked there. I pulled out of the lot and, after waiting for traffic to clear, headed west on the Ford Freeway. After going a couple of miles, I got off the freeway and pulled into the parking lot of a strip mall. I started to get out of the truck with the bag.

I was immediately surrounded by FBI agents who threw me against the truck and grabbed the bag away. An agent, who was obviously the one in charge, looked inside the bag.

"It's all here," he shouted to the others.

They hustled me into a black Chevy.

"What's this all about?" I said with the right amount of indignation.

I was sitting between the agent in charge and a second one who looked like a slab of corned beef in a suit. They put the bag of cash in the front seat. The Chevy pulled out into the traffic, which was sparse in this neighborhood, especially at this time of day.

The agent in charge turned to me and gave me 'the look'. It was supposed to intimidate me, I guess.

"Where is she?" he demanded and signaled to the driver.

He pulled the car over. I looked around nervously.

"Hey, this is a really bad neighborhood. We shouldn't stop here," I said.

"Shut the fuck up, you puke," Corned Beef said and punched me in the stomach. I doubled over.

Just then the tear gas bomb inside the bag exploded. The Chevy filled with choking fumes. I had taken the precaution of shutting my eyes and holding my breath, but I still found myself gagging. I threw up in Corned Beef's lap as Wilma, wearing a gas mask, smashed in the side window and Tased him. She reached in and unlocked the door. He flopped around in a familiar way and I pushed him out the door and crawled over him.

The agent in charge was trying to claw his eyes out.

I was blind from the tear gas. I felt Wilma take my arm and guide me to the car.

"Fuck, it burns," I cried as Wilma high-tailed it out of there.

My eyes were on fire. It felt like they had been poached over a pair of Bunsen burners.

We were parked a few streets away. Standing next to the car, I poured saline into my eyes and felt the searing pain subside a little.

Wilma had stripped off my jumpsuit because it was infused with residual teargas. She sealed it inside a green garbage bag so the fumes would not escape into the car.

"Next time, you're the decoy," I said between coughing fits.

We had needed a distraction for the Fibbies back in the parking lot. I was it. They focused on me with the DAC bag instead of the spot between the cars where it had been hidden.

That gave Wilma time to retrieve the money which I had dumped into a worn overnight bag and pushed under the car. The bag I carried was fitted with a tear gas bomb that was covered in stacks of counterfeit ten dollar bills.

A former client had tried to pay us with fake currency a few years back. His attempt at malfeasance cost him a couple of toes. We held onto the fake money in case it might come in handy some day.

It had.

I trusted that the Bureau's techs had fitted the DAC bag with some sort of tracking device and they had not disappointed me. It was probably hidden in one of the handles, but I did not have time to confirm that. Wilma was planning to scan for the signal from FBI's tracker in the bag, but she didn't need to. By pure dumb luck, they used the same Chevy that Wilma had tagged with the GPS during Barney's funeral. All she had to do was fire up her iPad and follow along.

After they stopped the car she activated the tear gas remotely and the rest, as they say, was history. The morons had not even thought to take off my gloves. They would have no luck finding any prints.

And the gas had fucked them up so badly I was willing to bet my Identi-Kit portrait would make me look like a cross between Brad Pitt and Jerry Lewis.

Now we were $500,000 richer.

A few minutes later, we completed the transaction by dropping the still comatose Cinnamon in a nice park along the river. I called Frame and told him where they could find her.

I thanked him politely for the money and hung up before he had a chance to respond.

LITTLE MISS JESUS

My skin felt like it had been sandpapered and soaked in iodine.

"I need a shower," I whined.

Wilma pulled into my driveway and helped me into the house. She went back out and retrieved the bag with the money in it.

I took a long cold shower to wash off any lingering tear gas. When I came out of the bathroom, Wilma had stacked the money on my coffee table. She had divided it into two neat piles.

"So that's what half a million looks like," I said as I sat down beside her on the couch.

She smiled as she stared at the money. At last I felt like I'd done something right.

"I'll add this to my 401K," she said as she tucked her share into a shopping bag.

I stared at my stack. It was a big score. I should have been happy with it, but sadly I wasn't. There were too many dangling questions.

"We still have to find Donald and the book," I told her.

I thought she might argue with me about it, but she nodded slowly. That was another thing that I liked about Wilma; she hated loose ends too.

"So what now?" I asked.

She frowned. "I hate myself for saying this, but I think we need to go back to Iron City," she replied. "There has to be some other connection, and if we're going to find it anywhere, that's the place."

The idea of returning to Iron City had no appeal to me whatsoever, but she was right. There were answers to be found there.

"Before we do that I need a couple of days of rest," I said. Then I had another thought. "Did we get Barney's Outlook files when you downloaded his computer?"

"Yeah, I exported them as PST files."

"Did you check them?"

Wilma nodded. "It was just a lot of work stuff. He sure went to a lot of meetings."

"Do me a favor and print out his agenda for the last six months, also his full contact list."

"No problem," she rose and picked up the bag with her share of the money.

"Feel a little better about this now?" I asked.

She shook her head. "Nope, just a little richer."

We reviewed Barney's appointments over the past six months. I was amused to see his initial meeting with me was listed as **M: RH/Marriott RenCen**. Then the realization of what that meant gave me a twinge in my stomach. Wilma saw my reaction.

"Don't worry. I erased the hotel's security footage for that week," Wilma said, "before the police had a chance to check it."

Thank God for the underfunded Detroit Police Department.

Wilma flipped the page and pointed to another appointment the week before Barney and I had met. It read, **M: DD**. I blinked in surprise. The address was Donald's shop in Grosse Pointe.

"Makes sense, I guess. If you were going to sell a first edition, Donald is the person you'd go to."

"But he didn't mention it to us," she said.

"We know Donald is discreet. That's why we love him so much."

I could see she was still troubled by it though.

The rest of the entries appeared to be routine work stuff, with the exception of his bowling nights which were highlighted in green.

I went through his contact list and stopped at **F**.

Ellen Fine.

It wasn't so much the name as it was the fact that she lived in Iron City. I circled her name and continued through the list.

Matilda Barnes was under **M** with her home address and phone number. I wondered if they had been more than just colleagues. I might have to pay Matilda another visit. Little Rip stirred in his bat cave at this thought.

Wilma looked over my shoulder. "Is that little Miss Jesus?"

I nodded.

"She worked for him so it makes sense he would have her personal contact details," I explained.

It didn't sound all that convincing, even to me.

I.C.U.

Iron City again.

It looked just as grimy as it did when we last saw it. Well, at least we could afford more bullets this time.

We figured it would be a good idea to find out a little about Ellen Fine.

"Wasn't one of The Three Stooges named Fine?" I asked.

Wilma looked at me in disgust. "I can't understand what the male fixation is with them," she said.

I was tempted to explain the aesthetic of The Stooges to her, but I sensed she would not be a very receptive audience.

I loved the chaos they created and the pointless mayhem they inflicted on each other and the world. For years, I believed their particular brand of violence was mostly harmless, until the first time I dragged the blade of a saw across the top of someone's head. The result was not all that hilarious.

The main branch of the Iron City Library was a good place to start. They would have excellent local archives and free wireless service.

I was surprised at the grandeur of the building. Its vaulted ceilings would inspire any pilgrim to imagine they had entered a cathedral of knowledge. A wide central hall ran its full length with polished wooden tables and brass reading lamps. Comfortable armchairs for patrons to linger and read their tomes were around the perimeter of the hall.

However, this being Iron City, the place was empty.

A series of alcoves along each side contained the stacks. Over each alcove, the names of the subjects contained within were carved into the marble in Roman style lettering.

I had a feeling that if you opened any book in the Iron City Library the first words would be "get out while you can". That was certainly the way we felt.

I sat down at one of the computer terminals, logged into local history, and ran a search on Ellen Fine. There was a long list of search results. Ellen Fine appeared to be a pillar of the community. There were links to newspaper clippings about her various charitable events. She was a strong supporter of the local arts community. The only surprising thing was that Iron City actually had an arts community.

I did another search using both her name and Randolfo's. Bingo! There was a picture from a local charity ball taken a couple of years ago. From the picture, I guessed she was in her mid-50s. Slim and elegant in her designer dress, she stood with her date – Walter Randolfo.

Wilma leaned over and looked at the picture. "Think he was her squeeze?" she wondered.

I was wondering the same thing. "We need to have a chat with her," I said.

Wilma booked us into the Holiday Inn Express on the edge of town. We decided not to press our luck and stay downtown in case somebody recognized us from the news. Anyway, the Holiday Inn had a salt water pool, which Wilma claimed was good for her complexion.

Our room was typical moderately-priced hotel chic with comfortable beds and soothing wallpaper – the kind of place where Willie Loman would have felt right at home.

I changed into an FBI-grade black suit. Wilma put on conservative duds as well. We now looked like a reasonable facsimile of a pair of Bureau weenies.

Ms. Fine had certainly done alright for herself. She lived in the penthouse of an expensive building overlooking Iron City Harbor. After we flashed our fake FBI credentials, she showed us into a living room that had more square footage than the Palace of Versailles.

"Can I get you anything?" she offered.

We declined and she indicated a long leather couch for us to sit on. She sat in a high-backed armchair which was covered in silk. I opened my briefcase and took out a file that I'd stuffed with Holiday Inn stationary. I opened it and pretended to read.

When I looked up, she had an elegant looking nickel-plated automatic pointed at the middle of my chest.

"Since you are the third team of supposed FBI agents to call on me in the last few days, I just want to start by saying that I didn't get to where I am today by being completely gullible."

Her gun didn't waver, and neither did her gorgeous steel blue eyes.

"So let me tell you what I told the other phony agents. I went out with Walter Randolfo a few years ago. He was a nice man and he treated me very respectfully. We were never intimate and remained friends.

"His nephew would call me every so often and ask me to look in on Walter to make sure he was alright. Walter would take me to dinner on the second Tuesday of every month. I was shocked and pained that he was killed when his condo was robbed."

"Actually, ma'am, we really are FBI agents, and I would appreciate it if you put your weapon away," I bluffed.

She looked at me and shook her head.

"Like I said, I'm not that gullible. The only reason I'm talking to you right now, and not to the police, is that I'm hoping someone might find Walter's killer. The police and the real FBI have been useless so far."

Wilma got up and stepped toward her.

"Put the gun down, Ellen. You know you're not going to use it," Wilma said in her most calming voice.

Ellen Fine sighed and lowered the gun. Wilma took it from her and examined it.

"This is very nice," Wilma said and held it up for me to admire.

It was a specially customized STI VIP, the .9 mm model.

"This has to be worth at least $1,500," Wilma speculated.

"It cost me $2,400 with the engraving," Ellen Fine said.

Wilma slid out the magazine and dropped it into her handbag. She ejected the round in the breech and handed it back to Ellen.

"We can help you find the killers," Wilma said.

Ellen looked at her hopefully.

"They are us," I said, "Randolfo's nephew contracted us to kill his uncle and steal his copy of *Moby Dick*."

I took her through the rest of our adventures since we got the book.

Ellen was absolutely right. She wasn't that gullible, and knew that we wouldn't have told her everything if she was going to get out of this alive. I admired the way in which she held onto her dignity.

Wilma put a firm hand on each of Ellen's shoulders and looked her straight in the eye.

"But we aren't the only ones who wanted to kill him. Just after we finished Walter, a couple of goons broke in and started shooting up the place. One was a tall man and the other was short."

"They sound like the second set of agents who visited me," Ellen said. "The short one was particularly obnoxious."

"I know he was, and he's dead now. Shot in the throat," Wilma said with a reassuring smile.

"Anyway, we think they're tied up with a guy named Felix Frame. Have you ever heard of him?" I asked her.

"Felix Frame? There's a fashion designer named Felix Frame. I think I have some of his company's stock in my portfolio," Ellen said.

I nodded. "That's him. Those two goons worked for him."

"That doesn't make any sense though. Felix Frame is a billionaire. Why would he want to harm Walter?"

I shrugged. "We think it has something to do with *Moby Dick*. Did Walter ever say anything about whales?"

A weird expression crossed her face.

"We were at a fund-raiser for Iron City University about two years ago. Walter cornered Jeff Hitchens and they huddled together for a few minutes. You know, the way men do when they have something serious to discuss," Ellen said. "I thought it was strange at the time. I couldn't imagine why Walter would be having such an intense conversation with Jeff."

"Why?" I asked.

"You see Jeff is a professor of biology at the University, he specializes in cetology, the study of whales."

We all pondered this for a few moments. If it had been a movie, this is where the scene likely would have faded. Wilma took the clip out of her purse and put it back in Ellen's pistol. She pulled the slide back and seated a bullet in the chamber.

She smiled down at Ellen and asked, "Would you like to leave a note?"

Iron City University sat on a bluff at the south end of town. The campus was obviously not Ivy League. Most of the buildings looked like big box stores. The place had all the charm of a Russian Gulag. That is to say, the campus was oppressive.

Students trudged to class burdened by the bleakness of their school, and the thought of the crushing student loans they would carry into middle-age. I wondered how many of them would even admit they'd graduated from old I.C.U.

We found Dr. Jeffrey Hitchens just finishing his weekly Biology 101 class. We waited patiently as his students plodded out of the lecture hall. Once the hall was empty, we joined him down front and produced our fake credentials. We assumed that he had not been questioned by two other teams of phony agents so he'd likely be more impressed than Ellen had been.

He was.

I explained that we were following up on the murder of Walter Randolfo.

"Yes, I read about it. It was quite tragic."

"I understand you knew Mr. Randolfo," I said in my politest Bureau manner.

He shook his head.

"I met him once or twice at fund-raisers. I think the last time was about a year ago."

"Did you have a conversation with him?" Wilma asked.

"No, I … Wait … Yes, we did," he replied. "He cornered me at a party with a number of questions about ambergris."

"Ambergris?" I said.

"Yes, it's an excretion from sperm whales. It comes from the whale's gallstones, but a lot of people think it's whale feces."

Whale shit, that's what the geologist said just before his head went splat. And I thought he was just being insulting.

"Why would Mr. Randolfo be interested in whale vomit?" Wilma asked.

"I don't know, but I have a suspicion that he might have had some," he said. "He asked me a lot of questions about its value and where the best ambergris markets were."

"So you think he was trying to sell ambergris?" I asked.

"I don't know for sure, but maybe."

"It's valuable then?"

"Yes, high grade ambergris is worth more than gold. I think the current price is around $30 to $35 a gram."

That's almost as expensive as printer ink.

I did a quick calculation. That rock we had tested would have been worth somewhere in the neighborhood of $3,500.

"So if he had ambergris, where would he sell it? Is there a whale feces exchange or something?" I asked with a smile.

"No, not at all. It's considered a by-product of whales and it's covered under the International Whaling Convention. It's illegal to buy or sell in most countries, including the U.S.

"So it's valuable, but there's no place to sell it," I said.

"No, there are plenty of black market dealers. It's highly valued as an ingredient in perfume. There's lots of European and Asian perfume manufacturers who would love to get a supply of it."

The stakes, as they say, had been suddenly raised.

FRAMED

We felt that we had gotten everything we needed from our trip to Iron City.

Not that you could ever get enough of a town like that. We headed back home.

Wilma spent a good part of the trip hunched over her laptop burning through data. Sitting in a horrendous traffic jam coming into Chicago, we started putting the pieces together.

"Uncle Walter collected a lot of this ambergris through the years," I said, remembering all those coded ledger entries and shipping receipts from places like New Zealand. Wilma's quick online scan about ambergris had told us that it was often found on beaches in the South Pacific.

"Then he stashed it somewhere and coded the location into his first edition copy of *Moby Dick*."

Old Walter had quite a sense of humor. Or maybe he was just being ironic.

"Frame's a fashion designer and most of them have some sort of signature perfume, so he needs the ambergris," Wilma added.

"And Barney discovers his uncle's secret and wants it for himself, but he needs the book to tell him where it is," I continued.

I know very little about cryptography, but I'd read somewhere that most codes were based on a grid. To decipher the grid, you need a key. The key could be as simple as shifting all the letters in the alphabet one or two letters to the right or the left, or as complex as a three hundred and fifty bit algorithm.

"I think we need to find out everything we can about Uncle Walter," I said. "Maybe something in his background will give us a clue."

"Gosh, I feel just like Trixie Beldon," Wilma said.

I stared at her for a moment, and then laughed in spite of myself.

After all the double-crossing and killing, we were finally starting to have some fun.

Felix Frame entered his hotel suite followed by Lurch.

As he walked past her, Wilma juiced the giant with her Taser. She held it up for Frame to see and pulled the trigger. A vicious arc of electricity shot from one electrode to the other. He looked down at his spasming henchman on the carpet. Frame got the message and slumped into a chair.

"I guess you haven't come to give me my half a million back?" he said.

I was sitting at the desk. I had just finished watching the concept spot for his proposed perfume, Framed. It was a stereotypical fragrance commercial. A slinky blond was dressed in black silk, purring about how she'd "been framed".

Offended by the sexist ad, Wilma zapped the Taser impatiently.

"I'd love to put this in your mouth and liquefy your fillings," she told Frame.

If he was intimidated, he didn't show it. Lurch continued to roll around on the floor.

"You weren't planning to buy the ambergris were you?" I asked Frame.

He smiled and it gave me the creeps.

Wilma and I are evil, there's no denying that, but Frame was at a much higher level on the villainous scale. He was somewhere between Adolf Hitler and Dracula. When he grinned, I checked his mouth for fangs.

He ignored me and looked at his henchman still writhing on the floor.

"You zap Mark once more and I'm going to have to sell him to Detroit Edison," Frame said.

"You should find a more efficient bodyguard than this clown," I told him.

"I had one until you blew his tonsils out," he replied. Frame looked down at Lurch in disgust. "Anyway, I can't get rid of him. He's my brother-in-law."

Mark *Slade?*

I stared down at the bodyguard, but couldn't see any resemblance to Cinnamon. He must have inherited the ugly genes. Not only was he very tall, but he had one of those long ski jump chins that made me think of Jay

Leno. His eyes were set wide apart and were slightly googly, though that might have been from all the electricity he'd absorbed over the past week.

His nose had been broken at some point and skewed slightly to the right. His mouth was full of widely spaced teeth. From the way we kept getting the jump on him, he must have had the cunning of a bowl of shit.

"How's Cinnamon?" I asked.

"She's feeling better. I sent her back to New York."

"Okay, so that gets the pleasantries out of the way," Wilma said. "Now we want you to tell us where you've stashed our friend Donald and Randolfo's copy of *Moby Dick*."

He sighed. "We've already had this conversation. I don't have your friend or the book."

I thought back to Ellen Fine's comment about us being the third team of FBI agents who visited her. I wished I'd asked her to describe them. It was a stupid oversight.

"How about shit-for-brains here and his little buddy; did *they* pose as FBI agents up in Iron City?" I asked Frame as I gave Lurch a kick.

Lurch screamed in rage. I put my right foot over his hand and crushed down on it to add injury to insult. That got his attention, and he momentarily went limp.

"How about it, Gort? Did you play FBI agent for the nice lady up in Iron City?"

I pressed harder on his hand, flashing back to the paper cutter in Randolfo's bindery.

"Yes," he yelped.

"So your two guys posed as agents, and we did as well. Now, who was the third team?" I asked Frame.

"Maybe they were the real FBI," he said.

Wilma shook her head. "The Bureau will take weeks to get around to questioning her. So where does that leave us."

The air went out of the room as we all realized that there was someone else out there dogging us from the shadows. Whoever it was had been playing us off against Frame. We were so busy shooting at each other we hadn't noticed there was someone else in the game. I had a strong suspicion that this someone had both Donald and the book.

I took my foot off his hand and Lurch rubbed it, trying to make the pain go away.

"Okay, let's stop fucking around," I said. "You need this whale shit to make pretty smells with, and we need our friend back along with a whole bunch of cash. So why don't we work together on this?"

Wilma looked at me in surprise.

Yes, it was like making a deal with a bunch of electric eels, but at least we'd have them off our backs and could focus on finding whoever was behind this. Also, when we did get the ambergris, Frame would be a built-in customer. We wouldn't have to take it to market.

"How much are you willing to pay for the ambergris?" Wilma asked.

"We tested a sample that Randolfo provided awhile back," Frame said as he helped Lurch to his feet. "It's the purest quality anyone has ever seen."

"Did he say how much he had for sale?" I asked.

Frame smiled again and I felt geese marching over my grave.

"Nearly four hundred pounds," Frame replied.

"Four hundred pounds?" I repeated. "How much would that be worth?"

"Somewhere between three and four million," he said.

"And you would pay us that much if we found it for you?" Wilma asked.

Frame frowned. It was obvious he hadn't even considered paying for it until then. He looked at us in disgust.

"Maybe, but less the half million I already paid you," he said.

Wilma shook her head. "Sorry. Not negotiable. That was payment for all the trouble you and your minions caused us."

Frame chewed his lower lip for a few seconds then put his hand out for me to shake.

I took it reluctantly, expecting fangs to sink into my palm. As we shook on it, I looked into his reptilian eyes. He was already figuring out how he was going to double-cross us.

Before this was over, I knew I was going to make him bleed.

"How much do you think he's going to make on that perfume?" I wondered aloud when Wilma and I were back in the car.

"At least twenty to thirty million," she said, "probably a lot more. Designer fragrances are really hot these days."

"Well, just as long as we don't get framed," I joked.

Wilma frowned. She didn't have much of a sense of humor.

"He's going to screw us," she said.

"Of course he is, but we'll be ready for him," I said. "Promise me one thing though."

"What?" she asked

"I get to shoot big holes in Lurch."

This time we both chuckled.

Then I had another thought. "I think we should take another look at Ben Candle and his relationship with Randolfo."

She looked wistful. I think she actually regretted helping Candle to the other side. Of course Wilma was not really capable of feeling regret, neither of us were. Perhaps she was feeling more like a fisherman who catches the big one and then feels badly for eliminating a worthy adversary.

THE END OF AN ERA

Lightbulb was enjoying a drink in a dive off Mack.

He sat in a corner by himself. When he saw us come in the front door, he waved us over to his table. From the look of the salty types in this shithole, I was glad my .45 was tucked under my arm. But no one seemed particularly interested in us as we made our way to the back.

We pulled out chairs and sat down across from him.

"Now I know where my next round's coming from," he declared.

"There were lots of two-tone wannabes back in those days, but none of them had the class of Ben Candle." Lightbulb sucked back a big mouthful of malt liquor and continued, "He was the genuine item, a real old school gangster. He owned these streets for twenty years until the Feds nailed him."

He held up his glass in salute.

"To Ben Candle," he said, and we clinked glasses.

Candle's 'suicide' had been reported in the papers. The *Free Press* declared his death was "the end of an era".

"Did you ever find him?" Lightbulb asked.

I shook my head. "No, we never did."

Lightbulb discreetly hadn't asked why we were looking for Candle in the first place.

"How about some of the guys in his gang?" I asked. "Any of them still around?"

He hesitated. I pushed a pair of Ben Franklins across the table, and Lightbulb put them in his shirt pocket. He pretended to concentrate while figuring out just how much info to give for my $200, and how much to hold back for future consideration.

"I think there might be one or two still in the city. I can check around for you and let you know tomorrow. Meet me up by the front gate of Mount Elliott about noon and I should have something for you."

I debated pressing him for the information now. I was sure he had it, but I kept thinking about my car parked outside.

I'd just picked it up from the body shop and they had done a terrific job. It had a great alarm system. If someone tried to steal it, they wouldn't know about the special entry code that used the radio preset buttons. They'd get about six blocks before a charge under the driver's seat turned them into Cream of Wheat.

If anybody tried to trace the serial numbers from whatever was left, they would find out it had been made up of parts from dozens of stolen cars. There was no way it could be traced back to me.

It was a nice car and I would regret losing it should that happen. Thankfully, it was still intact when we came out of the bar.

I dropped Wilma off and went home to curl up with a good game show.

THE KIND OF MAN
WHO MAKES A DIFFERENCE

A long funeral procession was going through the gates of the Mount Elliott Cemetery.

Wilma and I sat in her car, which was parked up the street, and waited for Lightbulb to put in an appearance. I anticipated he would be late and I wasn't disappointed. He strolled down Mount Elliott at about 12:15 and leaned into the car. He smelled like he'd showered in Colt 45 and Wilma pushed her seat back to get out of his way.

"Did you get anything?" I asked.

He shrugged and grinned. "Not much. Most of the guys that ran with him are either dead or still doing time. I did manage to get one name though. Derrick Barker."

"And where can we find him?"

Lightbulb's grin widened. "Well, he don't use that name anymore. He's known now as the Reverend Powell Edwards."

I recognized the name. Reverend Edwards was in the news all the time, usually in connection with one new community initiative or another.

Detroit was big on social activism these days; it's the only thing that might give the city a chance to claw its way back. Churches fill a huge void and provide everything from food banks to bus service for the elderly.

Edwards and his church had led the way and, as a result, he was always being honored as the kind of man "who makes a difference".

He also didn't try to hide his gangster past. Most of the news stories about him contained at least a passing reference on how at one time he'd been one of Detroit's most feared bad guys.

However, while serving twenty to life he'd undergone a prison conversion and reformed. He emerged from jail a changed man who renounced his outlaw past and worked hard to make himself a respected member of the community.

My cynical nature told me he was probably running some kind of scam and someday the headlines would scream about his disappearance with a large sum of money and a comely member of his congregation. And there's always that bastard 'co-inky-dink' because the Right Reverend Edwards was also the pastor of Blessed Resurrection Church, the very same place where Ben Candle spent a lot of his time during his final days.

That made Wilma's spidey sense tingle like a son of a bitch. We decided we would take Reverend Edwards at face value and treat him with the respect he seemed to have earned. That meant we were going to have to rely on our FBI credentials when we talked to him.

"Sure, I knew Ben Candle, but you already knew that," Edwards said after we were comfortably seated in his study.

He was sitting at a massive slab of a desk. His back was to the floor-to-ceiling bookshelves. Most of his books appeared to be old and well-worn. They gave off a slightly musty odor.

I wondered if he had a copy of *Moby Dick*. I was tempted to ask him.

Edwards was a big man who continued to work his way through a pile of documents on the desk in front of him while he talked to us. He read each document, making notations as he went along. His face had filled out since his prison days. The result of too many church dinners, I guessed. His hands were as large as hockey mitts, but handled the pen and documents with amazing dexterity.

"He spent a lot of time here at the church," I said.

He looked up impatiently. "Yes, for the last few years. I hired him to be the janitor here when he got out of prison. After a couple of years he wasn't able to handle the job anymore. He was too frail and the work was too physical. But he hung around and participated in some of our programs for the elderly.

"What's your interest in Ben anyway?"

"We're just trying to get a clear picture of what he was up to," I said.

"Why, are you writing a book?" Edwards stopped looking at the documents and stared at me skeptically. "Ben Candle died after he went to prison. Jail time has a way of doing that. It kills you a little more every day. You either come out stronger with the resolve to make a difference or you come out like Ben, old and bitter."

He looked at me and something must have made him suspicious.

"Now, I can make one phone call to Mike Magee, the special agent in charge of the Detroit Field Office, or you can start telling me the truth."

He sat back and waited for us to come clean.

I leaned forward, which I'd been told indicated sincerity.

"Do you recall a man named Walter Randolfo?"

He shook his head. "Name's not familiar."

"He and Ben did some business together back in the early 70s," I said.

"Lots of people did business with him back then. I was his right hand, but only on a portion of the shit he had going down."

When he said this, I had a brief flash of the man before me in his gangster days. He would have been formidable. I could imagine him dressed in striped bell bottoms, a wildly pattered shirt with wide collars, and a silver coke spoon on a chain around his neck.

"He ruled Detroit back then." Edwards smiled at the memory. "We had ourselves a huge set of offices downtown. We were real important businessmen. Way up in the Blanchard Building. He liked to look out the windows there and survey his domain, just like one of those kings back in the Middle Ages."

"Did he ever talk about it when he came out?" Wilma asked.

"Nope. Not a word. That life was history and we never talked about it."

He leaned in close and said, "I can tell you think this is some sort of scam I'm running, but it's not. I'm sincere in my beliefs and the work we're doing here. I was in hell once and I have no intention of ever returning there.

"It troubles me that Ben couldn't shake loose those demons. Despite the fact he died by his own hand, I expect the Lord will make a place for him."

I was tempted to reveal he could rest a little easier as Ben hadn't actually committed suicide, but that wouldn't have been the prudent thing to do.

"He's not telling us everything," Wilma said as we drove downtown.

I sat next to her and stripped off my false FBI mustache. I was hoping she wasn't going to suggest what I feared she might.

But she did.

"We're going back there tonight and ask him some questions after midnight."

"Questions after midnight" was Wilma-speak for torture. It was something she was particularly fond of, but didn't get to practice very often. I took a more moderate stance in these matters and tried to get the information out of folks by simple subterfuge. However, in the case of a hard nut like Reverend Powell Edwards, a dental pick inserted between the orbit of the eyeball and the socket often produced more satisfactory results.

HAMMER DRILL

Wilma gave the Reverend Edwards a little kiss from her Taser as he was about to get into his car in the church parking lot.

It was nearly 8:00 and the area was dark and quiet. I handcuffed him, put a wide swatch of duct tape over his mouth, and threw him into the trunk. It was all over in less than a minute. I drove my car and Wilma helped herself to the Reverend's six year old black Lincoln.

We headed out of town to a little place we had in the county. It was going to be a one-way trip for Edwards.

The farmhouse wasn't fancy, but it was miles from any nosy neighbors and had a large equipment shed out back where we could stash the cars. It also had a heavy duty electrical supply so Wilma could operate her power tools.

It was your classic prisoner interrogation. You've seen it a hundred times in old movies. A hanging lamp illuminates a single chair which has been bolted to the floor. Other than the tight circle of light cast from the lamp, everything else is hidden by blackness. It has a wonderful psychological effect on the subject.

Unfortunately for me, it brought back unpleasant memories of my hand trapped in the paper trimmer.

We used nylon ties to bind Edwards to the chair. I stepped up behind him and pulled the hood off his head. We had stripped him naked to increase his feeling of vulnerability. I remained behind him where he couldn't see me. I would be just a disembodied voice in the dark.

"I guess by now you've figured out we're not from the FBI," I began.

He twisted his head to get a glimpse of me, but I was only a shadow in the darkness.

"I get the sense you weren't completely honest with me earlier, so I feel a follow up interview is necessary."

"Look, I already told you everything I know." he was remarkably calm.

On the other side of the basement, Wilma tested her cordless hammer drill. It was a good one, contractor quality and quite reliable. It had never let us down.

"First, let me be upfront with you. I admire the work you and the church have done for Detroit. If it's any consolation, I think you've made a real difference in the community," I said sincerely. "However, you aren't going to get out of this alive. I'm sure you've seen the movies where they offer the option of an agonizingly slow death or a quick one. Well I'm making that offer right now. Take a minute and consider it carefully because it's the last important decision you'll ever have to make."

"I consider it a gift from God to be martyred like this," he said defiantly.

"I guess that's one way of looking at it. But from my experience, it can be quite messy and always ends with the person telling us everything while begging us to kill him."

Wilma stepped into view, covered head to toe in disposable painter's coveralls. She had her rose-tinted face shield down and his naked form was reflected in it. She held the drill.

"And here's a final thought. You are about to become a Detroit legend," I told him.

"Yes, like Jimmy Hoffa," Wilma added.

She put the drill bit against his left knee cap.

It turned out he did remember Randolfo from the old days. He'd even gone out to the airport with him to meet a courier coming in from Mexico City. The courier had handed over a large roller bag and Randolfo paid him off. Edwards had lifted the heavy bag into the trunk of his car.

Candle had been bribing customs officers for years to get his shipments into the country unmolested.

"Randolfo opened the bag to check it and I saw it was full of big white chunks, like rocks. They were wrapped in plastic.

"I thought it was just dope, but it had a funny smell, kinda sweet, like a really nice perfume." Edwards sobbed.

He couldn't tell us where Randolfo took the bag. He dropped him off at the Pontchartrain Hotel downtown and that was the last he ever saw of Randolfo or the bag.

I had fond memories of the Pontchartrain from years ago. My grandparents took me to lunch there once a year after the auto show at Cobo.

Wilma once tossed a guest from the roof of the Pontch. His wife had a problem with his obsession with transsexual hookers and paid us to make it look like he'd jumped out a window. He landed on the roof of a FedEx truck that was illegally parked in an alley behind the hotel. Since I had a fear of heights, I stayed down in the lobby and played lookout.

After the job was done Wilma, and I had a nice lunch in the hotel's bar.

Between screams, Edwards also suggested we speak to Mira Byrd, a former stripper who used the name Myna Bird and had dated Ben Candle back when he was king of the underworld. He had seen her only a few days ago. She'd been one of a handful of people who had gone to Candle's funeral. The Reverend told us she lived in a trailer park just south of Port Huron.

When we completed our interrogation, we rolled him up in plastic.

I went to get the backhoe from the equipment shed. I drove it out into the field behind the farmhouse and spent an hour digging a long trench. When I finished, it was seven feet deep and wide enough to fit both the Reverend and his Lincoln. I imagined him pulling up to the Pearly Gates in it and honking the horn for St. Peter.

An hour later there was no trace of the Reverend's grave. I drove the backhoe around a bit to flatten out things and then returned it to the shed. While I was out in the field, Wilma hosed down the basement and sprayed it with bleach.

Dawn was breaking when we drove down the lane and onto a country road. It began to rain heavily. A couple of good rains like this one and the tire marks from the backhoe would completely disappear out there in the field. Then the Reverend could truly rest in peace.

In a few weeks, the farmer we leased the field to would be planting his crop of organic barley and, within three months, the field would be covered in waving green. I wondered if the barley roots would reach the roof of the Lincoln. Since it was at least three feet below the surface, I doubted it.

Thanks to my liberal education, I'm an atheist. Though we had never discussed it, I assumed Wilma was as well.

I felt sorry for the Reverend. He'd endured all we had put him through because of his unshakeable faith in God. Imagine his surprise when death plunged him into dark nothingness. The thought made me sad. I felt melancholy all the way back to the city.

Since we'd been up all night, I suggested we grab a few hours of sleep before heading up to Port Huron to see Mira Byrd. I was getting kind of numb, and a short break would help pick up my spirits.

We went to Wilma's place and hopped into bed. We were too bushed to do anything else. To help me sleep, I began counting bodies. I was out by number five.

Just because we were sleeping, however, it didn't mean everyone else was.

STRIKE THREE, YER OUT!

Mira Byrd lived in what was referred to as a modular home these days.

In reality, it was just an extra wide trailer without wheels. Every year dozens of people die in these houses when tornados rip them apart. While they might look solid sitting there on a twelve by twenty lot, they really only have the tensile strength of a Black Forest cake.

It would have been merciful if Mira had been killed by a twister.

The door had been crudely jimmied, probably with a large screwdriver. Inside, her house was old lady neat. Porcelain figures lined little wooden display cases hanging from the living room wall. The television was so old it had been made in America. Magazines were stacked in a stand next to the couch and appeared to be mostly about gardening. The furniture was made of solid wood and must have been expensive when she bought it.

A small table beside the armchair held a television remote and a pair of dollar store reading glasses. It was quiet in the house, which was not a good sign considering her car was parked in the driveway. This didn't look like the kind of community where neighbors did a lot of socializing, so I feared the worst.

We found her body in a back bedroom. Seeing her like that brought back memories of Barney in the motel room and Samantha in her lab. An aluminum bat had been tossed in a corner of the room.

A single drop of blood fell from the ceiling. It had been a recent kill, likely only a few minutes before we arrived. We were looking through the doorway at the carnage in the bedroom when we heard the first siren. It wasn't that far away. I could hear the unmistakable sound of a car engine increasing speed and the squealing of tires.

This was not good.

"I didn't see a back door," Wilma hissed.

"There should be one somewhere."

I ran to the other bedroom and saw a solid wooden chest of drawers blocking the rear exit. I also glimpsed armed policemen crouched low in the backyard. They had their guns trained on the door. Gravel crunched out front and the house filled with flashing blue and red light.

Wilma slipped into the bathroom and looked around. I glanced at Mira on the bed once again, and was shocked to see her try to turn her head. I carefully stepped into the room, avoiding the pools of blood on the floor.

She was gasping and blowing bubbles of blood, trying to clear her mouth. I bent down close.

A voice shouted through a megaphone, "If there's anyone inside, throw your weapons out and follow with your hands over your head."

"Alton, Alton, see Alton ..." Mira whispered and then her head lolled to one side in death.

Wilma motioned me from the doorway and whispered, "Come on, for Christ's sake."

She had moved a small shelf in the tiny washroom. These homes were set on slabs of concrete and had no basements. What they did have was a small access panel in the bathroom so a plumber or electrician could get into the crawlspace underneath to do repairs. The entrance was secreted behind a low shelf unit that held extra towels and toilet paper. It was designed to swing out.

There was a fierce hammering as the SWAT team battered its way through the backdoor. I could hear the chest of drawers in the bedroom fall over with a solid thump.

Wilma swung the panel open and crawled into the hole headfirst. I followed her and pulled the shelf back into place so it concealed the access door. This might give us a few minutes while the police made a sweep of the place.

We crept along the ground under the house and reached the opposite side away from the porch.

Above us we could hear the thumping of heavy footwear as the SWAT team searched. The sound of their boots covered up any noise we might have made.

There was plastic lattice work that surrounded the trailer and covered up the crawlspace. On the other side we could see bushes. They would help to cover our escape. I was counting on the discovery of the body to draw most of cops inside so we could make a break for it.

When we heard muffled shouts and a lot of feet running I grabbed the lattice and pulled it inward. It snapped and opened up a space behind the bushes. We crawled through a gap in them and looked around. There was three feet between Mira's home and the next one. Her neighbors were out at the end of their driveway watching the action next door.

While they were distracted, we crouched low and ran across the lawn and into the darkness behind their home. We moved from yard to yard until we were six houses away. People were walking down the street toward Mira's unit. Wilma turned me around and brushed off the dust and cobwebs from my clothes. I did the same for her. Satisfied that our appearance wouldn't raise any questions, we casually walked over and joined them.

A couple of state cops, pissed off they were missing out on the action, held everyone back. One put his hands up and declared, "Move on folks nothing to see here." He had seen too many movies.

We continued walking down the street. The car was parked a few blocks over in the driveway of an empty house with a For Sale sign on the lawn.

I jimmied the back door lock. Inside the empty house we changed out of our dirty clothes and into the clean ones we kept in the trunk. I put on my mustache and horned-rimmed glasses and Wilma tucked her hair under a blond wig. As a final touch, we pulled on matching FBI nylon jackets. We looked official now.

I circled the block and approached the scene. The cop manning the rope line held up a hand for us to stop. I held up my phony Bureau ID and he snapped to attention.

"Who's in charge here?" I demanded of the cop standing guard at the door.

"Sheriff Hardy," he stammered.

"Get him, please," Wilma said firmly.

He scurried into the house and returned with a thin man who held out his hand as introduced himself.

"Ray Hardy."

I shook his hand and introduced myself as Special Agent Jim Phelps and Wilma as Special Agent Honey West.

"Mira Byrd is an important witness in a RICO case we're handling and when we heard the call go out we high-tailed it up here to see what the hell was going down."

That was probably too much information, and might have made a savvy lawman more than a little suspicious, but Hardy accepted it with a nod and led us back to the bedroom. I was pleased to see a dozen guys were stomping around the scene messing up any trace evidence.

"Hey, haven't you guys heard of forensics? We need to secure this scene," I shouted at them.

The dummies stopped picking their noses and, chastised, filed out of the room.

Wilma and I pulled on latex gloves and put booties over our shoes. I asked Hardy to keep everyone out while we did a preliminary search. I shut the bedroom door to assure we wouldn't be disturbed.

"I figure she was whacked no longer than ten minutes before we got here," I told Wilma. "So I don't think they had time to search the place."

"Well, we don't either. One of these morons is going to think to call the Bureau, or worse, some real agents are going to show up and then we're toast."

"Let's make it quick," I said.

Wilma searched the dresser while I went through the desk in the corner. There was no sign Mira had ever owned a computer so I looked for papers. I found a receipt for a safety deposit box from a local branch of Comerica Bank. I stuck it in my pocket. There was a safety deposit box key on a ring in her purse. I put it in my pocket too.

Wilma found a large padded envelop in the bottom drawer. It was stuffed with appointment diaries, and from its thickness I could tell there were at least thirty of them. I dumped a pair of shoes out of a box and dropped the diaries in. The sheriff gratefully accepted the box and carried it out to the car for us.

We finished our search, figuring we had pushed our luck about as far as we dared. I ordered the cop standing outside the bedroom to "Lock it until the crime techs get here."

We politely thanked the sheriff for his help and drove off.

Once again we were one step behind.

Whoever had killed Mira was out there in the darkness somewhere, just ahead of us. Not too far though. They had probably called the cops after we went in and told them that a murder was in progress. I guess they thought they could slow us down, possibly even get us killed. That meant we were getting too close for comfort.

"We need to get to the Comerica Bank in Marysville," I told Wilma.

I showed her the receipt for the safety deposit box.

"It's the middle of the night. I don't think they'll be open," she replied.

"Find a motel then. We'll go through some of this stuff and be there first thing when it opens in the morning."

Wilma found a Quality Inn just off the Interstate. Once we were in our room, she began to practice Mira's signature. Wilma was a passible forger and it didn't take her long to produce an almost perfect facsimile of Mira's handwriting.

I started to go through the diaries beginning in 1970. Mira Byrd used some kind of primitive shorthand that took me a few pages to figure out. She abbreviated Ben Candle as **B**^{C}. It wasn't some sort of code. She was probably just lazy.

Farther on there was a note that read **B**^{C}**/Rdy/PH**, which I deciphered as 'Ben and Randolfo meeting at the Pontchartrain Hotel'. There were a number of similar meetings through the early part of the 1970s, and then Walter Randolfo wasn't mentioned anymore.

There were also a number of entries that mentioned **Alt**. They were sprinkled through the 70s and into the 80s, ending around the time of Ben Candle's trial. Was this the Alton that Mira had mentioned just before she died?

I put the name Alton in a special box inside my head.

"It's strange that she didn't have any photos isn't it?" Wilma observed.

She had joined me and was leafing through the diaries.

"Well, we don't have photo albums either," I said.

"Speak for yourself. I have six of them at home," she said.

I looked at her in surprise and she laughed. Every so often Wilma says something absurd and I fall for it. This was one of those times.

I found the total absence of photographs at Mira's home strange. I'd taken the idiot sheriff's business card out of courtesy. I pulled it out of my pocket and I dialed his cell number.

"Sheriff Hardy, this is Jim Phelps again. Are you still at the scene?"

"Yes, I am." He sounded tired.

"Would you take a quick look and see if there are any framed pictures around. I'll wait."

He talked me through a guided tour of the house and confirmed there were no photos anywhere.

"While I have you on the line, Agent Phelps, we think we've discovered how the killer escaped from Miss Byrd's home," he sounded excited like Joe Hardy did when he and Frank discovered an important clue.

I cut him off.

"That's great, Sheriff, please put it in your full report and fax it to me in the morning."

I hung up before he had time to ask for my fax number.

"No pix anywhere according to Quick Draw McGraw, but he said there were some empty hooks on the wall in the living room where something might have hung."

"So we have to assume there was someone in those pictures the killer didn't want anyone else to see."

I gave it some thought. Pictures meant negatives, and we hadn't found any of those either.

"You don't think she might've had a storage locker somewhere do you?" Wilma asked.

I thought of *Storage Wars* and its wacky gang of vultures gleefully picking over the debris of peoples' lives as they looked for that big score. They end up chucking the most precious stuff – family mementos – into the garbage. It was heartless and sickening, but highly entertaining.

I looked up storage facilities in the local yellow pages and saw at least fifty listed in the Port Huron area. There was no way we would have time to check them all. I made a list of the ones within a ten mile radius of Mira's house, figuring she would probably choose someplace close.

In the morning we would look in the safety deposit box first, and then spend the rest of the day checking out storage companies.

I turned on one of the Port Huron television stations to catch the morning news. As I suspected, Mira's murder was the lead story. There was nothing new to report, though the sheriff mentioned the FBI was working in conjunction with his department to "bring those responsible to justice".

It was the second story, however, that made my heart sink.

"It was a busy night for firefighters as …" The anchor went on to describe a four alarm fire at a storage facility south of the city. The structure had been completely destroyed and damage was estimated to be over two million. I looked at my list and saw it was second from the top.

They were one step ahead of us yet again.

We stopped at a Tim Horton's for breakfast. The bank was across the street. At 9:30 on the dot, the front door was unlocked and a small line of people went inside. We waited a few more minutes and then casually strolled over to the bank.

Wilma went to the service desk and asked them to get her safety deposit box. No one raised an eyebrow when she gave Mira's name. It was obvious that no one here knew Mira Byrd by sight. Wilma showed them a fake Michigan driver's license with Mira's name and address on it.

I hoped the bank clerk had not watched the morning news.

Wilma followed him into the vault and signed the card. He took a few seconds to compare her signature with the one the bank had on file. Satisfied, he took out his key and inserted it into the lock. Wilma waited until he removed his key, and put hers in. She then opened the door of the safety deposit box.

He slid out the box and carried it to a small screened-off area and set it on a desk. I joined Wilma and we opened the box. It contained an out-of-date passport, a small notebook filled with Mira's abbreviations, and an American Airlines ticket voucher valued at $5,000. There were also a couple of pieces of expensive-looking jewelry and, best of all, an envelope crammed with negatives.

We took the notebook, the negatives, and the jewelry and left the rest. I carried the box back to the vault and signaled the official that we were finished.

It was time to call Frame and bring him up to date.

A CAGE MATCH WITH HANNIBAL LECTOR

We met Frame for a drink at Tom's Oyster House across the street from the Renaissance Center.

He was more relaxed than when we last saw him.

"I need you to be straight with us for about three minutes," I told him after the waiter took our drink order. "If that's possible."

Frame shrugged, "I'm not sure it's in my nature."

Telling the truth in our business is like breathing carbon monoxide, if you do it for very long you'll die.

"Did your guys do Grande in the motel?" I asked

He looked at Lurch sitting beside him and shook his head.

"No. Why would we? He was supposed to bring us the ambergris."

"But once he did, all bets were off," Lurch added with an evil chuckle.

This earned him a scowl from Frame. The henchman shifted uncomfortably in his chair.

"What about the woman who ran Golden Labs out in Inkster?"

"I'm not even sure who that is," Frame said with a puzzled look on his face.

"And the geologist, did you shoot him?"

Frame was getting impatient with all this truthiness.

"Look, when am I going to get my ambergris?" he demanded.

"We're working on it," Wilma hissed.

"Well, work harder. I've got a board meeting on the fourth and I want to announce Framed."

"Yeah, and then we can leak the news to *Women's Wear Daily* and watch the stock price go way up," Lurch said sullenly.

Frame shot him another harsh look.

He looked at his watch and got up.

"Well, that's enough truth for the time being. Go find my fucking ambergris."

After they left, Wilma got out her iPad and brought up the city map so we could see where they were heading.

The Mercedes stopped at the old Packard plant on East Grand. We cruised by to see what they were up to. The photo shoot had moved over here from Grand Isle and models strolled around the wreckage of America's great industrial past at the Packard plant. I looked for Cinnamon among them, but no luck. Frame must have been telling the truth when he told us that he had sent her back to New York.

Too bad, Little Rip thought.

Since Wilma was going to be busy for the rest of the day scanning the negatives into Photoshop, I had some time to kill.

I wondered what Matilda was up to.

Matilda was primed and ready to go when I picked her up. She suggested we get some takeout fried chicken and go back to her place. Later I tasted a hint of the Colonel's secret recipe on her.

Cuddling after sex had always made me a little tense. It was usually the time when a woman would bring up the deadly subject of us – as in "where do you think we're going" or "we should take this relationship to the next level."

However, Matilda seemed only to be interested in having as much sex as possible. For such a religious girl she was remarkably uninhibited.

"Anything new about your boss's murder," I asked.

Her head was on my chest and she circled my navel with a finger.

"Not that they're telling us. I think maybe it was a random thing, like a serial killer."

I didn't tell her that, for the most part, serial killers were the invention of television shows like *CSI* or movies like *Silence of the Lambs*.

Idly I wondered how I would make out in a cage match with Hannibal Lector. Her fingers started to glide down toward my crotch and I didn't give it much more thought.

"Haven't you killed her yet?" Wilma asked the next morning when I got back from Matilda's.

I shook my head and yawned.

"Oh Jesus, don't tell me you're starting to fall for her. You know that's a bad idea."

I nodded my head in agreement. "I know. It makes it harder to kill her," I said, annoyed she had brought it up. "Did you find anything in the photos?"

She tossed a bunch of eight by tens onto the coffee table. I picked one up. It was a picture of a much younger Mira Byrd arm-in-arm with Ben Candle. It must have been taken in the disco era. Candle was wearing a white suit with a shirt open to his navel and a shitload of gold chains hanging around his neck. From the tackiness of the background, I guessed that they were in a nightclub.

"You'll find some interesting folks in there," Wilma said.

And I did.

There were several shots of Walter Randolfo. He appeared to be in his mid-fifties. From the way the shot was taken, I wondered if Mira had used some sort of hidden camera. Perhaps she was collecting some protection for herself, or maybe a way to fund her retirement, though that didn't seem likely given her modest home and belongings.

The third picture from the bottom was really interesting. It looked like it had been shot through a car window. Ben Candle stood on the sidewalk with the Reverend Powell Edwards when he was still known as Derek Barker. However, what interested me most were the two men with them. One was a heavy guy in plain clothes, but the other was a very young uniformed officer named Delbert Newell.

"Del," I said softly.

DOCTOR SEUSS

Del walked across Jefferson Avenue.

I'd arranged to meet him in front of the UAW-Ford Building next to Cobo Hall. We strolled down to the river and stood looking across at Windsor.

"Fucking Canadians got it easy. Windsor's a shithole, but it's still a hundred times better than here. They don't even lock their front doors over there," Del said.

"I know. I've seen *Bowling for Columbine* and it's bullshit."

I passed over the picture. Del looked at it for a long time.

"Charlie Owens," he pointed to the fat man in plain clothes. "He used to ride with my dad. He plucked me out of patrol and gave me my first undercover assignments. He ate his gun down in Arizona a few years ago. Guess retirement wasn't all he'd hoped it would be."

"So?" I said pointing to the picture.

"What's it look like?" he replied. "Candle paid us to give him tidbits. Charlie set it up so I could get a taste."

"So why didn't you tell me this when I first asked about Candle?"

"My sordid past didn't have anything to do with it," he said.

He was right. Whether or not he was on the take from Candle really didn't matter, and I already knew Del was bent. That's how he got to know me in the first place. But I didn't like secrets, or the people who kept them from me.

"Where'd you get this?" Del asked.

He looked at the picture again, and his eyes narrowed. "Candle's skank," he said. "When he was top dog they lived in a penthouse across the street."

I resisted the urge to look over my shoulder to where the former Pontchartrain Hotel still stood.

"Anything else you remember from those days Del?'

"He had a piece of everything," Del said. "He got half the city hooked on crack, and it caused an implosion. If I'd known what his poison was going to do to this town I would have blown his head off."

"Very noble of you Del, but you were a part of it. You enabled him."

He nodded. "Yeah, me and a hundred others. When they finally put him down on those RICO charges, he took a lot of cops, and even a couple of judges, with him."

"But not you," I said.

He nodded. "Yeah they didn't go down that far. The courts were too busy."

He looked like he was going to crumple up the picture.

"Did she give you this? How much does she want?"

"She's dead. Someone beat her to death with a baseball bat the other night."

"I guess she stepped on someone's toes then."

"Does the name Alton mean anything to you?" I asked.

He looked at the picture again.

"Alton Geisel. He was another one of Candle's boys. He was smarter than most of the others, he stayed in the background. He didn't flash his gangster status. They used to call him Seuss on account of his last name."

"Yeah, Theodore Geisel, Dr. Seuss, I get it," I said impatiently. "Is he still around?"

"He disappeared years ago, just about the time Candle got busted. A lot of us figured he was the inside man for the Feds. He didn't have a sheet. I checked when it went down."

"Why don't you nose around and see if you can find anything more about him. He might have popped up on someone else's radar in the past few years." I tapped the picture. "You can keep that if you like. We have the negative."

I pulled out a padded envelop and handed it to him.

"What's this?" he asked.

"More photos for you to look at," I said. "I'd like to know who every person is in each of these. Write the names on the back. I want it done by noon tomorrow."

Hardly anyone lived off the grid these days, but Alton Geisel was a total cypher. Wilma spent hours online trying to find out anything about him. There was nothing. He'd fallen off the face of the earth.

Geisel must have picked up a new identity somewhere. Since he disappeared thirty years ago, our chances of finding him were remote. There was also the possibility that he was dead, or that he had disappeared into witness protection.

I put these last two possibilities to Wilma. Maybe she could work her online magic and find out for us.

"That's way above my pay grade," she said.

While Wilma could extract information from the internet, she was only a rudimentary hacker. To dig into Department of Justice high-security systems, you needed a real pro, someone who could drain your bank accounts, charge thousands to your credit cards, and fill your hard drive with child pornography.

That would be someone just like Blofeld-106.

The nice thing about our kind of work is we meet all kinds of interesting people.

Promod Sharma is one of them. He lives in a quiet cul-de-sac in Sterling Heights with his wife and daughter. He drives a three year old Lexus and has an office downtown in the Guardian Building. He's one of those nondescript guys who volunteers for school fundraisers and helps out at the food bank. When asked what he does, he tells people he's a life insurance broker, which is guaranteed to make their eyes glaze over and discourage them from asking any further questions.

Of course, Promod isn't what he seems. He's actually one of the world's top hackers, going by the moniker of Blofeld-106.

We first got to know him when he hired us to eliminate a competitor nicknamed Buzzkill 400. Buzzkill had somehow learned Promod's real identity and threatened to reveal it to the world unless he coughed up an algorithm that could defeat nearly every form of data security system. This algorithm was Promod's biggest trade secret. It had taken him years to develop.

Buzzkill 400 was a whiney little jerk who reminded me of the Comic Book Guy on *The Simpsons*. He enjoyed playing the role of hacker to the hilt;

living in a dirty, cramped apartment filled with a massive server array and latest technology doodads.

When we dropped by to see him, he was dressed in baggy shorts and a stained Deadmau5 T-shirt. He had no real sense of style, unlike Promod who favored Brooks Brothers suits and $200 neckties.

Buzzkill was extremely obnoxious. He was also quite stubborn. After he refused to reveal where he'd hidden his file on Promod, Wilma had to remove a couple of his fingers with a Dremel Tool in order to loosen his tongue. In the end he gave us the files, plus the access codes to the remote servers where he had stashed copies.

Wilma was an extremely effective negotiator.

She spent an hour or so cleaning up his digital dirt, and then we loaded Buzzkill into the trunk of our car. We threw everything, including Buzzkill, into a coke oven in a steel mill on Zug Island.

A grateful Promod called me on my personal cell phone a few weeks after the job to thank me. I was a little disturbed that he had my number. I only gave it out on a need-to-know basis, and Wilma was the only person who needed to know it.

However, you couldn't hide from Promod, and calling me on my personal phone was just his way of letting me know there would be no secrets between us. We thought about killing him, but decided it was better to keep him alive as a resource. You just never knew when a good computer hacker might come in handy.

This was one of those times.

I called his secretary and made an appointment to see him later in the afternoon.

DUMB TERMINAL

Promod was the antithesis of the media stereotype of a hacker.

A combination of three gym workouts a week and a strict vegetarian diet kept him in great shape. As always, he was impeccably dressed in an expensive suit and conservative tie.

Because Promod's office was on the fifteenth floor, I sat on a couch by the door as far away from the window as I could get.

The Blanchard Building stood directly across Woodward from his office. He stood by the window staring at it. It was shrouded in wire mesh and all the windows had been removed in preparation for its impending implosion.

Promod sat down and shook his head sadly, "If it keeps up like this, pretty soon there won't be a skyline left."

He was right. Since the downturn in the economy, half the real estate in downtown Detroit was sitting vacant, prey to squatters and copper thieves.

"There's no chance it will fall in this direction is there?" I asked.

"No, they've figured it out precisely. I took a look at the plans on the demolition company's server and their math is correct." He waved a hand at the laptop on his credenza.

I asked about the computer at one of our previous meetings. Laptops were not that powerful, and I assumed a hacker of Promod's skill would need a lot processor muscle.

He explained that most of his computer power was elsewhere. The portable PC was just a glorified dumb terminal. In the unlikely event there was ever a raid, the police would find no evidence on it. It wasn't much more than a prop.

"Now what can I help you with?" he asked.

I explained about Alton Geisel and the DOJ database. His mouth tightened momentarily and then relaxed into a smile.

"It might take a day or so, but I'll see what I can do. Are you at the same number or do I need to track you down?"

I admitted I had the same phone number.

On the way out, I thanked his secretary and wondered how much she really knew about Promod's business. Probably not much, I guessed.

As I walked along Woodward, one of my cellphones rang. It was my throw away, and I figured it might be Matilda. To my surprise, it was Cinnamon Slade.

"Rip?" her voice sounded strained and tentative as if she wasn't sure how I would react.

"Felix told me you went back to New York," I said coldly.

"Well, that's what he thinks," she replied. "I'm at the Dearborn Inn near Greenfield Village."

"Did he tell you we'd thrown in together," I asked.

"No, he doesn't tell me anything," she replied. "Can you come out here?"

"I thought you'd be angry with me," I replied.

"What, just because you drugged and kidnapped me," she said.

"Well, yeah."

"Not really. You made that bastard pay half a million to get me back and it looks good on him."

"So what do you want, Cinnamon."

Her voice took on a sultry tone that caught Little Rip's attention.

"I'm bored and lonely and I was hoping you would come out here and keep me company."

I thought about it for a couple of seconds and agreed to come. While my big brain warned me this was a really bad idea, Little Rip won out by a hair.

Lust comes in all forms. In silk or rubber sheets, bound and gagged, on top, doggie style – wined, dined and sixty-nined. In its most pure form, it ends with the gleeful ringing of a one armed bandit going off in your head.

My night with Cinnamon was all that and more.

I woke up at 6:00 the next morning to the rumbling of car transporters full of newly minted Fords rolling out of the storage yards next to the hotel. Cinnamon kissed me softly on the inside of my thigh, and I stroked her back. The top sheet was twisted around us. The rest of the sheets lay on the floor at the foot of the bed.

As we lay together, I reached over and slid down the sheet to reveal Cinnamon's perfect body. In the gloom I saw something that disturbed me. I turned on the bedside light and took another look. Cinnamon had greenish bruises on her inner thighs. I stared at them and she turned away.

"What the hell did he do to you?" I asked.

"I disappointed him," she said softly, "and I cost him money. He believes that I might be in on it with you."

"Why didn't your brother stop him?"

"Mark? He's a primate. Anyway he's only a half-brother. My mother was drinking a lot when she hooked up with his father."

"So why don't you just leave him?" I asked.

"Felix? You don't just leave Felix. Remember Connie Jackson?"

The name was vaguely familiar, but I didn't remember why.

"She was his top model and lover for five years. She'd finally had enough of him and tried to leave. He had Mark hold her while that little prick Perry bashed in her face with a steel garbage can lid."

I remembered now. It had been a big story about three years ago. She'd had her modeling career destroyed by a pair of muggers. The press dubbed her the "broken bird of the New York fashion scene". Apparently there was even an HBO film in development.

Overwhelmed by pain and fear, Connie Jackson had finally swallowed a bottle of prescription painkillers.

"So yeah, you don't leave Felix Frame," she said and began to sob.

I pulled her into my arms and kissed her tears away. Careful to avoid the bruises, I made gentle love to her.

"I think it's kind of ironic that the man who drugged and kidnapped me treats me better than my own husband," she whispered later.

Her head was resting on my chest and her breath stirred the hair there.

"Sorry, that was strictly business," I said. "We needed to teach Felix a lesson and taking some of his money seemed the best way. If I'd known he'd hurt you, I would have found some other way to get him."

"You mean shooting Perry wasn't enough?"

"No, that was just payback."

I thought of Perry laughing as he pressed the buttons on the paper trimmer and then when he sadistically bashed me with the two by four. Then I imagined him caving in Connie Jackson's face with a garbage pail lid. He deserved to die just for that.

"But after all that you partnered with Felix," she sighed.

"It was expedient. There are too many people after the same thing. I needed to narrow the field down a little. Anyway, he's the one with the cash to pay me once I find it."

She looked up at me. "You know he isn't going to pay you. He's just going to kill you and take the ambergris for himself."

"Probably, but I do have a few surprises left."

"I hope that isn't all you have left."

I felt her hand move down to Little Rip who happily cried, "Good morning!"

Driving back from Dearborn, I plugged in my iPod and turned up U2's *No Line on the Horizon* really loud. I needed something to drown out my thoughts and this fit the bill perfectly.

One of my cells began to buzz urgently in my pocket. It was my Del phone. I selected the phone on my Bluetooth.

"I'm finished with the pictures," he said.

"Ok, meet me at American Coney Island in an hour."

I hung up before he had time to protest that they didn't have any vegetarian options.

AMERICAN CONEY ISLAND

The two best hotdog spots in the civilized world sit side-by-side on Lafayette Avenue in downtown Detroit.

American Coney Island is in a flatiron building that comes to a point where Lafayette Boulevard meets Michigan Avenue. Lafayette Coney Island is located right next door.

Originally started by members of the same family, there was a nasty split between them many years ago, and for almost a hundred years the two restaurants have been the source of controversy for Detroit hot dog lovers.

You are either in one camp or the other when it comes to who serves the best dogs. I happened to prefer American Coney Island. In my opinion, they serve just the right combination of spiced chili, mustard, and sweet onions on top of a hot dog, which crunches when you bite into it.

I arrived before Del and managed to grab the point table at the front of the restaurant. It was a just before noon and the place was starting to fill up. Del walked in a few minutes later and dropped into a chair across from me.

I ordered a pair of full loaded Coneys and Del had a Greek salad. We ate in silence.

Del passed me an envelope after we'd finished. "Had any luck finding Seuss?" he asked.

"I'm working on it."

"Let me know if you find him. I know a few guys who would be willing to pitch in for a hit."

I took the envelope.

"So anything interesting here?"

"Yeah, but it took me half the night. The Commissioner's got us working overtime on the Powell Edward's thing."

HAIR TRIGGER

I feigned interest. "Any luck?" I asked.

The late Reverend Edward's mysterious disappearance had been top of the news for several days. The FBI had been called in and there was speculation that he might have become a tennis partner for Jimmy Hoffa.

"No, I figure he's in the wind. Probably took a shitload of his church's money and has gone somewhere warm to wipe the cobwebs off his dick."

"Anyway, what did you find?" I asked, bringing him back on topic.

"Another one of Candle's guys is still around. You'll find him in there. Johnny Oates. He was one of his bodyguards. They called him 'Steel Cut Oates' back in the day. We figured him for at least seven murders, but couldn't find any proof. He did a couple of years on an armed robbery beef. After he got out he bought a club off Atwater. He ran it for about fifteen years. His son owns it now. Oates retired a couple of years ago."

Del gave me Oates' address in Southfield.

"Most of the others in the photos are dead," he said.

Wilma slapped the GPS tracking device down on my coffee table next to the envelope full of photos. "We're getting stupid and sloppy," she said in disgust.

She had discovered a device on her car that morning when she changed her oil. Wilma liked to do all her own maintenance. When she checked under my car she had found another one.

"They put it exactly where I put ours on Frame's Mercedes and the Bureau's Chevy."

"So who do you think put it there?" I asked her.

"I'd bet it's our mysterious friends."

"It could also be Frame keeping tabs on us," I suggested.

She shook her head. "His unit's still operating, so he hasn't found it yet."

"We didn't think to check our cars either," I pointed out.

She picked up the GPS and was about to throw it into the fireplace. I stopped her.

"We can use this to our advantage," I said.

We put the GPS on the front seat and drove aimlessly around the city for a bit to fuck with whoever was monitoring us. Occasionally, we would stop and wait for a few minutes. I even hopped out a few times hoping that would draw them out.

No such luck. They were probably monitoring us from a few streets away. It's what we would have done. We were finally tired of playing with them. It was time to give the dog a stick to chase so we drove to Southfield and parked next to the Greyhound terminal.

A bus was leaving for Atlanta in fifteen minutes. It was easy to slip the GPS into the luggage compartment. I figured they wouldn't catch on until at least Bowling Green, so we might have twelve hours without them on our asses.

I waved cheerfully to the passengers on the Atlanta bound Greyhound. Then we went to visit Johnny Oates.

ROLLED OATES

The sound was turned up really loud.

Johnny Oates was sitting in the sunroom at the back of his house watching Ellen DeGeneres on a seventy inch plasma screen TV.

Wilma put the gun to the back of his neck while I settled into a chair across from him. He had half a bottle of Old Grand-Dad and a small bucket of ice on the coffee table in front of him. He was holding a full tumbler of whiskey.

"So this is what retirement is all about – daytime TV and bourbon. It certainly looks fulfilling," I said

"Fuck you," he muttered and took a long pull on the drink.

"One day just bleeds into the next," I continued. "Well, we're here to help you break the monotony. How about a trip down memory lane?"

He was a little resentful at first, but after a few more shots of bourbon he loosened up.

Oates wasn't really a bad guy, and he didn't strike me as a natural killer. He was more like a guy who just let things get way out of hand. I imagined he woke up many nights in a cold sweat tortured by the faces of the people he'd killed. He was a man desperate for absolution, and we were there to give it to him.

"Sure I remember him," he said when I asked him about Randolfo. "Randy Walter. That's what we called him. He'd come around once or twice a year. Ben would fix him up with some ladies at the Pontch and they'd fuck his brains out. He couldn't get enough of it." Oates chuckled at the memory.

"So how was he connected with Ben?" I asked.

He took another slow drink. "I'm not sure. I got the feeling he was some sort of supplier. A couple of times he hauled suitcases up to the office. He always left empty-handed."

"Any idea what happened to the suitcases after he left?"

"One time I took one out to Ben's place on the St. Clair River. It was fucking heavy. In them days they didn't have wheels on luggage like they do now."

"Where exactly was Ben's place?"

He thought for a few seconds. "Somewhere near Algonac. The Feds seized it when they popped him."

Wilma held up a pill bottle. It was his supply of Ambien. She shook a few pills out and offered them to Oates. He wasn't stupid. He got the picture and dutifully washed them down with a healthy dose of bourbon. She shook a few more tablets onto his palm.

It made sense that Walter Randolfo would team up with Ben Candle. Randolfo had the connections to obtain the ambergris. Candle had the muscle and could hide and protect it from the bad guys. They probably had a deal to split the profits when it was sold.

If the government had taken Candle's cottage as part of the *Proceeds of Crime Act*, there would be a record somewhere.

I fished some more. "Did he have any other spots, maybe someplace no one knew about?"

Oates' head lolled over. He was having a hard time staying awake. Booze and sleeping pills were a bad combination.

"Trout Lake …" he slurred.

I shook him. "Where's Trout Lake?"

"Ben had a cottage there," he said as he started to drift off again. "It's somewhere across the river."

In Canada?

Shit.

Wilma set the empty pill bottle on the coffee table next to what was left of the bourbon.

Oates would be taking an extra-long afternoon nap today, one he wouldn't be waking up from.

THEY PUT VINEGAR ON THEIR FRIES

I finally found it on a Google map of Ontario that Wilma brought up online.

Trout Lake was south of Lake Huron. On the map, it looked more like a large pond than a lake. That was a good thing because it would mean fewer cottages for us to check out.

Going to Canada, however, gave me the creeps. Unlike the FBI, the RCMP was actually quite efficient and always "got their man". Canadian law enforcement was well-funded and well-trained. Going into Canada would be like working without a net.

On the plus side, like Michigan, Canada had no death penalty.

Traffic was backed up at the Blue Water Bridge as we waited patiently to cross the border. At Customs, the agent took our phony passports and scanned them. After a few moments he handed them back with a smile and welcomed us to Canada.

Canadian weirdness started a few hundred feet from the border. A sign told me the limit was 100. I had just reached 85 when another larger sign politely explained that speed was measured in kilometers here.

I immediately slowed down.

Their gas, however, was ridiculously cheap – only a buck thirty a gallon.

Sadly, I found out about liters a little while later.

Even at sixty miles an hour, we made good time and reached Trout Lake in the late afternoon.

"You folks here for the fishing?" the clerk asked as he checked us into the Pines Motel.

"Nope, just the scenery," I replied.

He smiled and handed me a key. "Well, we've got plenty of that."

The motel didn't have a restaurant, but he pointed us in the direction of a place down the road.

Wilma looked around the restaurant in horror. "They're putting vinegar on their fries."

"Just relax," I cautioned.

The waitress brought my club sandwich and Wilma's burger. I shook a couple of drops of white vinegar onto my fries just to annoy her. She turned away in disgust.

Vinegar on fries wasn't that bad. "You should try it," I said offering Wilma the bottle.

She reached past me and took the ketchup.

"No thanks. I prefer the American way," she said.

Wilma did not travel well. She couldn't relax in unfamiliar surroundings.

"This is bullshit. If it is here, it's over twenty five years old, and probably no good," she said.

"Everything I read said that ambergris only gets better with age, and more expensive."

"It better be."

Wilma squirted a fry with ketchup and popped it into her mouth.

Like all Canadians we'd met, the lady in the county registry office was very polite. I explained I was a nephew of Ben Candle's and was trying to locate his cottage on Trout Lake.

She spent a few minutes on the computer and came back shaking her head.

"Sorry, nothing under Candle," she said. "Would he have registered it under another name?"

Of course he would have. He was a criminal after all, and would've wanted to keep it off the radar.

I had a thought. "Could you check under my aunt's name, Mira Byrd?"

It only took her a second get confirmation. She printed out the registry record. "It's from 1985. Sorry to be the one to tell you this, but it was sold back in 2003 as an abandoned property. The taxes hadn't been paid in twelve years, and it was in poor condition. Says here they tried to contact your aunt, but she never responded. The county petitioned the court and seized it."

"Well, that makes sense. My uncle died in 1995 and my aunt was quite ill as well," I explained.

I made a mental note of the lot number for the cottage. I had serious doubts that the original structure would still exist, especially if it was going to be condemned.

You can imagine our surprise when we discovered the original cottage was still standing. The new owners had fixed it up, but they retained a lot of its 1960s charm.

Ray and Helene Prescott were a nice couple.

I felt a little guilty as Wilma held a gun on them while I tore open the walls of their living room. We were dressed in our black Zentai suits, which covered our bodies from head to toe, and made us look like silhouettes. They helped us blend into the shadows, and had a terribly intimidating effect on our victims.

The cottage had no basement so if the ambergris was here, it was probably hidden behind the drywall. I tore out a few panels only to find pink insulation. It looked fairly new.

"Did you insulate the place?" I asked Ray.

He nodded. "A few years ago, so we could stay here in the winter."

"Did you find anything unusual in the walls?"

"No. Nothing."

Wilma leveled the gun at him.

"You're lying," she said.

He lowered his eyes and his wife started to sob in fear.

"Was it money or drugs?" I asked.

"Money," he confessed. "There was over $300,000 in US currency packed in the living room walls."

"And that was all?"

He looked confused.

"All? Isn't that what you're looking for?"

$300,000. They must have thought they'd gone to pig heaven when they found it. They seemed like nice people. Maybe they deserved their good fortune.

"Do you still have it?" Wilma asked.

Ray shook his head.

"There's not much left. I exchanged a lot of it when the US dollar was still high. It converted to almost $400,000. We used it to pay off the mortgages on our home and this place. We kept some for our children's education."

I imagined what would have happened to the money if they were Americans. They would have blown it on pickup trucks, jet-skis, flat screen TVs, and a trip to Vegas.

I felt that we should reward their financial responsibility.

We wouldn't kill them.

"I tell you what. We're going to leave now. I think it would be better for all of us if you just forgot that we ever dropped by. And I'm really sorry about the damage."

The Prescotts nodded in relief.

Wilma cut the nylon ties we had bound them with and we bid them a pleasant goodnight.

We decided to avoid the bridge and drove along the St. Clair River for a few miles. There was a regular ferry back to the States that ran across to Algonac. It seemed like a better bet than the bridge where illuminated signs warned us there was a three hour wait.

Since we wanted to check out Candle's other cottage, this would work out just fine. Compared to the stop and go traffic on the bridge, the ferry was quite pleasant. It held about twenty cars and customs on the other side was a breeze.

We drove north and looked for the address Wilma had found in the DOJ file. The cottage had been sold in 1995. I hoped the owners were as nice as the Prescotts.

Unfortunately, the Connors were real pigs.

Mrs. Connor looked pre-diabetic and screamed a lot when we tied her up. Our Zentai suits obviously scared the shit out of her. Mr. Connor tried to prove how macho he was by pulling a pistol when we first burst in. Wilma took it away from him and tossed into the river.

I took a quick look around. There were two jet-skis floating next to the dock, a pickup in the carport, and a large flat screen TV on the living room wall. A shingle-sized sign over the bar proclaimed **WHAT HAPPENS IN VEGAS STAYS IN VEGAS**.

They had none of the quiet dignity of their neighbors across the river.

"So how much did you find in the walls?" I demanded.

Connor looked up at me and frowned.

"Fuck you," he said defiantly.

Wilma shot off his big toe. His wife screamed, and then lost control of her bowels. She cooked up a really nasty smell.

Luckily, they were on a quiet section of the river and had no close neighbors.

"Four hundred thousand in small bills," he blubbered.

"Anything else?" I asked.

"A couple of pounds of coke. I threw it in the river."

I believed the poor sap. The dope might have been worth more than the cash. But if it had been in there since the mid-90s, chances were it hadn't been any good.

I looked at Wilma, "What do you think? Live or die?"

"I have an idea," she replied.

Being on a jet ski out in the St. Clair River after midnight is not only a really bad idea, it's downright dangerous. A steady stream of lake freighters sailed up and down the river all night long.

We strapped the Connors onto one of their ill-gotten jet-skis with nylon ties. I locked another tie over the throttle and turned the ignition key. The watercraft rocketed into the night with the Connors flopping around, and screaming like they were riding Space Mountain.

I waved farewell and wished them good luck. Hopefully the Coast Guard would pick them up before they hit Lake Huron. I sank the other jet-ski and trashed the flat screen. Wilma put the pickup in gear and we pushed it into the river.

For good measure, I used their phone and called the IRS tip line. I reported the Connors had hundreds of thousands in income they had not declared. That should make their life interesting for awhile – if they survived their little excursion out on the river.

Driving away, I felt philosophical about the entire affair.

The Lord giveth and the Lord taketh away.

PRIVATE JETS & FANCY HOUSES

While our field trip had been fun, we were no further ahead than before.

I was hoping Promod might have something interesting for us, but he called the next morning to let me know he was having no luck.

"Some kid from Latvia hacked into the DOJ mainframe, and they've changed all the encryption codes again. It's going to take at least a couple of days to get in."

One of Promod's many skills was his ability to use social engineering to get the information he needed. I had every confidence he would sweet-talk someone at the Department of Justice into giving up the new keys.

I had another favor to ask, and explained what I was hoping he could help us with. He laughed and told me it would be a "piece of cake" and to drop by his office at 4:00.

Since there was nothing else happening, I decided to spend a few extra hours in bed catching up on some sleep.

When I woke up, Little Rip reminded me I had not given him a good workout in a couple of days.

I called the Dearborn Inn and learned that Cinnamon had checked out the day before. She'd probably gone back to New York. I called Matilda at her office but she was at a dentist appointment. I left a message saying I would call back later in the day.

Little Rip was just going to have to wait.

I checked my messages and found several from Felix Frame who sounded progressively more pissed off. I contemplated just how much to tell him.

"Good morning, Felix," I said in my most pleasant voice.

"What the fuck have you been up to?" he growled. "Have you found my stuff yet?"

I felt like pointing out to him that technically it was not his stuff until he paid us $2.5 million. However, I didn't want to antagonize him any further.

"I'm getting close," I said. "I expect to have it in the next day or two."

There was a long silence. I didn't think he bought it.

"You'd better."

Was that an implied threat?

Actually, there was nothing implied about it, and it pissed me off.

The mashed-in face of super model Connie Jackson popped into my head. I fantasized about pulling out one of Frame's eyeballs and making him eat it. I would even put some vinegar on it for him. I just held onto that thought for now. I would make certain Frame paid when the time was right.

"Once I do locate the stuff, you have to be ready to move quickly," I told him.

"Don't worry about that. I have a G-4 standing by."

Ah, the idle rich with their private jets and fancy houses. I had done a little reading about Frame and discovered he owned six houses around the world. According to *Businessweek*, he had an estate on Majorca, a condo overlooking Central Park, a townhouse in Belgravia, a chateau in Provence, a lodge in the Austrian Alps, a private island in the Caribbean, and a mansion in Bel Air.

This was a guy who loved living large. I wondered if he would love to die large. Hopefully he would, and in the slowest and most painful way I could devise. Better still, I would let Wilma dream up something special for him while I watched.

I set the tracker from Wilma's car in front of Promod.

Across the street, the demolition crew was jack hammering away at the upper levels of the Blanchard Building. The vibrations made things hop around on Promod's desk.

"Christ, how can you stand this," I shouted over the din.

Promod concentrated on the tracker. "It's a pain, but they're just about finished prepping it. They sent out a notice that the demolition is scheduled for Sunday morning. They're shutting down the area for safety on Saturday night. We won't have access to our building until Monday morning."

I looked at the Blanchard Building. The skyline would look a lot different after Sunday morning. Another part of the city's history whittled away.

"Now let's see what our little friend has to say." Promod plugged one end of a UBS cable into the tracker and put the other end into his laptop. He studied the screen as letters and numbers flashed by. "It looks as if it isn't being actively monitored. It was up until two days ago, and then they stopped watching."

That made sense. It would have been around the time they reached Nashville and realized they'd been had.

"I'll check the logs to see if I can determine where they've been monitoring it from." Promod scrolled down the screen. "They were moving around a lot, probably following you. I'll plot it."

He brought a city map up on the screen and glowing red lines crisscrossed it. The lines painted a picture of our activities over the past week.

"I can change the variables and pinpoint where and when the devices were planted if that helps," Promod said.

He worked the mouse and keyboard for a few minutes. I watched the lines whip all over the map as he reversed through the data looking for the origin. At last he reached a point where there was only a single line on the screen. It began to recede until it was just a blinking dot.

"That's the point of origin," Promod declared.

Son of a bitch. The blinking dot was Wilma's car.

From its location on the map, I could see it terminated in Inkster near the hotel where I found Barney beaten to a pulp. The date on top of the screen matched that night.

Wilma must have been sitting in her car waiting for me to come out of the motel. Whoever planted it would have had to slide right under the car and carefully attach it to the tailpipe.

That took balls.

They had followed us everywhere over the next few days. My tracker was planted when we parked outside the bar on Mack where we met Lightbulb. That made sense. My car had been in the shop until then so there was no reason to cover it.

These guys were definitely not amateurs.

"It's too bad this thing doesn't work in reverse. I'd like to find out where those fuckers are hiding," I said.

Promod nodded. "Well actually, there might be a way. These things work on a 3G network, like a cell phone. This one uses AT&T as its primary carrier. I might be able to write a macro which will correlate this data with local cell towers, and then hack into their database to match it. It might be a little spotty, but it could give a fairly good idea of where they were monitoring you from."

And maybe where they lived, I thought hopefully.

"Give me a day," Promod said.

I was excited. There was a possibility that we might be able to shine a light into the shadows and get a look at these fuckers at last.

I gave Wilma the bad news that our mysterious pursuers knew where we lived and every move we'd made over the past week.

"That means they know about our safe houses and the farm and everything," she groaned.

I told her about Promod's idea for locating them and her mood brightened.

"If we can find out where they are, we can go after them," I said.

It was our only chance. If we didn't find them, they could expose our secrets to the world, and that would be the end of our business.

However, we had not survived this long without a few tricks of our own.

"They don't know about cold storage," I said.

FORT KNOX

Cold storage was our ultimate fallback.

Years ago we had invested some of our excess capital in a storage facility. I named it Fort Knox Secure Storage after watching *Goldfinger* on the late show. It's located off Twelve Mile near the Lodge Freeway in an area occupied by big box retailers and very few residents.

It had been built to our exact specifications. From the outside it looked like any other storage company – high perimeter fences topped with razor wire, lots of exterior lighting, security cameras, state-of-the-art alarm system, and a wide paved area between the fence and the building. Inside, it's a series of large storage lockers arranged along corridors wide enough to drive a truck through.

No one has ever been in the building except for me and Wilma, but if anyone did, they wouldn't see anything unusual. However, closer inspection would reveal a survivalist's wet dream – lockers filled with weapons and enough food to last a year, along with two fully furnished apartments so Wilma and I can hide out in comfort. There are also numerous escape tunnels. My personal favorite terminates behind a change room wall in the twenty four hour Target next door.

Batman would be proud of us.

When I arrived at Fort Knox, I was certain no one had followed me. I'd taken a meandering route around the city, and made a lot of sudden U-turns to shake off any possible tail.

The only way to open the gate was remotely with a special phone app. I pulled up and keyed in the access code on my cell, careful not to misdial.

One digit wrong and Fort Knox Secure Storage would instantly become a large crater.

The gate opened and I drove through. I waited for it to close securely and then drove up a slight incline. I keyed in a second number on my phone. A heavy steel door rumbled up and allowed me access to the building. I drove in and paused as the door came down, sealing me off from the world.

At last I felt a sense of security. Now, we could get to work.

I parked the car inside a large locker and walked down the corridor to our conference room. Wilma had arrived a few minutes ahead of me. She was already making notes with a blue marker on a whiteboard. She was a visual thinker, and it helped if she could sketch things out.

She had written three lists of names under the headings **OURS**, **FRAME'S**, **UNKNOWN**. These were the dead. Our column started with Walter Randolfo. We had a long list. Frame's was much shorter, but the unknown column was nearly as long as ours.

She had drawn lines between the victims to show their relationships. I wasn't getting much out of Wilma's exercise so I focused on a couple of things she had in boxes near the bottom of the board – ambergris and Alton Geisel. They both had question marks next to them.

She stepped away from the board and contemplated her work.

"Did that help get it out of your system?" I asked her.

"Not really. It's still a clusterfuck," she replied.

"Well, I have a suspicion that our friend Dr. Seuss here," I pointed to Geisel's name on the board, "is Mr. Unknown. And I don't think he's working alone."

"Frame?"

"No, I don't think so."

"The Grinch then," Wilma said with an unpleasant laugh.

I moved on to item number two, the ambergris.

"Frame said there was four hundred pounds of it. That's a lot to hide."

"For all we know, Candle might have stashed it in a place like this," she suggested.

"I don't know. You have to figure the Feds would have looked for it."

"Come on, the FBI? They didn't even check the walls of his cottage," Wilma snorted.

I had to agree with her, it was a possibility. I began to do a quick calculation of the number of storage facilities around Detroit, multiplied by the number of units inside, and divided by the number of ones in existence when Candle began his stretch in prison.

My mind boggled.

"God I wish Donald was here, he would help us clarify this," I said in frustration.

Donald was probably at the bottom of the river by now. It pissed me off that he was collateral damage in our little war. While he wasn't exactly an innocent, he didn't deserve to be tortured and killed.

I wondered if he had been able to crack the Moby code. I was betting he hadn't been able to, and that's why our mysterious friends were still pursuing us.

"So what do you think we should do now?" I asked Wilma.

"Hunker down here for the next seven or eight months and wait for it all to blow over," Wilma suggested. "Hopefully Frame and our mysterious friends will kill each other, and then we can get back to business as usual."

I had to admit that sounded good to me. We hadn't taken a decent break in all the time we'd been in business together. There were always people who needed to be killed, and folks who were willing to pay us to do it. Anyway, I was growing more and more uncomfortable now that we'd popped up on law enforcement radar. It might be a good thing to take some time off and build some more capital in the Bank of Lucky.

Wilma and I hadn't slept together in a while. After what we'd been through over the last few days, and a couple of large glasses of wine, we decided it might be a good way to take the edge off.

She screamed and clawed and generally let it all out. When we finished, I lay on top of her and she ran her fingers up and down my back. She seemed to enjoy being dominated in this way.

I'd gone light on the foreplay and it was obvious she hadn't gotten off. I kissed each nipple softly and watched as she closed her eyes and tilted her head back. Her lips parted as a little smile played across her face. Her moans of pleasure turned into gasps as I worked my way around her body. Then came the full-fledged cries of ecstasy.

Wilma seemed to experience sex, and most other things in life, with a determined intensity that was both exciting and upsetting. While we screwed, she was somewhere inside her head experiencing God knows what – racing down the side of a mountain in a bobsled, descending into the Marianas Trench, or parachuting from the edge of space. Whatever it was, it totally consumed her.

Her orgasm was punctuated by a long, sharp exclamation as her fingernails dug painfully into me. "Thanks," she whispered in my ear, then turned over and went to sleep.

Somewhere in the darkness I could hear screaming. Wilma was already out of bed, stark naked and holding her Kimber. The laser sight was steady on the center of the bedroom door.

I rolled out on the other side, and was feeling for my gun under the pillow when I realized it wasn't a person screaming. It was the ringtone of my phone, which I'd jokingly set to Johnny Weissmuller's Tarzan yell. Wilma jammed her gun under the pillow and crawled back into bed in disgust.

From the phone's display, I could see it was after four in the morning. Who the hell would be calling me at this hour? In fact, who would be calling me at all?

I answered the phone.

"What the hell have you gotten me into?" Promod demanded. He sounded panicked, which was really upsetting because he's the calmest guy I know. "Someone just put a bullet through my window."

"Are you at home?"

"No, at the office. I got caught up in your little problem and lost track of time. I'm pinned down under my desk."

"I'll be right there," I promised.

SHOTS FIRED

Downtown Detroit at 4:30 in the morning is a cemetery.

It took us fifteen minutes to make it to the Guardian Building from Twelve Mile Road. That might have been a land speed record, but it still felt like an eternity.

Promod called me twice on the way downtown to report more shots. We parked on Griswald behind the Guardian and surveyed the scene. There were at least half a dozen tall buildings where a shooter could perch and snipe away.

I called Promod.

"I need you to do me a favor and stand up."

"Are you crazy," he screamed.

I held the phone away from my ear.

"We need to get a line of sight on the shooter."

However he didn't need to stand up. There was a bright flash from the roof of the Penobscot Building next door.

"He got my laptop that time," Promod howled.

"Okay, we got a bead on him. I'll be right up."

Wilma was already on the move zigzagging up Griswald toward the Penobscot. I made a beeline toward the back of the Guardian Building. Of course at this hour, admittance was by card only.

I checked the security company badge on the door and pulled the correct access card for the system from my wallet. I had master key cards from each of the major security companies so getting into a building and operating elevators after hours was no problem.

The security desk faced Woodward and the guard didn't see me until I was right on top of him. By then it was too late. I took his uniform jacket and cap and headed for the elevators. When they reviewed the camera footage later it would be impossible to see my face under the hat's brim.

I turned off the lights in the corridor outside Promod's office so that I wouldn't present a target when I entered. The lights in the outer office were off. I lay on the floor and pushed open the inner door to his office. A bullet smacked into the back of his secretary's chair. I reached up and killed the lights. That would force the shooter to switch over to a night vision scope and might buy us a few seconds. I kept low and crawled to the desk beside Promod.

"You okay?" I asked.

Apart from being scared shitless, he was unharmed and busy prying a hard drive out of his shattered Dell laptop.

"Just stay down," I cautioned and peeked over the top of the desk.

Come on, Wilma.

As if in answer to my plea, there were multiple gun flashes from the roof of the Penobscot Building. It looked like a running gun battle was happening over there. Wilma had engaged the shooter. I could hear the sound of multiple gunshots reverberating off the buildings around us. If it had been anywhere but Detroit someone might have even paid attention.

Then there was darkness again. A few seconds later my phone rang.

Wilma was out of breath. "I think the shooter went off the roof."

"He fell?" I asked with a shudder.

"Well, he certainly disappeared," she gasped.

"Did you get a look at him?"

"Nope, he was wearing a Zentai suit."

I thought we were the only ones who did that. These guys were good.

"What about my family?" Promod asked, starting to panic.

"It's okay. They don't know where you live."

"How can you be sure? They found out where I work."

"That's because I inadvertently led them to you with the GPS tracker. They probably reactivated it," I said.

"So why shoot at me?"

Why indeed? Then I had a sinking feeling. I hit the speed dial on my phone.

"Watch out! I think it's a trap," I shouted to Wilma.

"I just found some sort of climbing tackle on the edge of the roof. These guys are crazy. I think they climbed down the side of the building," she said in wonder.

I had an image of Wilma standing on the edge of the building. I shivered as my acrophobia kicked in. My fear of heights isn't one of those little crawly feelings in the pit of the stomach. It's a full blown, paralyzing, can't breathe, Jimmy Stewart in *Vertigo*, irrational, fear. Wilma always handles the high altitude work; she has no problem with it. I'm okay *inside* tall buildings as long as I stay away from the windows. Put me on a roof or some other open space high up, however, and I turn into lime Jell-O.

"Take a look around," I suggested.

Wilma laughed. "There's some blood up here. Since it's not my time of the month, I must have winged one of them."

"Be careful anyway. I'll meet you out back in five. We'll have two to beam up."

There was silence.

"I don't think that's a great idea," she said coldly.

I scurried across the floor away from Promod.

"We need him alive. He's our best hope to track down these assholes," I whispered.

More silence. Finally she sighed in resignation.

"I guess, but we dose him."

I looked back at Promod who had succeeded in getting the hard drive from the remains of his machine.

"Just a light one," I said.

She disconnected.

I crawled back to Promod. "Keep low. We're getting out of here."

He nodded and followed me.

It took us a little while to get down fourteen flights of stairs to the lobby. Wilma was waiting in the car when we got there. I pulled a hood over Promod's head and led him to the car. Wilma popped the trunk and I helped Promod inside.

Rolling up his sleeve, I warned him, "This is going to sting for a moment."

I injected a small amount of sedative into his vein. He would sleep soundly for at least an hour.

"I don't like this," Wilma said as we pulled into Fort Knox.

"Why not? Superman took Lois to the Fortress of Solitude. Batman showed off the Batcave to Alfred."

We had argued about it all the way back.

The soundproof room was similar to the one in the house in Sunset. I dropped Promod's limp form on a cot. We had agreed that Wilma would stay out of the picture. Promod had only dealt with me and it was a good idea to keep it that way.

A couple of hours later, Promod was still groggy from the drug. I passed him a glass of green tea.

"Thanks," he said in a shaky voice.

"I need you to find those guys for me," I told him and held up the hard drive salvaged from his laptop.

"I just about had it when they started shooting," he said. "Now, I'll have to start from scratch."

"What do you need?" I asked.

He rubbed his face. "A computer lab with data retrieval software."

"Would you settle for a laptop with high speed access?"

"I need some way to get the data off this drive. The motor's probably damaged."

I led him down the hall to the room where Wilma kept her computer gear. He stopped in the doorway and admired the set up.

"Wow, this is really serious stuff," he said.

I wasn't worried about Promod learning anything from our system. It was completely virgin and had never been used. We kept a series of clean IP accounts for emergencies like this.

"I'm going to have to lock you in now. Sorry. If you need anything, just pick up the phone and let me know."

He was already transfixed by his new toys. "Give me a couple of hours," he said absently as he began to work on the drive.

"So is Bill Gates happy with his new home?" Wilma asked when I joined her in the kitchen for breakfast.

She'd gone to Target and picked up some groceries, including bacon and eggs. Some of Wilma's wonderful scrambled eggs were still in a sauce pan on the stove. Wilma made the best scrambled eggs I'd ever tasted. They were light and fluffy, with a silky texture. She claimed her secret was a little cream and just the right amount of cooking time. The one time I tried to cook them myself, she told me to take them off the heat before they were fully set, and let them finish cooking. I never got it right. My eggs came out like drywall compound.

"Yeah, he has everything he needs."

I sat down and dug into my eggs. "So what happened on the roof?" I asked when I'd finished.

"Whoever was up there was a pro. It took me a couple of shots before I located him. Just as I was about to pop him, he turned and began firing in my direction, as if he had sixth sense or something."

"Or night vision goggles and someone backing him up," I said.

She nodded. "Anyway, we had a little gunfight and he pinned me down behind the elevator housing." She chewed on the corner of a piece of toast. "When I came up for air, he'd disappeared."

"Down the side of the building," I said.

"I found his climbing stuff anchored to the window washer's winch. It takes real guts to rappel down the side of a forty story building at night."

I had to agree, and shuddered again just at the thought of scaling down the building.

"Those assholes went to all that trouble just for this." She held up another GPS tracker. "I found it under the car."

"Shooting at Promod was a distraction to lure us downtown so they could plant it. They figured that we wouldn't stop in all the confusion," I said. "That takes balls."

"Yeah well, fool me once ..." she muttered.

"So why go to all this trouble," I wondered.

"It's obvious they don't know where the ambergris is either," Wilma said. "They think we might lead them to it."

"That would mean that they didn't get anything out of Donald before they killed him."

"Maybe he didn't figure it out," she said.

I remembered the sprays of blood from the Louisville Slugger on the ceiling of Barney's motel room. It wasn't a pretty way to die. I hoped they'd made it quick for Donald.

I poured a cup of coffee and started down the hall to see how Promod was getting along.

My phone rang and our world changed once again.

IT'S A TRAP!

Donald was alive.

His voice was thin and shaky on the phone. "They keep beating me," he sobbed in fear.

I listened closely trying to pick up any background sounds that might help me find where they were keeping him, but that only happened in cheap crime novels.

Donald sounded traumatized. He didn't have the stamina for this level of mayhem.

"Where are you right now?" I said in a calming voice. "I'm coming to get you."

"I don't know, but they're going to kill me if you don't give them the book," he pleaded. "Remember, you promised to keep it *safe* for me. I have a buyer who's willing to pay *ninety eight fifty six* for it."

A cold mechanical voice came on the line. "Your friend is going to have a hard time walking for a while. If you want him to continue breathing, you better bring us the book."

Before I could answer, he disconnected.

I told Wilma the details of the call.

"And that's exactly what he told you, word-for-word?" she asked.

"Yes," I replied.

"Well at least Donald was smart enough to tell us where it is and how to get it."

Donald had been focused enough to put a subtle emphasis on the word "*safe*" and I flashed on the big walk-in vault down in the basement of his shop. The amount he said the buyer was willing to pay was, of course, the combination to unlock it. Was it *nine* to the left and *eight* to the right, followed by *five* and then *six*? It might take me a while to run a bunch of different possibilities, but I knew that I could find the right one.

We looked up in surprise at a sound from the kitchen doorway.

"I need a couple of 32 gig memory keys if you have them," Promod said looking in at us.

Wilma had her Kimber out and a red laser dot hovered on the tip of Promod's nose.

He walked in nonchalantly and picked up a piece of toast from a plate on the table.

"Sorry, but you guys really cheaped out on the locks in here." He dropped a twisted paperclip on the table.

The red dot dancing around his nose disappeared as Wilma put her gun away.

"You must be Wilma." He extended his hand. "Glad to meet you."

She turned to me in disgust. "Is there any secret of ours this guy *doesn't* know?"

I promised to pick up the USB keys he wanted on my way back from Donald's shop.

Along with guns and rations, we also store a few spare vehicles at Fort Knox. You never know when you might need a new car. We also have some more exotic forms of transportation. I decided that a bike might be a better way to travel. There was a good chance this was going to be an ambush, and a motorcycle would give me more flexibility if I had to make a run for it.

I choose my favorite, a Yamaha R1. It was a bit of a bastard to control, but it was lightning fast and agile once you got used to its quirks. Mine was custom-painted a flat gray and had a matching carbon fiber cowl.

For extra peace of mind I dropped a Steyr TMP machine-pistol along with a half dozen extra-capacity ammo clips into a box hidden under the seat. I also strapped a Beretta 93R under my leather riding gear. It was fully automatic and would give me a real edge if I ran into an army.

Now I felt confident that I was ready to retrieve the book.

Promod admired the bike. "Nice," he said.

Wilma shook her head. "I don't like this," she said. "You know it's a trap. Let me come along for backup."

I slapped the seat of the Yamaha.

"I'll be okay." I dropped my voice, "You need to stay here and keep an eye on him."

I nodded at Promod who had been distracted by one of our Segway scooters.

"Can I use this to get around?" he asked excitedly.

I waited until after dark before heading to Grosse Pointe. Ripping along the Interstate on the bike was exhilarating. I looked truly evil in my matching gray leather racing suit and helmet. However, this wasn't a pleasure trip and the fact that I might be walking into a trap tempered the joy I felt riding the bike.

I debated about parking a few blocks away and sneaking up to Donald's shop through neighboring backyards. I finally decided to park out front just in case I needed to make a quick getaway. Windows glowed up and down the quiet street. These were houses filled with everyday upper-middle classers watching the latest episode of *American Idol*.

I walked around to the back with a stride that told anyone watching I belonged there.

I picked the lock. Once inside, I used the alarm codes Wilma had given me to deactivate the security system.

The safe in the cellar was one of those old-fashioned models that looked like it would survive the second coming of Christ. I began dialing various combinations using the numbers Donald had given me. The third attempt produced a satisfying click. Inside the safe were metal shelves with Donald's rarest first editions. I spotted a couple by Edgar Allan Poe, and a copy of *Farewell to Arms*. I took it down and opened it. The signature on the inscription was almost as large as Hemingway's ego. There was also a first edition of *For Whom the Bell Tolls* beside it.

I hoped it did not toll for me.

Moby Dick sat on a shelf all by itself. Donald's grid lay beside it. I grabbed both and put them into the nylon messenger bag slung over my shoulder.

While I was concentrating on relocking the safe I missed a sound from above. It had been a soft footstep. I was just about to go up the stairs leading to Donald's office. A tiny puff of dust from the rafters caught my attention. I froze. There was a second creak as someone moved up there. More dust filtered down.

As suspected, it was an ambush. I slid the Beretta out and thumbed off the safety. I selected the three-shot-burst option, and folded down its fore-grip so I could keep the gun from pulling up when I fired.

It sounded like there was only one person. I had to assume he was a highly efficient killer.

From where the dust was coming down, I knew the attacker was positioned between the stairs and the back door. He would blow my head off when I emerged.

I'd left the lights off in the office so he must've had a night vision scope. Time to even the odds.

I snapped the cap off a Thunderflash grenade and counted off a few seconds. I lobbed it up the stairs. It exploded with a brilliant flash and thunderous bang, which shook a lot more dust loose. I ran for the stairs and threw a blue smoke bomb.

When I reached the top, I could see someone stumbling around in the smoke and darkness, stunned and temporarily blinded from the Thunderflash. I dropped to my knee, fired a couple of quick bursts in his direction, and then sprinted for the front door.

I chopped away the door's lock with another burst, and smashed into it at full tilt. As I hit the heavy oak door, I felt my left shoulder crunch inside and grow numb. I hoped I hadn't dislocated it. That would make it difficult to ride the bike.

On the front porch, I wheeled and fired another round through the shattered doorway to discourage anyone from following.

I ran to my bike, praying there wasn't more than one shooter. Throwing myself on it, I fired up the engine with a loud roar. That would certainly bring the neighbors to their front windows, if the sound of the gunfire hadn't already. As I twisted the throttle, I was relieved to see my shoulder was not badly injured. It hurt like a son of a bitch, but I still had full mobility.

My front wheel stayed in the air for almost a block as I raced away. No one seemed to be pursuing me. Regardless, I opened her up and put as much distance as I could between myself and Grosse Pointe.

Wilma and Promod were sharing a laugh over a cup of tea when I walked in. I slapped the book down on the table.

"Now we're right back where we started," Wilma said.

"Did you happen to remember my memory keys?" Promod asked.

I glared at him and shook my head. He was starting to get on my nerves.

He examined the book. "Nice. Is it a first edition?" Promod then picked up the grid. "What's this? A transposition cipher?"

"Transposition cipher?" we both asked.

"Yeah, it's the kind of thing kids do to send secret messages. It's pretty rudimentary."

"Can you read it?" I asked him.

"Sure. It should be easy. Do you have the key?"

From our blank expressions he quickly gathered that we did not. I explained about the book and the dots under the letters. He looked at the grid again. He opened the book and carefully flipped to the back page. Flipping forward a few pages, he compared it to the grid.

"Looks like he transferred all of it to the grid. Now, I just have to find the key."

"What's a transposition cipher?" Wilma asked.

"Say for example the word you want to encrypt begins with an A you might decide that you will transpose G for it. Now the alphabet would begin with the letter G and flow from there. Your key would be 7 because G is the seventh letter in the alphabet. That's how a kid would do it.

"However, to make it more secure you might add further layers of encryption by moving forward or backward a certain number of letters in the alphabet. Let's say you provide a key that is nine numbers long. That means you start at the last number and work backward. The first number will reveal the message."

"Sounds complicated," I said.

Promod rolled his eyes. "Yeah, well it is supposed to be a secret code after all."

"So you could decipher it?" Wilma asked him.

"Yes, I should be able to. Once I have the key, I won't know whether or not the numbers intend for us to move forward or backwards so there'll be thousands of possible combinations to work out. I can write a macro to run that. The challenge will be figuring out the key."

"Forget the GPS stuff right now," I said. "Concentrate on cracking this first."

Promod picked up the book and the grid.

"Should be fun," he said and strolled off down the hall.

PERSPECTIVISM

"Are you going to call Frame about the book?" Wilma asked.

"Nope. Right now it's the only advantage we've got. Anyway, I think we should make him sweat for a while. Let's follow the money," I suggested.

Wilma gave me a look as if I'd suggested we dance naked in the moonlight.

"The money?"

"Okay, the ghost of the money that's yet to come," I said. "We know Frame will pay us millions for finding the whale shit ..."

"Whale vomit," she corrected.

"Yeah, whale barf. But who else out there might want to buy it? And more importantly, will they pay more?"

"Since it's illegal to possess and sell in the US, as well as most other countries," she said, "maybe Russia or Japan? They both still actively hunt whales."

"And they both have large markets for luxury goods such as expensive perfumes."

"So you figure these other guys are some sort of Ninja gang or the Russian mob?"

"No. If they were Russian or Japanese, they wouldn't keep missing," I said. "I think these guys are just ordinary crooks."

"I don't buy it. They set up an ambush and send only one person," she replied, and then had a thought. "You checked the bike for tracking devices didn't you?"

I nodded, "I stopped downtown and gave the bike a thorough going over. It's clean."

"So how come they let us have the book?" Wilma asked.

"Maybe they want us to find the ambergris so we can lead them to it?" I ventured.

She shook her head. "How do we arrive at absolute truth?" she asked.

Oh Christ, she's going to introduce *Perspectivism* in the equation.

"Nietzsche? Really?" I groaned.

"Why not? Let's assume there are no objective facts or single point of view that leads us to the absolute truth. We have to take all points of view into consideration to arrive at the truth."

"Their point of view definitely is to kill us and get the ambergris," I said.

"And that's not any different from ours."

She'd always been a pseudo-intellectual, but she might have a point. I could see where she was going with this. Simply put, what would we do if we were out there in the shadows? We knew Frame's point of view. We knew our own. But what did we know about our mysterious friends' point of view? That was the missing piece of the equation.

What was their absolute truth?

The next morning I decided to let Frame know we'd recovered the book. I was curious to see what his next move might be.

"So where does the book say the ambergris is hidden?" he demanded.

I was getting sick of his commanding attitude. In my eyes, he was nothing more than a high-maintenance client who would pay well for our services. To him, we were nothing but a pair of thugs he'd hired to find his treasure.

In purely Nietzschean terms, both these points of view probably formed an absolute truth. But I just didn't give a shit.

Here was another absolute truth to consider: he was never going to get the ambergris because I was going to shoot holes in him for what he did to Cinnamon.

"We should have it figured out today."

"Once you do, I want to know," he said.

"And why would I tell you? We can arrange an exchange later after we have the stuff."

"Because you're going to need help moving it," he said in a tone someone would use when talking to a slow child, "and if you don't tell me, I'm going to have Mark slice up Cinnamon's face."

"What? You thought she'd gone back home," he said cruelly. "She hasn't paid me back yet for fucking you, and for costing me half a million."

"You hurt her again and I'll kill you," I said evenly.

"Get off the fucking pot," he shouted. "I want to be there when you find it. That way I can be sure any thought you might have about double crossing me is not going to happen."

I held my next threat in check. Why not have him and his henchman come along? They would be able to help carry the load, and once it was safe and secure in the trunk of our car, we could kill them both.

"Okay," I said softly in my best conciliatory manner. "Just don't hurt Cinnamon."

"I'll take it under consideration if you're a good little monkey."

I consoled myself by imagining the various ways in which I would carve him into small fashion accessories.

He had me agree to call him the second I knew the location of the ambergris.

Ten minutes later, I got a call from Mr. Mechanical Voice with the same basic demand.

Once the code was cracked, we were to tell him where the stuff was or we would become proud members of the body-part-of-the-month club and their first offering would be Donald's left foot.

"How do I get hold of you?" I asked.

The voice rattled off a cell phone number and I wrote it down. As it was probably a burner like mine, there was no point in trying to trace it.

When I told Wilma about Frame and Mr. Mechanical Voice and their demands she smiled. "When we finally find it, there's going to be quite a crowd," she said.

"I guess we'll just have to plan for that."

FUCKITY FUCKER

Guns made Dorsey Mason uneasy, which was ironic since he'd carried one for almost forty years.

I aimed a large pistol straight at his chest.

Earlier I'd trailed him to a Farmer Jack's and waited patiently in the parking lot. He finally came out carrying a couple of large paper bags filled with groceries. I got the jump on him, and pushed him into the trunk of his Cadillac.

I drove us to a remote state park where there weren't a lot of people around, especially at this time of day, and parked on a boat ramp.

I had remembered Del's comment about a few guys he knew who had a grudge to settle with Alton Geisel. I spent an hour online looking up old court records and discovered some ex-DPD guys who Geisel had ratted out. Most of these axe grinders were long dead, but former Detective Sargent Dorsey Mason was still with us. He was living out a bitter existence in a tiny apartment off Eight Mile Road.

"Fuck you, you fuckity fucker," he screamed when I opened the trunk. He tried to kick out at me, but his arthritic knees robbed him of most of his oomph.

"Dorsey, please. There's no call for such profanity. And by the way, I don't think there is such as word as 'fuckity'," I said.

"Fuck you. I'm an ex-cop, you fucker. I've still got lots of friends on the fucking force."

"Actually, you're a dirty ex-cop who got kicked off the force and, sadly, you have no friends," I said. "So when you turn up floating in this lake, no one's really going to care."

That settled him right down.

"Alton Geisel," I said.

"Is a fucker," he muttered glumly.

I nodded. "That's true. He certainly fucked you."

He kicked over one of the grocery bags. A plastic bottle of vodka rolled out and across the trunk.

"I could use your help to find Geisel," I told him.

"Fuck you. Why would I fucking help you?"

"Because I want to find Alton Geisel, and I'm betting that you'd like to find him too."

"I'd like to fucking blow his fucking head off. The fuck."

Dorsey certainly had a chip on his shoulder.

"Anyway, he disappeared years ago. So good luck with that," he laughed.

"Maybe you could tell me what he looked like before he disappeared," I said.

"You ever hear of plastic surgery? Because Geisel was a sure candidate for it. He had the worst acne I ever saw. His face was a real pizza pie. A new mask was probably part of his deal with the Feds."

"Oh, I'm sure it was, along with a whole new identity. I bet if you think real hard you might remember something that surgery and a new identity couldn't cover up."

He shook his head stubbornly. I put the barrel of my gun in his ear.

"What else do you remember about him?" I asked coldly.

"Not much. He kept to himself a lot. Ben Candle was a straight-up guy, but Alton was a sneaky fucker. I don't think anyone really trusted him."

"What about a girlfriend? Did he have one?"

"Not that I knew of."

"Did he have any hobbies?"

"Now that you mention it, he sang opera. Had a nice voice."

"Really?" I was surprised.

"You know what?" he said.

"Yeah." I nodded. "Fuck you."

He grinned defiantly in a way that told me that was everything I was going to get from him.

I thanked him politely for his help and received another "fuck you" in return, which helped mitigate any feelings I might have had for him. I closed the trunk and put the car into gear. A little nudge sent it down the ramp into the lake.

I thought I heard a few muffled fucks before the car belched out a huge bubble of air and sank out of sight.

Little Rip was feeling restless as I walked back to where I'd stashed the bike. It was a little before 7:00 on a Friday night. I wondered what Matilda was up to, so I called her.

She sounded like hell. "Sorry lubber, I had my wisdom teef out yesterday and I doned feel berry frisky."

Just my luck...

I promised her I'd call within the next week.

Back in Fort Knox I was stowing the bike away in its locker when I heard shots. I pulled my gun and ran in their direction.

Wilma stood beside Promod holding his hand steady. She had been giving him lessons. Just what I needed – a cagey hacker who knew how to shoot accurately.

He fired another burst at the paper silhouette target in our range.

"This is really fun," Promod said as he turned and gestured excitedly with the gun.

I pushed the barrel aside so it wasn't pointed at my navel.

"Glad you're having a good time," I said coolly. "Did you manage to crack the code?"

"I thought he should have a little break," Wilma said taking the gun from his hand, seeing I was in a foul mood.

"Yeah, well that's really great, but the bars are coming down around us. We need to know where the stuff is."

Promod looked a little sheepish and left.

"So why are you feeling so pissy all of a sudden?"

I told her about Mason.

It made her feel pissy too.

SQUEEZING RALPH KARNEÉ

That night she joined me in bed without being invited.

We tried, but my bad mood spoiled any chance of sex. Finally we settled for spooning. She fell asleep first, and I watched her snoring gently beside me. Wilma's features were softer in sleep, showing the beauty she fought hard to hide behind a barrier of bravado and toughness. There was a hint of a smile on her lips, as if she was dreaming of something sweet – like chopping up Frame with a hatchet.

I thought back to the beginning of our life together, when everything was possible, and we were still high on the excitement of what we were doing.

You don't just get up one morning and decide you want to get into the people killing business. It was a big jump from starting fires to committing homicides. First there was a nagging feeling, like a grain of sand inside an oyster. It took time before I graduated from arson and progressed into murder-for-hire.

It was fortunate Wilma came into my life when she did. There was an unexplainable attraction that led us to this place. It had been a little like seduction. It started with a conversation heavy with innuendo. Like prospective lovers, we quickly discovered we were on the same wave length as we progressed through "what if" and "perhaps we" until, at last, we were seriously contemplating the act and its consequences.

We knew no one would pay us unless we established ourselves. We decided to select a target that would have some visibility in our prospective marketplace.

I had someone in mind – a local political fixer named Ralph Karneé.

Karneé had been a thorn in the side of Michigan progressives for years. He spread money like lard on any conservative cause that took his fancy. His largess was not only confined to politics; Karneé was also a glutton.

A normal breakfast for him consisted of a pound of bacon fried extra crispy, half a pound of home fries, and a dozen eggs scrambled hard – and that was just to start the day. He got hungrier from there.

All that food had ballooned Karneé to over three hundred pounds by the time he was thirty. The only exercise he got was lifting his fat ass out of his Cadillac and onto a motorized scooter.

A saying used to go around in political circles that *Ralph needed a taxi to go to the bathroom.*

Over the years Karneé had used his money and influence to support regressive policies, including opposing any sort of environmental reform or equal opportunity legislation. When we decided he would make a great first target, Karneé had just bought and paid for a bill allowing bottled water companies unlimited use of the Great Lakes.

It irked me when I read in the *Free Press* that the lakes were up for grabs by any company with enough plastic to drain them dry and bottle them up.

I had a vision of Ralph Karneé swallowing the entire state in one gulp. I resolved that he had to die. It didn't take much to convince Wilma, especially after she discovered he had paid for a change in law that allowed a protected wetland to be redeveloped as a tire recycling facility.

Wilma had a soft spot for ducks and turtles.

To gain credibility in our mission, however, we needed a sponsor, someone who hated Karneé enough to pay for our services. This wasn't as hard as you would imagine. There was a quite a long list of political enemies and everyday citizens who hated Ralph Karneé even more than we did.

We settled on Hollis McAlpine.

He had once been the most liberal member of the Detroit city council until Karneé tangled him up in a scandal that involved everything from accepting illegal payoffs to child molestation. When Karneé finished framing McAlpine, he was a husk. He'd lost everything – his family, his home, his position, his freedom.

Worst of all, he lost the respect he had built up after serving the city faithfully for over fifteen years. Karneé's money had paid for witnesses, bribes, and newspaper column inches. In the end Hollis McAlpine went to prison for five years and emerged a bitter, defeated man.

This made him the perfect customer for our particular brand of retribution services.

This all happened in 1996, just when a new phenomenon called the internet was sweeping across the nation. Back then it was little more than a novelty to most folks. However, Wilma had taken some computer courses at U of M, and understood the potential this new technology had in our line of work.

This was the wild-west era of the internet, long before anyone thought seriously about securing their data archives from prying eyes. Wilma used her limited skills to hack into Karneé's computer system and rooted out all kinds of damaging information, including how he had engineered Hollis McAlpine's downfall.

Hollis McAlpine was working as a greeter in a Walmart in Livonia when I first contacted him. I borrowed one of my sister Jeannie's kids, my two year old nephew Aaron. I stopped at Dairy Queen and let the kid fill up on Blizzards and orange pop. Then I bounced him around in his car seat for a few miles. By the time we reached Livonia he was ready to blow.

McAlpine stood at the front door of the store with a plastic smile pasted on his face. The rest of him looked dead; especially his eyes. They were tiny beads set in deep craters. His hair was gray and so dry there was a danger of a brush fire starting there. I'd seen lots of pictures of him from his days on council – smiling, shaking hands, cutting ribbons. It was hard to reconcile that man with this one.

I felt a twinge of anger at what Karneé had done to him.

McAlpine barely got through his "welcome to Walmart" spiel before Aaron threw up on him. Apologizing profusely, I helped McAlpine clean himself up. In the process, I slipped a folded piece of paper into his left pants pocket.

The document I'd put in his pocket was a detailed account of how Karneé had framed him, including a list of the evidence we had. It ended with a call to action if he wanted to avenge his ruination and recover his respect. There were no throw away cell phones in those days, so I left the number of a phone booth with a specific time to call.

"Call me Rip," I said as I sat down across from McAlpine several days later.

We had agreed to meet in a Wendy's next to the dumpy motel where he lived. He was still wearing his blue greeter's vest from Walmart.

"You can do what you said in the letter?" he asked, his voice filled with more emotion than I would have expected.

"Yes," I replied.

McAlpine took the letter out and unfolded it. He read it through once again. When he looked up, I thought he was going to cry.

"This can happen one of two ways. The first is that you agree to hire us to kill Ralph Karneé and expose all his nasty little secrets, including how he framed you. Then you sue his estate and eventually make millions," I whispered. "You get revenge and get back your respect, and we get 50k when you've won your lawsuit. By the way, as an extra incentive, if you don't win, we'll waive our fee.

"The second option is that you don't agree. In that case, I get up from this table and you never see or hear from me again, and Ralph Karneé continues to practice his particular form of evil.

"This is a one-time offer."

It was quite a mouthful, but I managed to get it all out while keeping a smile on my face. He looked at me grimly.

"So you want me to contract you to kill him?"

I nodded and dipped a fry into my bowl of chili.

Even with all the rotten things that had fallen on him, I could tell he was struggling with it morally. I remained silent. He had to come to his own decision as to whether or not he could step into the darkness with us. After all, I wouldn't be the one who would wake up night after night agonizing over the guilt of having a man killed.

It was his own personal *Road to Damascus.*

Still, it was maddening to watch him. I had no such qualms myself. In fact, I was looking forward to sending Karneé to the all-you-can-eat special in the sky. It would be a pleasure, and if it ever woke me up at night, it would only be to laugh.

However, Hollis McAlpine had what I didn't: a basic sense of right and wrong. Again, I looked at it in purely Nietzschean terms as just one more vantage point to the absolute truth of Ralph Karneé's death.

Hurry up, I silently urged McAlpine as he looked down at the document once again.

Then his eyes met mine and they were on fire. "Let's burn the sucker," he said.

Wilma and I decided that Karneé's departure from this earth had to be spectacular. We wanted a real show piece to kick off our new enterprise. Over the next few days we went into serious planning mode. We printed out hundreds of incriminating documents, organizing and filing them neatly in folders.

Karneé had a shit mountain of proof on his computer in case his masters ever turned on him. With a little rudimentary hacking, we were going to show it the light of day.

There was enough material here to bring down dozens of corrupt politicians, jurists, and corporate executives. There was also documentation that would prove how innocent people like Hollis McAlpine had been maliciously prosecuted and convicted. Most importantly, there were accounts that showed just where all the money had come from.

Karneé's computer contained hundreds of smoking guns.

After a bit of testing, we finally agreed we had estimated just the right amount of C4 to do the job.

Wilma fashioned the plastic explosive into the perfect shape to reflect the force of the blast upward, not outward. This would help minimize collateral damage. She reprogrammed a stolen pager to act as a detonator and packed it deep inside the C4.

It was a cold evening in January.

Ralph Karneé waddled out of Joe Louis Arena after treating a couple of state senators and a federal judge to a Red Wings game in his private box. He huffed and puffed his way to his Caddy, which was waiting next to the curb. A red-jacketed valet was holding the door open for him.

"Thanks," he muttered, and pressed a greasy ten dollar bill into the valet's hand. I smiled, thanked him, and shut his door after Karneé had wedged himself in behind the steering wheel.

I watched as he drove away, and then let the ten bucks flutter to the pavement. With any luck, some wino would find it and think he had gone to heaven. As Karneé maneuvered his car out onto Jefferson, I walked away from Joe Louis pulling on a heavy parka over my red valet jacket.

Wilma was waiting in traffic near the entrance to the Ford Auditorium parking garage. We fell in behind Karneé and followed at a safe distance. There was a lot of post-game traffic around him, so it wasn't possible to detonate the bomb.

We were in no hurry. The bomb was secured under the driver's seat with no chance of being discovered. We figured he would head up to Greektown for a midnight snack.

True to form, he ignored the **NO LEFT TURN** sign at Beaubien, and went up a few blocks to Monroe. He pulled into a no stopping area in front of a Greek tavern on the corner. The hockey crowd hadn't reached it yet and Greektown was still fairly quiet.

I dialed the pager.

There was a sharp bang and three tons of Cadillac lifted four feet off the pavement. While the car did buckle in the middle, the brunt of the explosion ripped through the floor just behind the driver's seat and propelled it forward. Ralph Karneé was thrown head first through the windshield. It looked as if someone had stomped down hard on one end of a packet of ketchup and it had splattered all over the place.

The explosion blew out the windows in the tavern along with half the other businesses at that end of the block. A couple of waiters ran out onto the sidewalk and looked at the burning wreck. One of them went in and got a chemical fire extinguisher and sprayed it into the passenger compartment of the Caddy. It had little effect on the flames.

I was happy we had invested in sturdy a fireproof document case to protect the evidence we had planted in Karneé's trunk.

Detroit FD finally arrived and got the fire under control. The police arrived and cordoned off the area.

We drove along Munroe in the other direction.

Karneé's death was front page news in the papers the next day. However, many more interesting stories began to appear several weeks later. Yet again, Detroit was consumed by scandal.

Hollis McAlpine, who I'd code-named Richard Kimball, rose to the top of the heap of bodies who Karneé had thrown under the bus. He became the poster child for the crimes of Ralph Karneé. Media stories began to highlight the horrible injustice that had been done to him by Karneé and his confederates. With the media baying for blood, the Governor urged the court to quickly hear McAlpine's appeal.

In the light of all of the new evidence the Governor decreed that Hollis McAlpine's conviction be set aside. McAlpine was resurrected from the dead. A few years later, there was even a movement to draft him to run for mayor.

That was an honor he was smart enough to decline.

Hollis McAlpine gratefully paid us off years earlier than I expected when he was offered a million bucks by a film company for the rights to his story. Of course he left out the part about me and Wilma, but he did pass along a recommendation for our services to a friend in city hall who was having issues with an indiscreet mistress.

Our initial taste of murder for hire had been an auspicious first step into a much larger world. At the end of the day, we looked back with joy – a really bad guy had been punished, lots of other bad guys had gone to jail, some of their innocent victims had been exonerated and, best of all, we earned some cash.

Life was grand.

THE TARGET EXIT

Wilma stirred beside me.

At some point I'd drifted off and dreamed sweetly of the bullet-riddled and otherwise mangled remains of our numerous targets. When I woke up, it was back to reality and a feeling of impending doom that I couldn't seem to shake. I slipped out of bed, trying not to wake Wilma.

Son of a bitch; Promod was gone.

I checked all the rooms. They were empty. There was no sign of Promod or the grid or the book. I went back and woke Wilma.

Her first reaction was to track him down and kill him.

"He's figured out the where it's stashed," I told her. "How the hell did he get out of here without setting off the alarms?"

Stupid question; with his skills, it would have been easy.

"He likely went out the Target exit," Wilma said as she brought the store's security cameras online. She wound back through the footage, and discovered Promod leaving the store three hours before.

I checked our arsenal. He had taken several pistols.

"Looks like he's going to make a run at the treasure all by himself," I said.

Wilma tried to keep the panic out of her voice. "You have any idea how we're going to find him?"

"I've got nothing. But if he tries to make a deal to sell it, they're going to grind him up."

We took a little time to think through our actions.

"We need mobility," I said, and Wilma agreed.

We had a panel van stashed in one of the back lockers. It had been painted to resemble a Fiber Vibe van. Fiber Vibe was a local tech company that installed and repaired fiber optic cables all over the city. They worked under contract with the phone and cable companies. Their vans were always blocking traffic. Our modified model had hidden racks for weapons, sophisticated surveillance and monitoring devices, a microwave, fridge, and chemical toilet for long stakeouts.

We packed all the necessities, including lots of guns, eavesdropping equipment, and explosives. When I was finished loading the van, I felt like we were ready to go to war. We were both dressed in Fiber Vibe coveralls to complete the deception.

It was 5:30 on Saturday morning when we pulled out of Fort Knox Secure Storage and the gate closed behind us. We headed downtown.

We had unfinished business with Frame.

And I was going to get Cinnamon back.

THE LOUSY AIM OF AN
IMPERIAL STORM TROOPER

I parked the van in front of the Marriott.

Wilma had hacked into the hotel's registration system while I drove and found out Frame et al were still in residence. He had several suites on the top floor of the hotel.

The Marriott had excellent security, but no one stopped us as we entered the hotel.

"I'd be surprised to find her there," Wilma said as we rode up in the elevator.

She was wrong. As the door opened, we saw Cinnamon, Frame, and Lurch hurrying along the corridor. We aimed our automatic weapons at them and they froze.

"A little early for breakfast," I said. "McDonald's doesn't open until 7:00."

Frame held up his hands in exasperation. Lurch brought up a mean looking Scorpion machine pistol and began to fire in our direction. Wilma pulled me into an alcove next to an ice machine. Bullet holes tacked along the hallway walls. Luckily he had the lousy aim of an Imperial Storm Trooper.

Wilma poked her machine gun around the corner and fired a blast in return.

I grabbed her arm. "Careful," I cautioned, "Cinnamon's with them." She shook my hand off and fired another burst.

"That's right. She's *with them*," Wilma growled.

It dawned on me that she was right. Cinnamon didn't appear to be in peril.

"Someday I'm going to do us both a favor and shoot your pecker off."

There was the sound of thumping footsteps as they retreated around the corner.

"The stairs," I cried, and put down a stream of covering fire as Wilma stepped out into the hallway.

"Clear," she shouted.

An annoying bell began to clang. They had pulled the fire alarm to cover their escape.

In the stairwell, the sound of footsteps came from several floors below. I hugged the wall and tried not to look over the edge, which would have made me freeze from vertigo.

It was a long way down to the lobby, and the stairwell began to fill with hotel guests panicked by the alarms. We hid our machine guns inside our coveralls. There was no hope of catching Frame and the others. I had a strong suspicion that our good friend Promod had called them and made a deal.

Oh well, that's what you get when you deal with a den of thieves.

The lobby was chaotic. It was crowded with firemen, and police who along with hotel security, tried to control the crowd and evacuate everyone safely from the building.

Sooner or later somebody was bound to discover the top floor walls were peppered with bullet holes, and they'd start to put two and two together. Of course, we were dealing with hotel security and the Detroit PD, so it would probably be later.

I had a thought, "If they take the Mercedes and they haven't discovered the GPS, we might have a chance."

We fought our way through the throng and got to the van. After a few minutes of maneuvering, I managed to break free of the crowd around the front of the hotel and headed along Jefferson to I-75 north.

"They're haven't found the tracker yet," Wilma called from the back.

"Where are they?" I asked.

"They're on the Lodge heading north."

I did a quick calculation. I could cut off at I-94, head east, and pick up the Lodge south of them. It really didn't matter because we had the GPS, but if they met up with Promod, he might tell them about the device. If that happened, we would lose our only hope of finding them.

We had to get eyes on them as quickly as possible.

Wilma crawled through the access hatch into the front seat. She balanced the iPad on her knees. "They're still going north."

Where the hell are they heading? Southfield? And then I got it.

"He's still up there," I leaned over and pointed at Twelve Mile Road on the iPad's display.

"Shit. He must be holed up in one of the other stores," she said. "There are at least half a dozen."

"How many of them are open at this hour?"

She got busy online as I pushed the van up to eighty. I prayed there weren't any state cops watching for speeders, but we needed to get close enough to see them. I couldn't go as fast as I wanted to because the Lodge was in terrible shape and I was afraid we might break an axle.

Promod was clever, I gave him that. Instead of putting as much distance between us and him as possible he just walked into another big box store nearby and called Frame. It would have been easy for him to extract Frame's name and number from our system.

When this was over, I would have to speak to Wilma about wiping our data trail clean.

My kidneys were screaming from the pounding they were receiving as we rocketed along the freeway. Even though I avoided the bigger potholes there were still enough little ones to shake you up good.

"We're close; they're only about a quarter mile ahead. We should be able to see them in a minute," she said, never lifting her face from the screen.

Then I saw the taillights of the Mercedes directly ahead and cut my speed back to a reasonable rate. As we thought it would, the Mercedes exited at Twelve Mile.

My cell phone rang.

I pressed the Bluetooth button on the visor.

"Rip?"

It was Promod.

"Yeah," I said coldly.

"I bet you think I double crossed you right?" Promod sounded worried.

"It crossed my mind," I said.

The Mercedes turned into the parking lot of a twenty four hour Meijer's and slowed down.

"You guys weren't going to cut me in on this even though I was the one who came up with the location of the ambergris."

"You think you can trust these assholes?" Wilma asked.

"No, of course not. That's why I want to make a deal for twenty five percent if I lead you to the stuff and you cover my back. You've got about fifteen seconds before I have to ditch this phone and go out to meet them. If you agree, I won't tell them about the GPS you put on their car."

"I'll give it some thought," I said calmly.

"You're about to run out of time," he said desperately.

It didn't hurt to make him sweat a little.

"Oh, and one more thing. There's a time limit on this. If we don't get the ambergris within the next eighteen hours, we can kiss it goodbye."

Eighteen hours? What the hell was he talking about?

Before I could ask, Wilma leaned in. "Okay we agree," she told Promod.

"Good," he said and disconnected the phone.

The Mercedes pulled up in front of the store and stopped. A few seconds later Promod walked from the store and jumped in the back seat. We watched from a safe distance as they turned back onto Twelve Mile and headed back to the Lodge.

I was pissed. "Twenty five percent? Don't you think we could have discussed it first?"

"Why? They're going to kill him as soon as he leads them to the stuff," she replied. "Anyway, he's right. We were shorting him. We should have offered him a share."

"I don't know. I figured saving his ass is payment enough."

"*Perspectivism*," she pointed out.

There were many vantage points to get to the truth.

I knew that they wouldn't head back to the hotel. There would be a lot of embarrassing questions to answer if they did. Instead, they got off at I-94 and headed west and then north. They didn't seem to be in hurry so we just followed at a distance. If they caught an occasional glimpse of the van they wouldn't give it much thought. I figured it was Lurch doing the driving, and he struck me as someone without enough imagination to recognize a tail.

Just to be certain, I used a neat device I'd had installed in the van. The flip of a switch would make it appear as if a headlight was burned out. Hit the switch again and a second set of running lights would come on. Anyone glancing in their rear view mirror would think there were two different vehicles behind them.

When the Fab Four stopped in Troy for lunch at an expensive Italian place, where Wilma and I had once poisoned a mob boss, we pulled into a nearby Arby's and ordered a couple of cardboard sandwiches.

"They're just killing time," Wilma said.

Actually they were killing more than that.

HITSVILLE U.S.A.

After lunch they were on the move again.

"Looks like they're heading back downtown," Wilma said.

They looped around again and headed back on I-94 and then got off at the Lodge once again. This time they were going south and had picked up speed.

"Where the fuck are they going now?" she said.

I goosed up our speed to keep close to them. They got off the Lodge at West Grand and headed east toward Henry Ford Hospital.

"Maybe they're going to take a tour of Hitsville USA," I said.

Hitsville USA was the tiny house where the original Motown Studios were located. It always impressed me how much big music had come from such a small place. It was practically across the street from the hospital. We pulled into the parking lot of a KFC and waited to see what Frame was up to.

The Mercedes pulled into the east parking lot of the hospital. As soon as the car stopped, Lurch went around to the rear and opened the trunk. He leaned in and lifted out something wrapped in what appeared to be a white bed sheet. We could see large red stains spreading on the sheet as the giant dropped it to the ground.

He turned around and flipped us the bird. They knew we were there.

I went cold looking at the shape on the ground.

Lurch got back behind the wheel of the Mercedes and they roared out of the parking lot. I gunned the van, fishtailing across West Grand and into the parking lot. I had an awful feeling that they'd left us a powerful message.

By the time we got the sheet untangled, Promod was making tiny gasping sounds as he struggled to breathe. He had been stabbed in both lungs, the blade of the knife inserted sideways between his ribs. He was drowning in his own blood. He also had a nasty abdominal wound.

The bastards wanted him to die slowly and painfully.

We lucked out. The emergency room was at the end of the parking lot. As I picked up Promod and carried him to the back of the van, Wilma slid behind the wheel. I put him gently inside.

Wilma knocked down the parking lot barrier as she sped toward the emergency entrance of the hospital.

Promod continued to struggle for breath.

"Hang on, we're almost there," I told him.

His eyes rolled back, and his dusky skin was turning an unsettling shade of blue-gray.

The van screeched to a halt and Wilma ran into the hospital.

"Stay with me, Promod" I pleaded. "We need to know where it's hidden."

He seemed to have stopped breathing. I was talking to a dead man.

The van's back doors swung open and a pair of burly orderlies pulled Promod onto a hospital gurney. As they moved him onto the stretcher, something fell onto the ground. Wilma scooped it up when they rushed him into the hospital.

I moved to follow, but she grabbed my arm. "No," she warned, "there'll be cops here any second. We have to go."

I looked in the direction they had taken him, and then slammed the van's doors in frustration.

Off in the distance came the approaching sound of multiple sirens. It was Saturday afternoon in Detroit and there wasn't a lot happening in the world of law enforcement. If this had been a Saturday night, our overworked PD might have taken hours to arrive.

We faded into the maze of streets near the hospital. When the police got around to actually interviewing the orderlies, there was a pretty good chance they wouldn't even be able to describe the van let alone tell them what we looked like.

Wilma held up the object that had fallen when Promod was loaded onto the stretcher. It was our GPS tracker. They had discovered it. Now they knew where the ambergris was.

Worst of all, they were in the wind and we had no way of finding them.

"I assume you didn't get anything from him," Wilma said dejectedly.

"No. He could barely breathe, let alone speak. I think he was going into cardiac arrest."

"So where does that leave us?"

"In the middle of fucking nowhere," I snapped and banged on the dashboard.

THE PERFECT MOMENT

Back at Fort Knox, I changed out of my blood-stained overalls and put the van back in its storage locker.

Wilma went through the motions of making dinner, though neither of us was particularly hungry.

This whole thing had started bad and gotten worse. We weren't ready to tell each other what was obvious, that we needed to give up and cut our losses.

Our losses.

I thought about Donald, who was probably singing with the choir invisible, and Promod, who was gravely wounded and not likely to survive. Both had been an important part of our support network.

Donald had given us an edge in more than one bad situation. In our business, knowledge was gold and he'd provided a wealth of it. Best of all, he had never betrayed us. It was not fair that he was buried in a shallow grave somewhere.

Promod knew where and how to find things, to pry into systems and extract the information we needed. He glided through cyberspace like an Olympic snowboarder manipulating the half-pipe. In this digital age, he'd been indispensable. Unfortunately, he had allowed his greed to overcome his common sense and had been fucked over as a result.

I couldn't imagine going forward without either of them backing us, but that was the reality we were now facing.

Then I had an ugly thought, which I shared with Wilma. "Do you think he told them about this place?"

She looked up from the vegetables she was cutting. "I've been monitoring the security cams around the perimeter, and in front of Target. There's no sign of them."

I secretly wished there had been. I longed for revenge and the idea of making Frame eat his own ears had a real attraction. After I finished with Frame, I would turn my knife on that tall asshole Lurch and turn him into the sum of his parts.

And then there was Ms. Cinnamon Slade – or Mrs. Felix Frame, if you prefer.

What part did she play in all this? Was she the abused wife who was searching desperately for a way out of the marriage from hell? Or was she the proverbial wicked enchantress who used her stunning body to get men to do her bidding. Either way, I would be merciful with her and just cut her throat.

Contemplating payback, while sweet, was not the way we did business. Hard vengeance was a luxury we could not afford. It doesn't put food on the table. So I pushed thoughts of slicing and dicing from my mind and decided to enjoy the delicious dinner Wilma was preparing.

It was time to forget about white whales and other things cetacean.

If he ever launched his new fragrance, we'd know Frame had been successful in his quest. And we would know exactly where to find him. I just hoped that he didn't know where to find us. At any rate, if he stood any chance of getting the ambergris, he'd probably have to deal with our friends in the shadows. They seemed to be far more ruthless than either Frame or us. One glance at Barney or Mira would tell you that.

Wilma had two porterhouse steaks thawing on the counter. She was chopping fresh garlic to combine with salt and butter for a garnish. A pair of potatoes was baking in the convection oven. I poured us each a glass of a particularly fine 2001 Pichon-Longueville. It would be perfect with the steaks. They would be rare of course. We both liked our meat bloody.

To help lift our mood, I put on *Rhythm of the Saints* by Paul Simon, which held a special place in our hearts because it had come out around the time we first met. The syncopated drumming of *The Obvious Child* thundered through the kitchen and I watched as Wilma swayed to the music.

Life, I decided, was only lived in little moments.

Joy was a pure essence that rose to the top of the crap and chaos of everyday life. I stopped to savor this perfect moment – the wine like nectar, the steak melting in its own juices, the music stirring us, and Wilma swept up in it. If someone stepped up behind me and put a bullet in my head, this would be the perfect time. My final thoughts would be rapturous ones.

Let them have all that whale vomit and money; I had this.

And then I felt the danger of suddenly having something to protect – even if it was just as simple as a feeling.

I'd let something intrude.

Was this what happiness was like? Unfortunately, it was not an emotion I could afford.

I chased it away reluctantly. Gloom descended on me once again, and my defenses went back up.

After dinner Wilma switched on the local news.

"Maybe they'll have something about Promod," she said.

If it bleeds it leads.

"Local landmark about to be no more ... A stabbing victim fights for his life at Henry Ford Hospital tonight ... The Tigers snap a four game losing streak in Toronto ..."

The anchor rattled off the rest of the headlines. I picked up the remote and switched channels as footage of the soon-to-be-demolished Blanchard Building came on the screen. I stopped on PBS where they were showing a nature special on white lions. Wilma got up and walked to the door.

"I'm going to pop a few caps," she said. "Keep an eye on the security cams."

She went down to the range. A minute later I heard a series of dull pops that told me she was shredding a target. Earlier I'd seen her earlier preparing a series of silhouettes by pasting a picture of Frame's face on them. This was how Wilma coped, by shooting things with a gun.

I had a hard time concentrating on the white lions. Finally I gave up and switched over to AMC. They were showing *Die Hard* for the millionth time that month. It was a film that never failed to amuse me. I loved the sight of Bruce Willis, feet all bloody, running around the office tower blasting at terrorists with a machine gun.

I dozed off.

Just about the time Willis was blowing up the entire top of the building to save it, I woke up.

Call it an epiphany, call it the Lord's telegraph, or call it whatever you want. Suddenly in my mind three thoughts came together – Promod's warning that we only had eighteen hours, Ben Candle ruling Detroit's underworld from his lavish office suite in the sky, and the Blanchard Building which was about to be imploded.

I sat bolt upright as if someone had pushed a cattle prod up my ass.

It was nearly 9:30.

I screamed for Wilma and she came running.

"What the fuck!" Wilma said in alarm.

"Come on, we've got work to do," I said, "and we're running out of time."

SPEAKING OF BALLS

The clock was running.

Unfortunately, it was running away from us. The Blanchard Building was due for implosion at 6:30 in the morning and Frame was probably already there removing the ambergris.

As I frantically loaded the van with whatever I thought we would need, Wilma worked her way through the Wayne County records looking for any information on Ben Candle's suite number. His office was high up in the building. We knew that much from our conversation with the late Reverend Edwards.

"If worse comes to worse, we'll just go floor to floor," I told her.

"They're going to blow the building in a few hours. Isn't that going to attract attention?" she pointed out.

Security would be tight. The guys who blow up buildings for a living are not like Bruce Willis. They're real anal-retentive types who want to be sure it doesn't fall where it isn't supposed to. Or even worse, throw debris in the air that could come crashing to earth and kill altar boys on their way to church. Either scenario would be bad for their business, but might be fun to watch.

That still left the challenge of what we would do when we found the ambergris. Four hundred pounds of petrified whale vomit wasn't going to be easy to move. The elevators would have already been taken out as part of the demolition process. Frame would have the same challenge; he'd have to find a way to move it as well.

"They've probably got a hoist going down the elevator shaft," I said. "Put the stuff in hundred pound bales and it won't take them that long to get it down."

"Well that's it then," Wilma said dejectedly.

I had a thought.

"Maybe not," I replied, "because I bet they haven't moved it yet. They're going to wait until security clears the site. Then there'll be no one around to see them take it.

"The demolition company will pull everyone back to a safe location an hour or so before they bring the building down."

Wilma was nodding. "And that will give them the window they need to get the ambergris out without being discovered."

"That takes balls," I said in admiration.

Speaking of balls, I was worried about mine – as in being blow off.

It kept getting more insane. I flashed on the view of the Blanchard Building I'd seen from Promod's office.

All the windows had been removed in preparation for the demolition. On some of the higher floors they had also taken out large portions of the walls to weaken the structure. Getting the ambergris away from Frame held the potential for the two things I hated most – high places and being shot at.

My fear worm began wiggling down deep in my belly. I could feel the wind whistling through the exposed floors. In my mind I was already free-falling from the top floor, tumbling over and over in the air.

Forget it, I thought.

But I couldn't.

We headed downtown. I could see the office buildings clustered there and I shuddered. We had a sort of plan for getting the ambergris and dealing with Frame and the other baddies. Wilma finally found the exact floor where Candle's office had been in an old story in the *Free Press*. The reporter had mentioned it covered the entire twenty fourth floor.

The challenge was finding the ambergris. We knew the floor number, but had no idea exactly *where* on that floor it was hidden. The Moby code would have provided Frame with the exact coordinates.

Our only choice was to evade security and get up there before Frame and company arrived. We'd wait for them to come and do the dirty work. Then we'd kill them, take the stuff, and get it and us the hell out before the building went boom.

That sounded simple enough. There were only about a million things that could go wrong.

Before we left Fort Knox, I'd changed the signage on the truck. It was now a reasonable facsimile of a Detroit Edison vehicle, complete with an emergency light array on the roof.

Even though it was only shortly after 4:45 in the morning, the police had already shut down the area within a quarter mile radius of the Blanchard Building. On the news they had also mentioned both the Ambassador Bridge and Detroit Tunnel would be temporarily closed to traffic during the implosion.

The bored looking cops at the Shelby Street roadblock didn't even blink when they saw our fake utility truck. They just moved a sawhorse out of the way and let us pass.

I guess no one messes with the electric company.

I turned on the roof flashers and pulled into a side street a couple of blocks away from the Blanchard. Wilma had located a useful diagram of Detroit Edison's underground conduit network. It ran straight north under Woodward, with various service access tunnels forking off to the office buildings along the street. One of these tunnels ran straight into the basement of the Blanchard Building.

I pulled on a yellow hardhat and pried up a manhole cover. Wilma erected a small safety barrier around the opening. To the casual observer, it would look copasetic. I dragged over a large plastic toolbox and lowered it into the hole. It was full of guns and ammo, and was damned heavy. We pushed a ladder into the hole and climbed down into the conduit.

It was now 5:10.

One hour and twenty minutes before the building was due to drop.

The electrical conduit smelled like Mr. Shit lived down there. It must have been all the standing water. I wished I'd put on rubber boots, but that would've been impractical once we started to climb. My New Balance sneakers were a far better option. Sadly, I would have to throw them away afterward.

I pulled a nylon day-pack from the toolbox and threw in a couple of dozen spare magazines. We'd brought identical .9mm Glocks with us so reloading wouldn't be an issue. There's nothing worse than trying to sort out different clips when you are in the middle of a gun battle. For extra punch, we loaded them with Teflon-tipped ammo. These do a good job piercing body armor.

Speaking of body armor, we decided to wear some on this outing. Normally we never wore it because it was bulky and uncomfortable. I dreaded having to climb all those stairs with it on, but dreaded being shot even more – and there was a real possibility we would be.

Wilma bitched about how it rubbed her in all the wrong places. She was getting on my already frayed nerves and I felt like testing the bullets on her to see if they really worked.

We found the feeder tunnel into the Blanchard's basement. I confirmed the number on Wilma's diagram with a rusty plate over a sagging wooden door in the conduit.

The door was secured with an ancient padlock. I levered a small pry bar under the hasp and gave it a pull. It ripped away from the doorframe with a loud screech and splashed somewhere behind us in the dark water.

The hinges were rusted and I had to put my full weight behind the bar to finally get it to move.

The access corridor to the Blanchard smelled even worse that the main conduit.

Wilma sniffed. "Think it's methane?"

"Why don't you light a match and find out," I suggested.

She frowned and gave me a gentle push. Ahead I could see a solid door. It looked like it was in much better shape than the other one. It also looked as if it had been opened at least once in this century. The door was secured by a formidable deadbolt, and a sign in large, unfriendly, red letters warned **DOOR IS ALARMED**. As I suspected, the lock was a good one. It took me almost forty seconds to pick it. I kicked door open and we were inside the basement of the Blanchard Building.

One hour and ten minutes to go.

All the interior basement walls had been knocked down, exposing a cavernous space. Bundles of cable, which were connected to blasting charges throughout the building, had been taped securely to the walls. The remaining supporting pillars were wrapped in wire mesh. I knew from various Discovery Channel programs that they had been pre-weakened and had charges planted inside to sever the rebar.

The sight was awesome, and terrifying. Charges had been planted everywhere down here. The scene looked strangely benign, but when the button was pushed all hell would break loose in a carefully orchestrated chaos that would use physics to bring the building down.

In a matter of seconds, charge after strategically placed charge would systematically weaken the building in key spots until it could no longer support itself. Once that happened, it would collapse inward.

The demolition crew had spent a lot of time cutting through the thick walls around the elevators. It was almost like a building within a building, and notoriously tough. They had removed as much of the wall as they could; exposing the dark cavity inside the shafts.

I walked over and looked in. When I shone my flashlight down, I could see there was a deep area to allow maintenance workers room to work. The flashlight beam only reached a hundred feet up the shaft before it was swallowed by the darkness.

I tried not to think about what was up there.

The staircase leading down into the basement had been removed so there was no way up to the first floor. I prayed they hadn't done this on all the floors or we were going to have one hell of a climb.

We looked around and found where the stairs had been. Twelve feet above us was an open doorway. A cross of two by fours blocked it so workers wouldn't accidently fall.

The dust was horrendous. Every step we took raised clouds of it. My nose began to itch and I could feel a sneeze coming on. We should have thought to bring dust masks or respirators.

Luckily, though, we had brought a lightweight folding ladder with us.

Not long ago we did a cat burglar who had double-crossed his partner. While I wasn't impressed by his sniveling and pleading, I did admire his tools and helped myself to them once we'd sealed him in a barrel. While Wilma banged on the lid and shouted at him to "be a man", I took his ropes and picks.

He had this custom folding ladder – at least I've never seen one for sale at Lowes. It came packed in its own convenient carrying case. The whole thing weighed less than the Sunday edition of the *Detroit Free Press* and unfolded to fifteen feet. Although strong enough to hold the weight of an average-sized man, it shook.

A lot.

Wilma went up first. I reluctantly followed. Halfway up, the flimsy ladder began to vibrate and I was scared it would collapse under me. Then I realized the shaking was coming from me. I paused and took some deep breaths to try and calm myself. The ladder finally steadied and I continued to climb. When I reached the top, I pulled myself through the doorway and lay panting on my back. Wilma pulled the ladder up after us and folded it back into its case.

The main floor smelled like damp cement and piss. I'm sure the workers hadn't bothered to use the on-site Porta Potties; they just peed wherever they pleased.

I glanced at my Timex. We needed to get a move on. Zero hour was less than an hour away, and I had a feeling that Frame wasn't too far behind us.

Wilma picked up a handful of the blue detonation cables.

"Put them down," I told her. "You might accidently disconnect a charge."

"I hardly think it matters," she responded.

I pointed around us. "All this shit is precisely designed to explode on cue. If they misfire it could really fuck things up."

"Define "fuck things up"," she said.

"The building's rigged to collapse in on itself, not topple over. That'll leave one neat pile of debris to clean up. If it explodes out of sequence, it could be like falling dominos all the way to the river. Only instead of dominos, it would be office buildings."

I had to admit that sounded pretty cool, but it would really mess up Detroit's attempt to attract new businesses to the downtown area.

Wilma replaced the cables respectfully and we started to climb.

Luckily the rest of the staircases had been left intact to allow the workers easy access to the upper floors.

Around the eighteenth floor I really began to question my sanity. This was nuts. I was in a building that was about to be imploded so we could retrieve whale vomit that had been hidden for decades. And there was the very real possibility we would have to shoot it out with one or more gangs of bad guys. And I was high up in a tall building.

Even though I didn't look down, I could feel my acrophobia kick in. My heart started beating wildly, and I felt that familiar unpleasant clutching in my crotch as my testicles ascended. I forced myself to focus, not to think about how far up I was. However, acute awareness that each step was taking me higher and higher started to slow me down. My growing panic was increased by the large floor numbers in dripping black paint conveniently left by the demolition crew.

"Move your ass," Wilma hissed when I hesitated between the twentieth and twenty first floors. I looked at my watch yet again.

Forty five minutes.

WE'RE ALL RUNNING
OUT OF TIME HERE

This was going to be close.

We heard the sound of voices coming up the stairs. They were too far below to be clearly audible, but one of them was female. Cinnamon Slade was coming to get her reward. Only it wouldn't be the reward she was expecting.

We hauled ass to reach the floor where Candle's office had been located. From the sound of their footsteps they were less than a floor below us.

There was no time to look around. We needed to find a spot to hide. I could see that it wasn't going to be easy. With the interior walls removed, it was just one open space. The elevator shaft walls were the only cover we could find. We dove behind them just as Frame and his cronies reached the floor and powerful flashlight beams stabbed into every nook and cranny of the room.

"Keep the lights low," Frame ordered.

Hugging the wall next to the shaft, I could feel a strong breeze from below and fought to control my panic. Less than a foot from where we hid was a giant hole in the floor over twenty stories deep. It was the only thing between them and us.

Heavy footsteps approached the hole from the other side. I guessed it was Lurch. It sounded like he was dragging something heavy. He dropped it with a clunk next to the shaft.

I jumped at the sound of a loud bang. The floor vibrated from the shock. He was firing anchor bolts in the concrete. There was a second and then a third bang.

I tried to lean out so I could see what he was doing. Wilma elbowed me in the ribs and shook her head.

A rhythmic pounding came from the other side of the floor. I ventured a look. Frame and the missus were smashing through the drywall. Cinnamon was swinging a sledgehammer, shattering the wallboard while Frame was knocking the pieces loose with a crowbar.

A loud whooping sounded from below. It was a siren. My first thought was that the cops were on to us. It blasted again and I realized it was a warning to clear the site.

I saw Lurch hurry over to the wall and start chopping away. They had left it way too close.

Wilma and I continued to watch while they did all the work.

I took a moment to glance at the device Lurch had assembled. It was a sophisticated rig attached to the outside supports of the elevator shaft and bolted to the floor. The top of it had a winch wound tight with thin steel cable wire, and a hook dangling down into the shaft. A large cargo net lay next to it.

We heard an excited cry and turned our attention back to them. Frame was on his hands and knees reaching into the hole. It got really quiet as they waited to admire their treasure. The timing was unfortunate because I could feel a sneeze coming on from all the dust. I desperately tried to suppress it. Wilma could see what was about to happen and looked at me in panic. I turned away and buried my face in the crook of my elbow to muffle it.

Frame pulled a hunk of chalky white stone from the wall and examined it in the flashlight beam. He wore a wide smile of satisfaction.

And then I sneezed loudly.

Lurch turned toward us bringing up his automatic weapon while Cinnamon dove to the right and started firing wildly. Frame dropped the ambergris and pulled a Mac-10.

Things seemed to slow down right about then. Bullets blew out large chunks of concrete just above our heads. Cinnamon wasn't much of a shot, but she pinned us down. I could see Lurch circling around trying to flank us. I fired a couple of shots in his direction to make him think twice about it.

He knelt and fired a burst back at me. I felt the slugs whiz between my ankles and I plunked a shot into the floor just in front of him. Razor-sharp shards of cement splattered his face.

Outside the siren blared again.

The five minute warning.

"I have a proposal for you," Frame shouted, "because we're running out of time here."

"Yeah, what is it?" I yelled back.

"We stop this nonsense and work together before they bring this building down and we lose our chance."

I hesitated, which is exactly what he wanted me to do.

Cinnamon came around the other side of the shaft and Wilma turned to face her. She fired, knocking Wilma into the open shaft. I didn't wait for the sound of her body to hit below. I dove to the side and fired a quick burst at Cinnamon. Luckily one of my bullets caught her in the shoulder. She dropped her gun and grabbed it in shock.

I whipped around. Lurch was standing over me smiling. His weapon was leveled at my head.

"Throw him down the shaft," Frame ordered as he turned and began pulling chunks of ambergris from the wall.

Lurch kicked my gun away and grabbed my ankles. As he dragged me across the floor, I caught skewed glimpses of the Detroit skyline in the early morning light. It was going to be a beautiful day, but I wouldn't be around to enjoy it.

"Jesus! Hurry up," Frame shouted at Lurch. "We have to move this shit."

Frame had piled the ambergris on the floor and was leaning in to get more.

They say that in the moments before death life takes on a magnificent clarity. I became hyper aware of even the minutest things – the raw smell of the concrete, the sound of my body crunching along the dirty floor, the feel of the grit grinding into my skin.

I took a final look over toward Frame. The section where he'd been digging looked clean, unlike the wall around it which was gray and faded. There must have been something in front of it.

Lurch hauled me up and dangled me over the edge of the shaft. There was nothing solid under my feet. I looked down into the darkness and realized this was it. I sucked in a deep breath as he began to push me forward.

Wilma's arm snaked out of the shaft and stabbed a hunting knife into Lurch's left eye, at the same time she used her forward momentum to push me back from the edge. I caught a glimpse of her hanging upside down from a piece of rebar sticking out into the shaft as I grabbed desperately at the wall. I hauled myself back into the room by a handful of the blue cables and landed hard on the floor next to the winch.

Lurch was roaring in pain while trying to claw the knife from his eye. Wilma's legs shot out of the shaft and closed around his neck like a scissor. She dragged him along as she swung her legs back into the shaft. I watched him dangle there for a few seconds before Wilma released him and he fell screaming into the blackness.

She was quite athletic and all her years of gymnastics had certainly paid off.

There was a series of short siren blasts.

The two minute warning.

Someone was running toward me through the cloud of dust. I looked around for my gun. I couldn't find it.

I was still gripping the cables and froze when I saw blasting caps were at the ends. I must have pulled them out of the explosives. While dynamite, C4, and most other modern explosives are relatively stable, blasting caps are extremely sensitive and can explode if you breathe on them the wrong way.

I turned to find Cinnamon standing over me with her automatic weapon aimed at my head. I held up the caps as if I was offering her a bouquet of roses. She almost batted them away until she realized what they were and froze. Her eyes widened in fear and her finger tightened on the trigger.

I saw a tiny red dot appear on her forehead. The beam of the laser sight was coming from outside the building. Cinnamon didn't see it.

I dropped to the side and watched as most of her head disappeared in a cloud of blood and bone fragments. She staggered to the edge of the hole and toppled in.

Wilma was beside me and stitched a row of bullet holes in the ceiling just over Frame's head to get his attention.

"Too late," she screamed.

Frame tried to pick up as much of the ambergris as he could carry.

There was another short wail of the siren.

The one minute warning; the final one before the big bang.

Frame staggered toward me cradling the load in his arms. I swung the blasting caps in an arc and let them fly in his direction.

A couple hit the ambergris and detonated. Frame was enveloped by a large ball of flame. I saw each leg fly off in a different direction.

What an interesting front cover for *Women's Wear Daily*. I almost laughed at the absurdity of the thought as I moved automatically toward the pile of ambergris.

Wilma dragged me back to the shaft.

"We're out of time," she shouted and attached the cargo net to the cable hook.

She held the net open for me and I realized what she was proposing. I froze just imagining the drop.

"Get in."

I hesitated and she stunned me with a hard rap on the side of the head. Wilma threw me into the net and crawled in next to me. She pushed off with her feet and I felt the net swing into the shaft. She banged the lever on the side of the winch and it released the cable with a high-pitched whine.

"I sure hope they set it properly," she said.

The steel cable screamed as it played out. Although the fall seemed to take several hours, it was actually over in a few seconds. The arrestor on the winch stopped with a jolt, and we bounced up and down on the end of the cable in the basement.

Wilma crawled over me trying to get out, but the net was tangled around us. "Knife," she cried as she clawed at the cargo netting.

I frantically searched my pockets looking for my knife. I couldn't find it.

"Thirty seconds," said an amplified voice from outside.

Desperately I looked around for something else to use.

I saw Lurch's body a few feet away. It was hanging upside down where he'd been impaled on a piece of rebar. I reached out and grabbed at the knife handle sticking out of his eye. It was slick with blood and eye goo. I had trouble getting a grip on it.

"Fifteen," the voice from outside announced.

I yanked the knife loose and slashed at the netting.

"Ten, nine, eight ..." the thundering voice continued as we ran across the basement floor and into the access tunnel.

I slammed the door shut behind us just as the first charges began to detonate.

We fled down the tunnel and reached the main conduit just as the pressure wave from the explosion popped the steel door on the other end like a cork, slamming it into the wall across from us. The conduit filled with a choking cloud of dust. I fell into the water in the center of the tunnel as pieces of concrete tore loose from the ceiling and fell all around us.

I felt something hard bounce off my head and everything went black.

WE HAVE A DIRTY JOB

It was quiet when I woke up.

It felt like I was waking from a long, deep sleep. Miraculously my flashlight was still in my pocket and it worked. I shone it around the conduit. It was in good shape other than the pile of debris next to the tunnel leading from the Blanchard Building. A few pieces of concrete had fallen off the ceiling. It was one of these that had knocked me out.

Wilma sat ten feet away looking stunned. She shook some of the dust from her hair. Her face was so caked with it that she looked like a ninety year old with a bad make-up job.

"You okay?" I asked.

"My chest hurts like a son of a bitch."

I could see two tiny craters in the center of her body armor as she tore it off.

"I just want to sit here for a few minutes," she continued, "and enjoy the silence."

"So that's what it feels like to have a building dropped on you," I said.

She shot me a dirty look, but I couldn't resist adding, "Do you think we have a chance of finding the whale barf under all this debris?"

We both laughed – and it hurt. But laugh was all we could do. This whole thing had been a slapstick comedy, albeit with a lot more blood.

I'd lost count of the number of people who had died, including our friends Donald and Promod. It definitely wasn't worth it.

I decided to take Wilma's advice and just enjoy the quiet for a while.

When we crawled out of the manhole a couple of hours later, large dump trucks were already rumbling up Woodward Avenue to remove the remains of the Blanchard Building. I looked at the gap in the skyline where it had once stood. Detroit now had one less heritage building, and one more parking lot.

I turned to find a cop staring at us from the sidewalk next to the van.

"Man, you guys are really dirty," the cop said.

Wilma returned his smile. "Yeah, we have a dirty job."

Back at Fort Knox we took long showers and then tended to each other's wounds. Wilma had two pitch-black bruises from the impact of the bullets on her body armor, one under each breast. I offered to tape them in case her ribs were cracked. The pain was too much for her to bear, so we finally decided sleep would be the best cure.

Sure there were loose ends, like who our mysterious friends were. Again I thought of the red dot on Cinnamon's forehead. The sniper had to have been on one of the nearby rooftops. It was one hell of a shot by any standard.

Now that the ambergris was gone, I hoped that would be the end of it. But I had a feeling it wasn't over. They, whoever *they* were, would be coming for us.

We were their final loose end.

I slept until 8:00 the next morning. When I finally managed to crawl out of bed, my entire body ached and it took four Advil just to knock back the pain enough to stumble to the kitchen. Despite her bruises and possible cracked ribs, Wilma looked great, but moved slowly as she made a huge breakfast of pancakes and sausages.

I slumped down and took the coffee she handed me. Jamaican Blue Mountain. It was delicious. Between the coffee and the Advil, I felt my pain start to ease. Once I began eating, the world felt almost right again.

My second cup was luxurious. This was the first time in what seemed like forever when we weren't chasing after something or somebody. The only blot on the horizon was that someone was going to come after us, but this wasn't the time to think about it. It was time to stop and smell the roses.

Smell the roses?

"You know, Frame had an armful of that stuff when the blasting caps went off," I said.

"Yeah, well it didn't do him any good," she said.

"One of the tests for the quality of ambergris is to heat a needle and stick it in. The ambergris should release a fragrance."

"Then the heat from that explosion should have made the place smell like a Chanel factory," she said slowly.

But it hadn't. Maybe he wasn't holding *real* ambergris.

I flashed back to the portion of the wall where they'd chopped the hole. It looked different from the rest of the area. It was too clean, like it had been freshly painted.

I set my coffee down.

"Someone got there first, took out the ambergris, put in fake stuff, and replaced the drywall," I said.

"That's a lot of trouble to go through."

Then it dawned on me. "It was a trap. They were planning to take us all out at once. It would be a neat package with all the bodies buried under tons of debris."

"No crime scene," Wilma added.

Gloom descended over us once again, wiping away our post-pancake bliss.

There was one piece of hopeful news that morning. According to Eye Witness News, Promod's condition had been upgraded from 'grave' to 'critical'.

He might make it after all.

RESTING COMFORTABLY

Wilma had hacked into Henry Ford Hospital's patient record system so we could monitor Promod's progress.

After three days of touch and go, his condition had been bumped up from 'critical' to 'serious'. They had moved him out of the ICU and he was resting comfortably in a private room.

There was a note on his file indicating the Detroit PD had requested the hospital post a security guard outside his door.

I hoped he was up for visitors.

Wilma cooked up some official-looking hospital IDs. I was Dr. Len McCoy and she was his associate, Dr. Bev Crusher. I hoped Promod's security guard wasn't a *Star Trek* fan, although that was a pretty remote possibility since most security guards are hardcore *Babylon Five* fans.

In the end it didn't matter. We weren't stopped by anyone at the hospital, not even the guard who sat outside the room reading a tattered issue of *Car and Driver*. He didn't even look up as we went in.

Promod looked like shit. There was no other way to put it. He had tubes in both arms and an oxygen mask over his mouth and nose. There were deep blue circles under his eyes. He appeared to be sleeping peacefully.

Too bad.

I shook him while Wilma turned off his oxygen.

"Morning, Sunshine," she said in the cheerful voice she reserved for those people she was about to eviscerate.

Promod looked at her in alarm. When he saw me standing beside her, his eyes widened. Then he realized he couldn't breathe and ripped at the mask.

"I … I …" he gasped.

Wilma put a finger to his lips. "You listen, we speak," she said firmly.

He nodded.

"What did you tell the cops?" I asked thinking of Deputy Dawg sitting out in the hall.

"I said that I was mugged."

He wheezed alarmingly when he talked.

"And did they buy that?"

He frowned. "I don't think so. Detroit PD isn't that dumb. I still had my wallet and Rolex when they brought me in. If it was robbery, why would muggers leave those? They told me a couple of people dropped me off at the emergency room – a man and a woman. You guys?"

I nodded.

"Thanks …" he said softly. "Anyway, they haven't come back to follow up on anything."

And it wasn't likely they would. For us it's one of the strategic advantages to living in a city like Detroit with its high crime rate and low tax revenues. Resources are spread too thin.

"How about Frame? What exactly did you tell him?" I asked.

His eyes darted from Wilma to me.

"And if you even think about lying to us, I'm going to put something really nasty in your IV." Wilma held up a syringe and squeezed a drop of bile green liquid onto the tip.

"I told them … I told them about the book," he struggled, "and that I'd discovered where the stuff was hidden." He reached for the mask. His fingernails were turning a deep shade of blue.

Wilma turned the valve on the green tank and we heard oxygen hiss back into the mask.

Promod slapped the mask gratefully to his face taking deep, greedy breaths. Once his breathing returned to normal, Wilma turned off the gas again.

"That's why you should stick to hacking. You played your ace way too soon. Why did you give them a reason to kill you before they had to?" I asked.

He lowered the mask. "Did they get it?"

I ignored him. "You gave up the book and the grid as well. So why would they need you?"

"I didn't," he gasped. "I didn't give them the book or the grid. I didn't have them with me."

I shrugged. "They didn't need them. You gave them the exact location in Candle's office where it was buried."

"No, I didn't. I gave them the floor number. I was saving the exact location until we got there. I figured you'd have my back."

I thought about the carnage in the Blanchard Building. He was lucky Frame had decided he didn't need him anymore and left him for dead. Well, if you define 'lucky' as being stabbed in the lungs.

That left the glaring question of how Frame knew where in Candle's old office the ambergris was hidden. There was a lot of wall space, and somehow Frame knew *exactly* where to go.

I got Promod to take me through the sequence of events after Frame had picked him up. It played out just the way I remembered. One thing did catch my attention, however. While they were having lunch, Frame had received a call and walked away briefly while he talked. After lunch, they stabbed him.

"The big guy held me while the woman used a switchblade on me. They wrapped me up in something and threw me in the trunk."

"So we have to assume that whoever called Frame gave him information that made you redundant," Wilma said as she turned his oxygen back on.

It was obvious that we had all been played. Our invisible friends had manipulated all of us into going to the same place at the same time, knowing we'd end up killing each other. Everything would be in a neat little package all tied up with string.

They would have the ambergris and, best of all, no one would be coming after them.

Except us.

"You said you didn't give them the grid or the book." I said.

He was sucking at the oxygen mask and nodded.

"So where are they?"

Even though the mask was frosted with a thin coat of condensation, I could see him smile. "In a safe place," he said after lowering the mask.

"I'm sick of this shit," Wilma said. She took the syringe and stabbed it into one of the IV lines.

Promod looked at it in horror.

The door opened and a candy striper stood there holding a tray.

"Is it okay to give Mr. Sharma his lunch?" she asked cheerfully.

"It sure is, honey. I'm just giving him his medicine," Wilma said with a wicked smile.

I stayed her hand and she pulled the needle out.

"Let's just wait a moment, Dr. Crusher. I want to ask the patient a few more questions," I said to Wilma.

"Dr. Crusher?" the candy striper repeated.

"Yes, I know, just like in *Star Trek*," Wilma responded.

"Yeah, not the first one. Y'know, the second one, with that foxy bald captain. My boyfriend has them all on Blu-Ray."

"Make it so," I said in my best Patrick Stewart impression.

We all laughed. Well, all of us except Promod. He just continued to look terrified.

After the candy striper left Wilma reinserted the needle.

"Look, I know you guys are pissed. I made a big mistake and I'm really sorry. I can make it up to you. Honest, I can."

"And just how do you propose to do that?" Wilma asked.

"You know what I can do. Just give me another chance. Please," he begged.

I looked at Wilma. She was ready to push the button on Promod.

"You know, dear, he just might be able to help us after all."

I spent the next few minutes explaining what I was thinking. When I was finished, I dropped an iPad on the bed beside him.

"Now get to work. You have five hours."

He looked at the iPad.

"I can't work with this," Promod protested. "It's a toy."

"Five hours," Wilma reiterated as she put the syringe back in her pocket. "Not a second more."

She looked disappointed, but sensed I was right. Promod could be of use to us. Just how long we would continue to need his services depended on what he found out in the next few hours.

Part of me was relieved we didn't have to kill him. I personally liked the guy and, until this recent unpleasantness, he had done excellent work. However, like many people, when given the chance for some easy money, he proved he could be tempted.

I nodded at the guard as we walked out of Promod's room. He still didn't look up from his magazine.

KEEP YOUR HEAD DOWN

We left through the main entrance of the hospital.

To anyone who might have been watching, we looked like a couple of medical colleagues going for lunch.

"Do you think we can trust him?" Wilma asked.

"Probably not."

A few minutes later we were back on the Lodge heading downtown again.

"I think we should go home," I suggested.

"Yeah, I'm tired of all this slinking around," Wilma agreed.

I dropped her off at her condo and headed to my place. I hadn't been home in a couple of days and my goldfish had probably starved.

My place smelled stale so I opened a couple of windows to air it out even though it was cool outside.

A thick pile of mail was stuffed in my box. Ninety five percent of everything the U.S. Postal Service delivered these days was junk so I gave it a quick scan and dropped most of it in the garbage. The only thing of importance was a renewal notice from *The New Yorker*. I put it with my other bills in a holder on the counter.

It felt good to return to normal life once again, or at least whatever semblance of normal this was.

My stomach told me it was lunch time. I went to the refrigerator to see if there was anything to eat. The milk smelled off so I dumped it down the drain. Some cold cuts were curling around the edges, and didn't look very appealing. Finally I settled on a can of spicy tuna mixed with some elbow pasta. I carried it into the living room, so I could watch my afternoon shows while I ate.

The buzz of my cell phone woke me up. I'd dozed off during *Ellen*.

"Hi there," Matilda said in a low voice that told me she was probably calling from the office, and didn't want her fellow cubical rats to hear.

"How are you feeling?" I asked.

"Oh, the swelling's gone down and my mouth's starting to feel better."

Little Rip reminded me just how good her mouth could feel.

As I bent over to pick up my plate, I noticed a red dot on the coffee table. I dropped to the floor just as the back of my couch exploded in a cloud of cotton stuffing. My head had been in the way only a second before.

"What was that?" Matilda asked.

I kept my voice calm. "Sorry, I dropped a plate."

A second bullet ripped through the couch. The shooter was using a suppressor so the shots wouldn't attract attention.

"I was going to call to see if you wanted to go out this week," I said as I crawled along the floor toward the front of the living room and the safety of its thick walls.

"I'd like that," she said enthusiastically. "You're always so much fun."

"I can't do it tonight, but how about tomorrow? I know a great brew pub up in Auburn Hills near the Silver Dome."

A third shot hit the sofa.

"Look, I've got to go into a meeting right now. How about I pick you up at your place around 7:00 tomorrow?"

"Sounds good. I'll see you then," she said.

I hung up and immediately called Wilma. When there was no answer, I had a bad feeling they'd gotten to her first. I left a desperate message for her to call me.

The hits just kept on coming.

Across the living room, my plasma screen exploded as Ellen was boogying with her guest. I wondered if my extended warranty from Best Buy would cover that sort of damage. Maybe I could deduct it, along with my couch, as a business expense. I'd have to speak to my accountant about that.

My phone buzzed again.

"What's up?" Wilma asked out of breath.

"Well, let's see. I'm pinned down by a sniper in my living room right now."

"At least that answers the question," she said.

"What question?"

"Whether or not they've given up," she replied.

"Yeah, well keep your head down. You're probably next on the list."

"Shit. I was trying to get my laundry done. So much for that." Wilma sounded disappointed. "I'll meet you back at Fort Knox," she added and hung up.

Getting out of the house wouldn't pose that much of a challenge with the escape tunnel in the basement. I just needed to get there without getting my head blown off.

The sniper had to be in the house across the street. The Hutchisons, a nice retired couple, lived there. Mrs. H. had a great garden, and she always gave me lots of tips for mine. I was pretty certain they were still in Arizona for the winter. Whether or not they were there, the shooter had a good blind.

I cursed myself for opening my bullet resistant windows. Instead of impacting in the glass, the bullets had sailed straight into my living room.

Someone's going to pay for this, I thought as I totaled up the cost.

I crawled along the front wall, staying low under the windows until I reached the front hallway. My armor-plated front door protected me there. I got to my feet and hurried into the kitchen. Down in the basement, I grabbed a couple of guns and headed out through the tunnel.

Ninety minutes and three cabs later, I arrived at the Target across the parking lot from Fort Knox Secure Storage. I grabbed something off a rack and headed for the change rooms in the back. I noticed I'd picked up a pair of women's jeans when I got there.

"You look lead-free," Wilma quipped when I walked into the kitchen and sat down.

I was breathing heavily and sweating profusely.

"You weren't followed were you?" she asked.

"I almost wish I was."

I put my gun on the table. I was pissed. This thing was just going on and on.

"I thought maybe they'd give us a pass once they had the ambergris, but obviously we're an obsession for them," I said glumly. "I just hope Promod comes up with something."

The man behind the curtain had to be Anton Geisel. He'd been protected by the Feds first and then by the passage of time. He was just another faded photograph in a dusty album.

Geisel was not totally forgotten though. There were still guys around like "fucking" Dorsey who remembered him. He'd hurt a lot of people and some of them had long memories. I thought back on that defiant old man, bitter and angry as he lay in the trunk of his car waiting for his final baptism.

A bee began to buzz inside my head. It was something that Dorsey had said. I just couldn't remember exactly what it was. I tried to recall our conversation, to play it back in my memory, but I was getting nothing.

Promod called at 5:00.

"Well, that was a real challenge," he said, his voice full of enthusiasm.

Solving a problem seemed to be good medicine for him.

"I had no luck finding that copy of *The Cat in the Hat*."

Promod got off on speaking in code. I was tempted to tell him not to bother, that our phone was heavily encrypted. However, I decided to let him have his fun and play spy.

From his *Cat in the Hat* reference, I assumed he was still locked out of the DOJ database and hadn't been able to learn anything about Geisel.

"But I did locate FF's cell phone records. Whoever called him while we were in the restaurant used a disposable, and only made that one call from it."

Another dead end.

"I pinged that phone to see which towers it had accessed. Whoever made the call was stationary and it only used one tower. The phone was within a quarter mile radius of that tower. I overlaid the possible location on a Google map and sent it to your phone."

A quarter mile radius? It might as well have been on the moon.

I opened the file and looked at what he sent me. When I realized what I was looking at, it all fell into place. A big flyswatter came down on that bee in my head. I remembered what was nagging at me from my conversation with Dorsey.

I stayed quiet for almost a minute.

"You still there?" Promod asked. "Did that help?"

"Promod, you're brilliant," I replied.

I heard him suck in some more oxygen.

"Brilliant enough to get a few points of the action?" he wheezed.

"Nope, but brilliant enough that you won't have to look over your shoulder for the rest of your life."

I hung up and told Wilma where we'd find Anton Geisel.

And the ambergris.

A CLASSIC MEXICAN STANDOFF

I sat in the dark and waited for Geisel.

Chewing on a Butterfinger, I reflected on how what had started out as a simple task had morphed into such a complete mess; one I hoped was coming to an end.

I heard footsteps on the floor above.

He came down the stairs slowly. I watch him swing the gun back and forth in wide arcs. It reminded me of a cobra in the hands of a snake charmer.

The nickel plated Smith & Wesson .44 Magnum he was holding had an eight inch barrel and was engraved. It was a work of art.

A single light illuminated an area at the bottom of the stairs. Geisel stepped into it and looked around. I was far back in a corner, my black Zentai suit blending into the shadows. He lowered the wicked looking weapon and strode across the basement toward the safe.

I stepped forward and extended my gun.

"Hello, Donald," I said and he froze. "That sure is a nice looking piece."

He didn't respond.

"Toss it away and down on your knees," I ordered.

To my relief, he tossed the gun into a pile of cardboard boxes along the wall. It would've been a shame to scratch that beautiful finish on the concrete. He knelt down and slumped forward.

"What is it with you bibliophiles anyway," I said. "You just can't walk away from those first editions."

I moved around and stood between him and the safe. I pulled off the black hood so he could see my face.

He smiled. "Just obsessive, I guess. I'd spent so many years collecting them."

"Too bad you couldn't have taken them earlier," I said, "but then that would have made me suspicious when I went to get the copy of *Moby Dick*, so you had to leave them behind. What's the matter, four million not enough to buy replacements?"

"That was for my retirement," he replied as his eyes flicked away.

I looked at the red dot that had just appeared in the center of my chest.

"And I thought we were alone down here," I said as I kept the gun pointed at his head.

A figure wearing an identical black Zentai suit stepped into the light holding a large assault rifle. The laser sight under its barrel did not waver.

"We have a classic Mexican standoff."

I recognized the voice instantly.

"No choir practice tonight, Matilda?" I asked.

Wilma put a gun against the back of Matilda's neck. She reached around and took the rifle.

Matilda pulled off her hood and sank to her knees in surrender.

"We could spend a few minutes reviewing all your crimes," I said, "but after seven hours of waiting down here, I'm tired."

"So am I," Wilma added.

"Here's the executive summary. Alton Geisel infiltrated Ben Candle's mob and then rolled over on him, his cronies, and a bunch of dirty cops. For your service to the federal government they rewarded you with a new identity, some plastic surgery, and set you up in business as a book seller in Ann Arbor.

"Do you remember a dirty cop named Dorsey Mason?"

He nodded.

"I had a talk with him the other day. He really hated Geisel – *a lot*. He couldn't tell me that much about him though. However, he did mention that he had bad acne."

Donald touched his scarred cheek with a frown.

"Not much that a plastic surgeon could do about that short of using a belt sander," I said. "You just couldn't stay clean. So you hired me burn down your store, but not before you skimmed off the finest first editions."

"Well you have to admit, it is a wonderful collection," Donald said. "The signed Hemingways alone are worth more than two hundred thousand."

"Yes, it is a nice collection," I continued, "but let's skip to the part where we walked in the door with our copy of *Moby Dick*. The code might have been a bit of a challenge, but I'm betting you already had it solved when you showed it to us.

"That gave you plenty of time to get to the Blanchard Building, dig out the ambergris, and then make a deal with Frame to buy it from you."

Donald smiled up at me and shook his head.

"Of course not," I said. "He paid you to tell him where it was stashed. That's why you put the wall back up. You had Frame pay and then figured you'd set us both up to take each other out. How much did you get from him?"

"Five hundred thousand," he said.

"And that would leave you with all the ambergris to sell on the open market." I turned to Matilda. "And you were up on a nearby roof as insurance. Thank you, by the way, for taking out Cinnamon before she whacked me."

"I never understood what you saw in that cold-blooded bitch," she spat. "I'm just sorry I missed you."

"Speaking of cold-blooded," I said, "the way you used the baseball bat on Grande and the others was pretty brutal. I should have put it together when I saw all those softball pennants in your room."

"Too bad you didn't look in the closet. You would have seen the trophies I won for shooting."

"You seduced Grande and he told you about his uncle's treasure."

"He thought he would impress me," Matilda said with a laugh. "He was such a pig – and a lousy lover. Not like you."

"When you learned about the book and Donald here, you decided to go for it," Wilma added.

"Not quite," I continued. "She was supposed to wipe Donald's slate clean."

Matilda smiled again. "He had a lot of enemies. They spent years tracking Anton Geisel with no luck. It took me two weeks," she bragged.

"What were you, Bureau or Company?" I asked her.

She shook her head. "Delta."

"I didn't think Delta Force had any women."

"I was the only one," she said with pride. "A gal can come in handy in certain situations."

"So you got out of the army and decided to go freelance."

"That's right."

"And you found Donald and he persuaded you not to kill him."

"His offer was better," she replied.

"That's so unethical," I told her.

"So where do we go from here?" Donald interrupted.

"That depends on where the ambergris is," Wilma said.

"It's safe," Matilda said coldly.

"I'm guessing you're right in the middle of making a deal. That's why you came back to get your books. They were safe enough here, but once the deal was done you were going to disappear again, and wanted to take them with you."

"I did have somewhere warm and quiet picked out," he said. "My Japanese buyers are paying top dollar, nearly six million. That's a lot of years on the beach."

"You don't strike me as the beach type," I told him. "You're more of a culture vulture. I expect that we'd find you exploring museums in Europe. Maybe stealing an illuminated manuscript here or there."

"I repeat my question," he said. "What now?"

"Since you've already gone to the trouble of arranging a deal, I think you should go through with it," I answered. "However, I have a couple of stipulations."

"How much?"

"Sixty percent."

"And what do I get for that?"

"Three things. You get a shitload of money for your retirement, and you get to live to spend it."

"That's only two things," he said.

Wilma stepped forward and cracked Matilda across the back of the head with the assault rifle. She went down in a heap on the floor.

"And no one else to share it with," I finished.

He thought for a few seconds and then put out his hand. I helped him up. Wilma bundled up Matilda while Donald and I cleared the books out of the safe.

He looked at the empty shelves with regret. "You don't happen to still have that copy of *Moby Dick* do you?"

Promod had been smart enough to stash it under a bench in the Target change room before he went off to meet Frame. We'd recovered it after he told us where it was.

"I think I'm going to hang onto it. Maybe I'll start my own collection of first editions."

We hauled everything upstairs and packed it into the van. I went back to the basement and set a small charge next to the gas line. I blew out the pilot light and turned up the gas.

I had a final thought and scooped up his .44 Magnum. It would make a lovely souvenir.

THAT'S ALL ANYONE
CAN HOPE TO BE

Wilma and I covered Donald's back when he delivered the ambergris to the Yakuza.

I didn't like the location he'd chosen. It was on a farm in the middle of nowhere with no cover. Wilma and I stood two hundred feet apart in an unplowed field. We each held a high powered rifle and made no attempt to hide. We wanted them to see us.

The ambergris was in the back of a stolen van we'd parked down the road. The Japanese arrived at precisely the agreed time. I love Asian gangsters. They're so punctual and polite.

Donald greeted them with a traditional bow and led the leader of the group to the van. The man spent a couple of minutes inside the van and then came out and nodded. One of his men went around to the trunk of their car and took out two large suitcases. He lugged them back up the road and put them down. Donald opened one and examined the money. Satisfied, he handed him the keys to the van and bowed once again.

The man took the keys, got into the van, and drove off. The others followed in the Ford. Donald stood at the side of the road with the suitcases and waited patiently while we retrieved our car.

We went back to the Hyatt in Dearborn. I put the **DO NOT DISTURB** sign on the door and we spent the next few hours splitting up the cash.

Donald packed his into a pair of expensive bags. He loaded them onto a cart and wheeled it to the door. I could see he wanted to say something.

I held up my hand to stop him. "We've got nothing more to say to each other. You've run out of things we need. Go. Disappear. If we ever see you again, we'll kill you. Understand?"

He hesitated, then shook his head sadly and shut the door.

We gave Promod a $100,000 along with the same message we had given to Donald. I left out the "disappear" part. I think he was a little disappointed. He enjoyed the challenges we'd brought him. For now, we would just put a scare into him. You never know when he might come in handy again.

I never asked Wilma what she did with Matilda. I imagined it must have been something extreme, probably involving power tools or a baseball bat.

Felix Frame's disappearance was a national news story until the next celebrity scandal pushed it from the front pages. In time, Frame and his disappearance would become a legend to be trotted out every few years in a new feature on famous people who'd disappeared without a trace. He would join a pantheon of the vanished along with Ambrose Bierce, Amelia Earhart, Jimmy Hoffa, and the Reverend Powell Edwards.

We decided to use a little of our new-found wealth to take some time off. Wilma booked a six month around-the-world cruise. I decided to finally deal with my fear of heights.

I continued to wake up every night screaming from vivid dreams of falling down the elevator shaft. My phobia had almost gotten us killed.

I'd been doing some research and discovered there was a private clinic in Interlaken having great success helping patients deal with acrophobia. I decided to go for it.

The cure could take up to six months and would cost me six figures, but what the heck. It would make me a stronger person.

And in the end, that's all anyone can hope to be.

ABOUT THE AUTHOR

After receiving a degree in film, Peter worked on various movie and television productions. He was head writer and show runner on two popular Canadian entertainment shows. He also wrote and produced numerous radio and television commercials.

The author of two travel guides, Peter writes extensively on film and tourism for a number of different publications. Peter lives in Toronto with his family.

Dark Sunset, Peter's first mystery novel, is available from Cliff House Publishing.

Look for Rip and Wilma to return in ***Double Tap***.

Made in the USA
Charleston, SC
17 April 2014